FOR THOSE IN PERIL

Romulus Hutchinson
Book One

David Clensy

SAPERE
BOOKS

FOR THOSE IN PERIL

Published by Sapere Books.

24 Trafalgar Road, Ilkley, LS29 8HH

saperebooks.com

ISBN: 978-0-85495-719-4

Dedicated to the memory of all those who served amid the peril of the Second World War.

Eternal Father, strong to save,
Whose arm hath bound the restless wave,
Who bid'st the mighty ocean deep
Its own appointed limits keep;
O hear us when we cry to Thee,
For those in peril on the sea.
William Whiting, 1860

CHAPTER ONE

Liverpool, 1939

Romulus Hutchinson sat with his head in his hands, his legs kicking idly at the edges of the quayside. His twin brother Remus sat beside him, looking out across the granite waves of the Mersey that had been reluctantly corralled into the dock and were now complaining with a choppy grumble as they slapped and hissed against the concrete face of the quay. A clock struck nearby, neatly clipped chiming notes that echoed through the air. Four o'clock. The ship was already half an hour later than the time they had been told she was expected by Old Jim on the gate. Other children were gathering, playing restlessly in the dirt of the dockside.

Rom recognised a few — the second engineer's eldest boy, Harry, was sitting on a nearby wall, fiddling with a conker on a shoelace. Then there were the ship's cook's three boys, the Charltons. John, the eldest, was a year or two older than Rom and Remmie. Tom, the middle lad, who was the same age as them, was a vicious little thug. He was currently trying to trip up first his younger brother, Daniel, and then his elder brother. Rom looked across and saw a smear of blood seeping out from the grime on the youngest boy's knee.

'Cut it out, won't you?' Rom called across at the young bully.

A frown creased Tom's face, and he laughed, spittle gathering around his yellow teeth. '*Ee-ah doh,*' he spat. 'Who do you think you are?'

Rom, who was still sitting on the edge of the dock, turned his body a little, so he was facing Tom. 'You just need to leave your brothers alone and sit quietly, like the rest of us.'

'Just 'cause your da's the captain, doesn't mean that you're any better than us,' Tom said in his distinctive screech, which rattled in his throat like tuberculosis.

'I didn't say I was.' Rom took a deep breath as he attempted to keep his cool.

Tom shuffled his feet and looked down at the little cloud of dirt he was kicking up before him. 'Yeah, but you thought it, didn't ya? Just 'cause you go to the grammar school, you think you're all la-di-dah.' Tom turned to his brothers and performed a grotesque little mime of a lady holding a handbag up to her chest with two tightly clasped hands and giggled gratingly.

Rom shrugged and turned his face back towards the river. He heard Remmie sigh deeply beside him.

'You two think you're *dead* posh.' Tom turned back to his own brothers — both of whom had once again been transformed into allies rather than enemies. 'Deese lads think that we're shite because our da's a cook and their da is a captain.'

The two brothers sniggered conspiratorially, Daniel already having forgotten the gash across his knee that was congealing into ink-black scum.

Rom heard three sets of feet shuffle across the dockside towards him. Remmie sighed again. Rom was the first to move, lifting himself up from the edge of the dock wearily and brushing the dirt off his hands.

'You lads got a problem?' Rom muttered. He could hear his brother rising to his feet beside him and Harry giving a comical little whistle from his perch on the wall.

The three brothers stood line abreast — Tom, the chief troublemaker, at their centre. Tom led the way in squaring up to the twins, his shoulders arching a little, despite his scrawny frame. Rom felt the muscles tensing in his legs and nervously calculated the proximity of the dockside behind him.

'Yeah, we've got a problem all right.' Tom gave a sly snarl. 'You want to know what our problem is? Our problem is that your ma's got a face like a robber's dog and seeing her makes us vomit.'

Rom's fist landed squarely on Tom's nose. Tom wailed like a cat and held both hands up to his face, lifting them aside after a moment to stare down in disbelief at the fresh blood that coloured his palms.

'Yous are dead,' Daniel hissed as his head flashed between the bloodied nose and the identical twins, while John stared in disbelief at Rom's fist.

Finally catching his breath, Tom glowered at Rom, and started lurching towards him until his attention was caught by a policeman running towards them, truncheon held aloft and a whistle to his lips.

'The dock bobbies!' Remmie said.

'Leg it!' John bellowed, as he turned on his heel.

The boys scattered like rats, each taking different routes through the accumulated goods and ropes and wooden cases that populated the quay.

The twins stopped running as soon as they got out through the gates and on to the dock road. They sat against a high brick wall and concentrated on getting their breath back. Rom was the first to speak, answering Remmie's unspoken remonstrance with a shrug. 'Well, he was asking for it.' Then he peeked over the wall and watched as the policeman stood at the dock gate, hands on hips, with his truncheon swinging from the leather strap that was looped around his wrist. The officer looked to the left and to the right, and with a shake of his head regained his composure and ambled back towards the docks. 'He's gone,' Rom muttered to his brother.

The rich, deep bellow of a ship's horn filled the air around them, and from high beyond the brick wall, the boys could hear the distinctive sounds of ships' chains. The twins ran back to the gate and peered through to see the distinctive low-slung silhouette of the SS *John Holt* edging towards the quayside.

Remmie reached into his pocket and pulled out a handkerchief. He held it out towards his brother's scratched and bloodied face. 'You'd better tidy yourself up, Rom. Dad's home.'

There was certainly no mistaking the silhouette of the man standing at the top of the gangplank an hour later. The peaked cap, the broad shoulders that effortlessly took the weight of the enormous canvas bag that contained all his luggage — clothing, personal possessions and doubtless special gifts from Africa's west coast markets. The twins smiled to see their father as he emerged from the shadow of the ship and strode towards them, his face looking remarkably sun-burnished beneath his neat square-cut white beard.

'Welcome home, Father!' they greeted in unison.

Captain William Hutchinson was still a Victorian at heart and insisted his sons not use the increasingly popular but less formal moniker, "Dad".

'Thank you, boys,' he said gruffly. 'You're both looking well,' he added, carefully examining the twins. A smile emerged, dimpling the sides of his beard until he took hold of Rom's chin and tilted his face towards the light. 'You've been fighting again, son.'

Rom knew better than to deny it. He turned his eyes to the ground. 'You should have seen the other lad, Father. And anyway, he was asking for it.'

'You need to keep your temper,' Hutchinson said, his frown creasing in the watery light that was glinting up from the dock. 'A decision made in anger is never sound, no matter what the other lad was saying.'

Rom nodded, his eyes still focused on the ground remorsefully.

'But look at the pair of you,' Hutchinson said. 'You must have both grown a foot in the last six weeks.'

'We're doing well, thank you, Father,' Remmie said. 'You've caught the sun.'

'There's plenty of it about down there,' Hutchinson said.

'How was the journey?' Rom asked his father.

'Oh fine, fine, no problems.' Hutchinson looked back over his shoulder at the ship. 'She runs like a dream. So much more efficient than my last ship. Pity I'm being transferred off the *John Holt.*'

'Why's that?' Remmie asked.

Hutchinson shrugged. 'They wanted someone with more experience on its sister ship, the *Robert Holt.* It's a pity. I liked this ship. She has soul. But tell me, how's your mother?'

'She's well,' Remmie said. 'She'll have the tea on.'

His father smiled. 'I'm sure she will.'

The three walked in silence for a few moments towards the gate until they saw Old Jim standing with one hand on the doorframe of the gatehouse, to support his perennially tired legs. He had worked as a gatekeeper, porter, watchman and general odd-job man at this dock for as long as Rom could remember, and even decades before that when his father had been a young man. Hutchinson was fond of exchanging a few pleasantries with the old man whenever he was in port.

Old Jim gave a comical little attempt at a salute. 'Your taxi is here, Captain Hutchinson.'

'Good man, Jim, and how's the wife?' Hutchinson asked.

'She's holding up, thank you, sir.'

'Pleased to hear it,' Hutchinson beamed, giving the elderly man a pat on the shoulder.

'She'll have a pan of scouse bubbling away on the stove, ready for my tea when I get home.'

'Jim!' Hutchinson laughed. 'You're making me hungry just thinking about it!'

An Austin London was idling beside them, its engine rumbling as Remmie opened the vehicle's door for his father, before turning to help Rom, who was wrestling the luggage into the back of the cab. The two boys squeezed themselves in, and the cab gave a growl and a shudder before setting off along the cobbled road.

A gang of navvies were filling sandbags on the far side of the road. Rom frowned towards them, his head turning slowly as the cab rumbled past the scene.

'There's so much talk of war. Do you think it might really come to that, Father?' Rom asked, raising his voice over the sound of the engine. 'Sometimes it seems like people are willing it to happen.'

Hutchinson leant forward and looked out of the car window, as if checking for rainclouds. 'It's coming all right,' he muttered, casting his eyes across the red-brick terraces as the cab swept through the city. 'It's a question of when, not if. The Jerries can't be allowed to carry on doing as they please. We'll have to make a stand at some point. You mark my words — this kind of an uneasy peace cannot last.'

Rom nodded sombrely, still staring out of the window. 'That's why I was thinking you might give me permission to join up, Father?'

'Join up?' Hutchinson's white eyebrows knotted into a frown. 'Give up your studies and join the Army?'

'No, the Navy. The Royal Navy.'

Hutchinson's expression turned serious. 'I'm not sure, Rom. The Navy? You're not old enough.'

'I am, with your permission. I'm sixteen,' Rom insisted.

Hutchinson sighed. 'And what about you, Remus? Will you stay on at school?'

'I'd like to go to sea too, Father,' Remmie ventured. 'Merchant ships, like yourself.'

'Well.' Hutchinson's distinctive smile emerged once again, flashing a row of white teeth at the two boys. 'What *will* your mother say?'

'She'll understand,' Rom said after a moment.

The cab pulled up outside a neat, modern detached house, with a clipped front lawn and rows of roses standing sentry along the gravel path that led towards the front door. Hutchinson looked out of the window at the home he hadn't seen in weeks. 'She'll understand that there's salt in your blood,' he agreed, as he waved at the woman who was already opening the front door while simultaneously removing her apron. 'But she'll blame me for that. Still, I suppose it was inevitable really.'

The next morning Rom woke up to the smell of eggs and bacon as he did every Sunday morning. By the time he got downstairs, his father was already seated at the kitchen table with a half-eaten fry-up on the plate before him, mopping up the leftover grease on his plate with a piece of toast. His mother, Eileen Hutchinson, was prodding at a pair of fried eggs in a splattering frying pan.

'Yours will be ready any moment,' she smiled at Rom. 'Is your brother awake?'

'He's on his way down,' Rom muttered as he yawned and stretched.

His father looked over the top of his newspaper and took a bite out of his piece of toast. 'What time do you call this then?' he grumbled. 'You won't be getting a Sunday morning lie-in once you join up, you know.'

'Yes, I know Father,' Rom replied, taking his usual seat at the table.

Remmie skidded in and sat beside him as their mother put down the two plates, each heaped with food.

'All the more reason why he needs the extra sleep now, I'd say,' she said, waving a metal spatula playfully towards her husband. 'They're growing boys.'

'They certainly are,' Hutchinson agreed, folding the newspaper before him and looking over his reading glasses at the twins. 'Anyway, there is to be an announcement on the wireless at quarter past eleven, boys. We should tune in. The Prime Minister is to address the nation.'

Rom nodded as he chewed on a mouthful of sausage. 'That can mean only one thing, I suppose,' he said through the meat.

His father frowned.

'I do hope you won't be eating with your mouth full once you get to your officer training,' Eileen quipped, softly whipping Rom around the back of the head with a tea towel.

Rom laughed. 'I'll be an officer and a gentleman, Mother, don't you worry. I'll be on my very best behaviour.'

Remmie giggled. 'You've a way to go before you achieve that, if you ask me.'

Their mother took a seat opposite them, clinging to a mug of tea.

'Have you told Charlotte?' she asked, her eyes following the steam that was rising from the mug.

'About the Navy?'

'Yes — she has a right to know your plans.'

'Not yet.' Rom took another mouthful of breakfast, before adding, 'But I will. I just need to find the right moment.'

His father was busy tapping his wristwatch. 'It's nearly quarter past now,' he muttered. 'Remmie, go and turn on the set.'

They all took their mugs of tea to the front room to listen to the Prime Minister. They stared at the front garden through the window as they listened to the crackly voice coming from London: '*I have to tell you now ... that this country is at war with Germany.*'

Rom eventually broke the silence that followed. 'Well, that's that then, I suppose.'

'I suppose it is,' his father muttered. 'I suppose it is.'

Rom walked along the sands of Crosby beach later that morning, the fingers of his right hand intertwined with those of his sweetheart, Charlotte. The late summer sunshine was beginning to disappear behind the rolling storm clouds that were sweeping up the river.

'What do your parents think about it?' Charlotte asked, her long, auburn hair blowing across her face in the salty breeze.

'I think my father's pleased I'm up for going to sea, rather than joining the Army. But he would have preferred me to go down the route that Remmie has taken.'

'Following in his own footsteps?' Charlotte said.

Rom nodded and looked out towards the waves. 'He sees it as the safest option, I suppose, and of course it's the world he knows best. You can't blame him for wanting that.'

They walked on in silence for a few moments. The sound of the waves and wind and the crunching of the sand beneath their feet was punctuated by the occasional solemn cry from a gull high above.

'What about your mother?' Charlotte asked.

Rom shrugged. 'I've heard her crying when she thinks we are out of earshot. I suppose she thinks I'll be torpedoed within days of joining up. I wouldn't be surprised if she's picked out her funeral dress.'

'Rom, don't say such things,' Charlotte said with a frown. 'You can't blame them for worrying. It's a big thing for them — their only two boys going off when the world is looking bleaker than ever.'

Rom stopped walking for a moment and looked at Charlotte. There was always something relaxed and natural about her — a quiet confidence in her every movement. It was what had first attracted him to her at school — this gentle, poetry-loving girl, delicate and pale, yet always somehow intense and passionate. The attraction had never faded for a moment, which was why he now felt like he had swallowed a boulder. He knew what he had to do and was trying to find the right moment. As she smiled at him, the sea breeze buffeting her hair, he knew it had to be now.

'What about you?' Rom asked her. 'What do you think about me going to sea?'

'You have to do what you think is right, of course,' she said, her brow knitting thoughtfully once more.

'But you'll worry about me?'

'Of course I will,' she said softly. 'But you'll be all right.'

'I might not be.'

The young couple's eyes locked on each other.

'I think,' Rom said, taking a deep breath to prepare himself, 'I think maybe it would be best if we stopped seeing each other, for a while anyway.'

'Why would you say that?' Charlotte's face hardened. 'Are you fed up with me?'

'No, no, nothing like that,' Rom said. 'I just think it'd be best.'

'Best for you? Girl in every port and all that?'

'No.' Rom tilted her face so her eyes met his once again. 'Best for you. Christ, Charlotte, anything could happen. You'd be better as a free agent for now. Don't you see that?'

'Nothing's going to happen, Rom. I'll wait for you. However long it takes.'

There was a long pause before Rom spoke again. 'I'm sorry, Charlotte. It's for the best. It really is.'

He looked down at the ripples in the sand, and listened to the sound of Charlotte's shoes crunching away into the wind.

The twins had never really argued like most brothers, but they seemed to grow closer still in their final few days at home. September had brought a biting chill to the wind, and even inside the house there was an autumnal hue to those final quiet days of togetherness. Their mother devoted herself to endless cooking, their father to pensive monitoring of the headlines. The twins themselves were ready to go into the big wide world, and were now waiting restlessly for the opportunity.

'My teacher cried when I told her I was joining up,' Rom told his brother as they sat together in the back room one evening. Remmie raised his eyebrows at the thought. 'Extraordinary, isn't it, how everyone has me all measured up for my coffin.'

'I don't think it's that,' Remmie replied. 'I think it's the shock. The realisation that the war is already affecting people around them — the children in their own classes are about to be fitted out with a smart uniform and sent off to fight for King and Country. It's the ones who were around for the last war who seem to feel that shock instinctively. They assume this war will be the Western Front all over again.'

'I wouldn't be surprised if it isn't a damn sight worse,' Rom said, his lips twisting a little with concentration. 'Last time round we gave the Bosch a bloody nose. Now that stings and they are looking for revenge.'

Remmie broke the tension in the room with a little laugh. 'How is Tom these days?'

Rom smiled at his brother. 'Tom Charlton? That idiot?' he muttered. 'Actually, I've not seen him since I landed him one.'

'I've heard he's also signed up for the Royal Navy.'

Rom raised his eyes to the heavens. 'You're kidding me! That shrimp?'

'Him and his older brother.'

'Well, hopefully the Seven Seas are big enough to keep him out of my sight,' Rom muttered.

'You never know,' Remmie teased. 'You lads could end up on the same ship. Bunk buddies.'

'Well, I don't think that little squirt will be squaring up to me again any time soon. I didn't half land him one. My fingers are still bruised.'

'You wouldn't train alongside the ordinary ratings anyway, would you?'

'No, I think it'll only be officer cadets.'

'Where will you go for training? Somewhere local?'

Rom shrugged. 'I don't think so. They're churning RNVR officers out like hot cakes at the moment. I suppose you train wherever there's a space.'

Remmie got to his feet and walked to the window. He looked out at the suburban street and the neatly clipped front garden. 'All of this is going to feel like another world, another lifetime when we get out to sea.'

Rom nodded and a silence engulfed the room, creeping in through the lace curtains and settling among the shadows.

'You all ready for training then?' Rom asked. 'You know, you could probably still change your mind and join me for RN officer training.'

'I'll be happier on merchant ships, I reckon.' Remmie shrugged. 'And I don't think I'm officer material somehow. I'm happy joining up as a deckhand, and Father didn't seem to mind.'

'He thinks it's good policy to start at the bottom and work your way up.'

Remmie nodded. 'I'm quite happy being one of the lads, if you know what I mean. I'm looking forward to it — getting on the train down to Sharpness Docks and stepping aboard that training vessel for the first time. I reckon it'll be brilliant.'

Rom nodded. 'You're probably right.'

'How did Charlotte take the news?'

'About me joining up?' Rom paused for a moment. 'I finished with her.'

'You didn't! That seems a bit harsh, Rom.'

'It's the right thing to do. She doesn't need me as an albatross around her neck, if anything happens.'

Remmie thought for a moment as he silently watched the dust motes circling the lampshade. Finally, he broke the tension in the room once again. 'You needn't worry,' he said with a grin. 'If anything happened to you, I'd be happy to comfort her.'

'Don't even think about it!' Rom laughed, flinging a sofa cushion across the room at his brother. It was his first bombardment of the war.

CHAPTER TWO

The following week, Rom was at Liverpool Lime Street Station with his parents to wave off his brother, as Remmie prepared for the long journey down to Gloucester to start his training. Nobody said anything as they walked along the platform, a wisp of steam already rising from the engine ahead. Remmie climbed up into a carriage and lowered the window. He leaned out and smiled at the three concerned faces that looked up at him.

'I'll be absolutely fine, Mother,' he said. 'You needn't worry about me.'

'Of course you will be,' his father agreed. 'Best thing you could possibly be doing, seeing a bit of the world. You won't regret it.' Hutchinson reached into his pocket, produced a small box and handed it to Remmie. 'It's a going-away present.'

Remmie opened the box and took out a shiny new watch. It had a leather wristband and a long rectangular, face divided into two separate clockfaces.

'It's dual time zone,' Hutchinson explained. 'So you'll always know the time where you are and the time back home.'

Remmie smiled and swiftly put the watch on his wrist. 'It's incredible,' he said. 'Thank you very much. I shall cherish it.'

'It'll make sure you always remember us back home, wherever you are in the world,' Eileen chipped in.

A guard blew his whistle and the platform suddenly came to life with banging carriage doors and the hiss of the engine.

'Good luck then, Remmie,' Rom called out over the hubbub.

'Good luck yourself, Rom!' his brother shouted back with a wave. 'Next time I see you, I suppose I'll have to salute.'

Remmie laughed at the thought, and Rom could hear his laughter blending into the cacophony as the train pulled noisily away. He felt a sudden pang of regret deep in his belly. It felt like he was being separated from the other half of himself. He turned his head to follow the carriage until it had disappeared out of sight.

The following morning, it was Rom's turn to fly the nest. From the moment he awoke, he felt quietly terrified. Over a subdued breakfast, it was agreed that he would say his goodbyes at home and head for the bus on his own in an attempt to save his mother's already shattered nerves. As he hugged her and received a firm handshake from his father, it quickly became obvious that Eileen's attempt to preserve her stiff upper lip wasn't going to prove successful.

His father handed him a small leather box, just like the one he had presented to Remmie.

'I bet you can guess what it is,' Hutchinson said.

Rom opened it and put the watch on his wrist, just as Remmie had done. 'It's wonderful,' he said. 'Thank you both so much.'

Eileen attempted to speak, but her words descended into a sob.

'I know, I know,' Rom said. 'It'll ensure I remember you at home, wherever I am in the world.'

'That's right,' Eileen whispered, giving her son one final hug.

Rom had barely reached the end of the path, when he turned to see his mother crumple with deep sobs into her handkerchief. His father's reassuring arm came to her aid, and with his other hand he gestured for Rom to carry on. Closing the garden gate behind him, Rom gave one final wave and strolled along the road towards the bus stop.

He had already visited the Royal Navy's recruitment office in the city centre a couple of weeks previously, but today's return felt more formal, as he was asked to swear an oath of allegiance to King and Country in a room crowded with eager young recruits like himself.

'In an ideal world you'd do your training a bit closer to home,' the recruiting officer said, with a weary sigh. 'But it's wartime and you get what you're given, I'm afraid.'

Rom nodded.

'So, you'll be travelling by train down to East Sussex — a place called Hove, near Brighton, to join the HMS *King Alfred* training establishment, under the command of Captain John Pelly.' The officer looked up at Rom and smiled warmly as he lit a cigarette. 'Don't worry, old boy, Pelly's a decent sort. You'll like him.' He reached down and stamped a couple of documents. 'Just do exactly as you're told, keep on the right side of everyone, and you can't go far wrong.'

He handed the top document to Rom and gave him a wink. 'Good luck, son. My colleague in the far corner will furnish you with your rail ticket and they'll kit you out with your uniform in the next room.'

The journey down to East Sussex was long, and Rom's carriage was populated entirely by fellow new recruits. They all looked terrified. Rom looked down in bewilderment at his new dark blue sailor suit. He felt slightly ridiculous, as if he was about to take a lead part in *HMS Pinafore*.

The young men travelled together in silence for some time, listening to the rattle of the carriage, conscious that with every rumble of the wheels on the rails, they were being carried further and further from home and everything that was familiar to them.

After the first half hour, the more confident of the young recruits started chatting. Rom managed to strike up a halting conversation with a round-faced boy of about his own age who was sitting mournfully beside him. He introduced himself as Eric Smith, known to all as "Chubby".

'Good to meet you, er, Chubby,' Rom stammered, uncertain about the etiquette with the nickname.

'It's all right,' Chubby grinned, sensing his dilemma. 'I'm so used to it, I don't think I'd even respond to my real name anymore.'

'So, what do you know about King Alfred?' Rom asked, keen to move the conversation on.

'He was the first king of Wessex to make use of ships in defending his realm,' Chubby said, leaning back.

'I don't mean the king himself, I mean the training establishment.'

'Oh, I see,' Chubby said, a little disappointedly. 'And I haven't even had the chance to mention his burning the cakes. All I know about HMS *King Alfred* is that it's not been around very long. The Admiralty requisitioned the town's brand-new municipal swimming baths a few weeks back to set the place up, apparently.'

Rom laughed. 'That'll make us popular with the locals.'

'It's the least they can do for the war effort if you ask me,' Chubby said primly, before turning to the window and muttering, 'Bloody civilians.' He rested a cheek on his upturned fist, distorting his face a little as he gazed out pensively.

The first few days in Hove felt very peculiar — like a sort of surreal trip to the seaside. Rom and Chubby, along with a few dozen other young men, were billeted in the rather dour

Langfords Hotel, and their days were mostly spent helping Captain Pelly and his small staff to convert the building site into suitable training accommodation. The first week passed with them all decked out in overalls rather than uniform, labouring to clear the site of builders' rubble and help put the finishing touches to the spaces that would be their classrooms for the next twelve weeks.

An underground car park was swiftly converted into a series of unconvincing representations of different parts of a ship — a bridge, an engine room, a fo'c'sle. It took a bit of imagination, but with a few suitable props the transformation was complete. The swimming pool itself, empty of water, was covered over with wooden floorboards to create the main instructional hall, while the neighbouring restaurant and dance hall became the officers' wardroom. A small side space, originally intended for spa bathing, was rather piously converted into a sort of makeshift chapel.

A nearby school had been requisitioned and the first couple of weeks of formal training were spent in its classrooms, with Rom and the other recruits squeezed onto little wooden chairs that had been designed for children. By the time they arrived back at the main HMS *King Alfred* site on the seafront of Hove, the transformation had been completed and the men were able to knuckle down to the real business of learning about life at sea. There was so much for their brains to take on board in just three short months.

Some of the recruits had been members of the pre-war Royal Navy Volunteer (Supplementary) Reserve, which had been formed in 1936 for young men who were interested in yachting with half an eye on the potential for another global conflict just over the horizon. This gave them a pass for a fast-track course, and they quickly left their ordinary RNVR friends behind.

Despite his family's rich maritime heritage, Rom had never been sailing in his life. The closest he had come was a summer's afternoon rowing a little wooden boat on the lake at Sefton Park, and he hadn't been the most co-ordinated rower even then. Now he was expected to sit behind a desk and, by gazing at a blackboard, develop a thorough understanding of the sea and its ways, of navigation and manoeuvring, of the strange alchemy of sailing that seemed to involve an understanding of the wind's intentions and a deep comprehension of advanced physics.

The men were divided into four classes of 'officers under training', each class comprising thirty men — two classes of midshipmen and two of sub-lieutenants. Rank was determined by age — those under nineteen-and-a-half became midshipmen, those over became sub-lieutenants. Rom eyed the older members of the group with a pang of envy. It seemed absurd to him to base rank purely on age — especially such an arbitrary age as nineteen-and-a-half. Upon receiving their commission, the new officers also received their badges of rank — midshipmen wore a maroon lapel flash while sub-lieutenants wore a single 'wavy' gold stripe on their jacket cuffs. This was the origin of the RNVR's nickname of the "Wavy Navy".

Rom quickly got over the slight. After all, he told himself, in just a few short weeks all the men would emerge from the course as Temporary Acting Probationary Sub-Lieutenants, and they would be sent off for a few weeks further training at the Royal Naval College, Greenwich, before being posted operationally. Assuming they all cut the mustard, of course.

Captain Pelly himself was an endearing character, with a round, moonlike face and a balding head beneath his pristine cap. He seemed to have a fixed expression of concern — a combination of anguish and benevolence painted into his grey, frowning brows and the deep-set bags under his eyes. He had once been a first-class England cricketer, and was always keen to drop it into conversation — though he was less keen to mention he only ever played in one first-class match. In his defence, he had left behind a promising sporting career after joining the Navy before the First World War — a conflict in which he had seen plenty of active service, as well as losing a brother. As he got to know the old, tender-hearted captain, Rom realised that it was this loss and the reality of having lived to see another world war that had painted the worry lines deep into the old man's face.

It was Pelly himself who taught the cadets about the strategic intricacies of hunting U-boats — which had proven to be such a scourge to merchant shipping during the Great War.

'This time, things will be different,' Pelly assured them, rocking backwards and forwards as he lectured them. 'This time, you will have the great benefit of ASDIC. Who can tell me what ASDIC is?'

Chubby raised his hand. 'Sonar, sir?'

'That's right, Smith,' Pelly went on. 'The Yanks simply call it sonar. We call it ASDIC — an acronym for Anti-Submarine Detection Investigation Committee. The committee was set up after the last war to try to ensure that we would never again be held hostage by an unseen foe. An Anglo-French scientific group was formed, and all our top boffins put their heads together and spent twenty years developing this clever piece of kit.'

Pelly produced a large diagram that represented the basic components of the ASDIC system, and pinned the sheet to the wall behind him. He stood back, looked up at it and smiled, as if he was seeing it for the first time.

'The apparatus consists of an electronic sound-transmitting and sound-receiving unit, encased in this metal dome, which is fitted to the bottom of a ship's hull. The transmitter sends out high-frequency impulses — audible pings — that bounce back when they strike an object. Are you with me so far, chaps?'

There was a general murmur of assent across the room.

'These echoes, if you like, are picked up by the receiver, which is monitored by an operator who wears headphones to listen to the pinging of the machine. He also watches the fluctuations of a line traced on a moving sheet of paper. The time that elapses between transmission and reception indicates the range of the object, while the pitch tells him whether the object — the U-boat — is approaching or moving away.'

Rom looked across at Chubby, who was desperately scribbling down notes as Pelly spoke.

'It means, my boys —' Pelly leaned forward for dramatic emphasis — 'that one destroyer in this war, equipped with ASDIC technology, can do the work of a whole flotilla from the last war.' He smiled proudly and clearly enjoyed the appreciative murmurs that followed. 'But there are limitations,' he added, raising an apologetic hand. 'For a start, the ASDIC system only supplies the bearing of the U-boat, not its submerged depth. Also, the echoes bouncing off a U-boat can bear a striking resemblance to the echoes striking off a rock, a sunken wreck, a whale or even a school of fish. Even difference in temperature between the different layers of water can cause soundwave echoes. A decent ASDIC rating is worth his weight in gold, because he will develop a sort of sixth sense that allows him to recognise a real threat when it is pinging back at him through his headphones. But even with a veteran operator, ASDIC has a useful range of just one thousand five hundred yards, and its transmission operates in a narrow horizontal cone forward of the ship. So don't get too cocky, boys — these U-boat captains are clever, and they're already learning to simply operate outside that cone of detection.'

Rom took a long breath as the key messages of Pelly's ASDIC lesson percolated around his brain. What had begun as an uplifting lecture on how modern technology would neutralise the U-boat threat seemed to have fizzled out and culminated in a list of disappointing limitations. It was always like this with Pelly. He was forever attempting to make the prospect of naval warfare sound appealing, but when it came to it, he could never stop himself from revealing little glimpses of the horrors that lay ahead of the boys.

Rom looked around the room at the other cadets. Even Pelly seemed to have talked himself into a fit of ennui. He walked slowly to the window and gazed out for a moment at the trees that were waving in the wind like the masts of a ship pitching and rolling on the ocean. Eventually the old man broke the silence with a little cough. 'Did I ever tell you boys about the time I batted at Lords back in twenty-six?' he asked wistfully.

It was a small staff of training officers who worked under the benign leadership of Pelly. His general air of benevolence seemed to have rubbed off on all of these easy-going men, with one notable exception. Lieutenant Jeremy Sneyd was a grim, weasel-faced man with slick, jet-black hair combed back in such a way as to give his forehead undue prominence. The cadets' first experience of physical training — a merciless ten-mile cross-country run up to the Sussex Downs — had all the hallmarks of Sneyd's particular brand of sadism. From the start, his tactic seemed to be to pit the cadets against each other.

'Look at the state of you!' Sneyd shouted, already inexplicably angry as the cadets fell in on that grey, drizzly morning. 'We'll get you into shape and make men out of you.' His eyes studied the line of cadets with menace, pausing triumphantly when they reached Chubby. 'Are you up to the challenge, Fat Boy?' Sneyd spat out each word with venom, edging close to Chubby's already sweating face.

'Yes, Sir,' Chubby muttered.

'Pathetic,' Sneyd laughed to himself as he continued along the line of cadets. 'You will be running up to the Chattri Memorial. You can't miss it. Big thing on the Downs that memorialises the boys just like you who joined up in the last war and didn't make it home.' The two black beads of his eyes ran along the line. 'To make it interesting, lads, this will be a race. Five miles there, five miles back. Last one back does it again, while the rest of us eat lunch. Understood?'

The cadets gave a nervously muttered chorus of 'Yes, sir.'

'Well, go on then, girls, off you go,' Sneyd said. 'And remember, last one back is the Sissy.'

The cadets started to jog out towards the road.

'Don't forget you're racing each other!' Sneyd shouted after them, before adding a sly, 'Good luck, Fat Boy,' to Chubby, who was already at the back of the pack.

Rom was not unfit. He had been the star winger for his school's rugby team and had plenty of experience of cross-country running. But the steep climb up away from the coast in the rain made the run a truly miserable experience. By the time he reached the edge of the Downs, leaving the town below, he was struggling to find any additional energy in his leg muscles to make the final mile or more across the long, slippery grass. Some of the boys had raced on ahead; some he had long since left behind. When he reached the memorial itself, he was entirely alone, and knowing he was in the middle of the pack, he was happy to give himself a moment's rest before beginning the laborious descent back down the hill. He stood with his hands on his knees, his head stooping towards the grass as he tried to get his breath back. The stitch that had been twisting his abdomen for the last mile or two gradually eased, and at last he was able to lift his head and look out towards the bleak grey line of the sea far below. Even from this distance, it looked like a fearsome place to spend your life and he wondered how he could possibly have been so stupid as to volunteer for a life at sea.

Rom turned towards the memorial with its peculiar white domed roof and ornate columns. It looked like a chunk of the Taj Mahal had been bitten off and spat out here in the unlikely setting of the South Downs. He walked a little closer and read the words: *To the memory of all the Indian soldiers who gave their lives in the service of their King Emperor in the Great War.*

Rom rested against the memorial and looked back towards the sea. What a thing to do, to come all the way from the sun-kissed shores of India to fight in the mud-soaked trenches of the Western Front. 'Poor bastards,' he said under his breath. 'It must have felt like being transported to another world.'

Rom stretched the muscles in his legs and took a few deep breaths as he prepared to start running back towards the sea. But just as he was about to set off, a calm voice stopped him. 'My boy, my boy, you'll tire yourself out.'

Rom turned to see an elderly Sikh with a long white beard and a neatly folded orange turban on his head. 'At least finish catching your breath before you set off again. You know, I've watched all you poor boys race up here this morning. But you're the first one to stop and read the words engraved on the memorial.'

'I was just recovering from that hill,' Rom said.

'I know you were catching your breath, but it is a good sign that you stopped to look at the details. You showed compassion.'

Rom gave the old man a quizzical glance.

'You are training for the Royal Navy, are you not?'

Rom nodded. 'The RNVR.'

'Yes,' the Sikh said. 'If you are to be an officer in His Majesty's Royal Navy, taking note of the details and showing compassion are two things that will stand you in very good stead. One day, these qualities will save your life or the lives of those around you. Take it from one who knows about such things.'

Rom smiled. 'Good to know, sir.' He cast his eyes over the man once again. 'I had no idea that the Indians fought in the trenches last time around.'

The old man nodded. 'People quickly forget such things. Many fought, many died. Some came back and died here — in the hospital at Brighton. A funeral pyre was held up here on this very spot where the memorial was later erected. Hindus, Sikhs, Muslims, Christians, all dying for King and Empire, just like you British boys.'

Rom nodded. 'I had better get back down that hill or my officer will have my guts for garters.'

The old man laughed. 'Guts for garters, yes indeed. But remember,' he added, his laughter stopping as suddenly as it had arrived, 'remember the details. That is where you will see the face of God — the eternal Waheguru. Compassion is the place where God is. And, of course, the devil is in the details.'

Rom reached out and shook the little old man's hand. 'Thank you, sir. Sound advice,' he said, before turning and starting the run back down the hill.

By the time he skidded back through the gates of the training centre, Rom was once again panting hard in an attempt to catch his breath. He could feel the muscles quivering in his mud-splattered legs. But he was relieved to look up and see Sneyd surrounded by just half a dozen of his fellow cadets, all looking similarly dishevelled.

They waited there at the front of the building as each cadet returned, panting and resting his hands on his knees. There was sinister malevolence in Sneyd's eyes.

'He's loving this,' Rom whispered to Thompson, the cadet standing beside him.

The young man frowned. 'Too bloody much, if you ask me,' he whispered back.

Finally, all the cadets were back, bar one.

'Surprise, surprise,' Sneyd grumbled. 'It's going to be Fat Boy who is going to miss his lunch. No harm there then, eh, lads? He's probably got enough fat on him to keep him going for a year.'

The wait was interminable from when the penultimate runner arrived back to when poor Chubby appeared at the gate, his face an alarming crimson, and his hair caked back against his scalp by the rain. He stopped halfway through the entrance and slipped down onto his haunches as he struggled to catch his breath.

Rom gathered his courage. 'I think Smith is unwell, sir,' he said with brisk confidence. 'Shall I take him to the sick bay?'

Sneyd laughed. 'Sick bay? What do you think this is, bloody prep school?'

Rom looked at the floor but seethed inside.

'No, Fat Boy has a promise to keep, doesn't he, lads?'

None of the cadets were joining in with the lieutenant's sadistic game, which only seemed to anger him further.

Chubby staggered across to join the group. 'Sorry, sir,' he gasped. 'I fell a couple of times. Twisted my ankle. It was slippery, you see.'

Sneyd tutted loudly. 'No, that'll never do. You see, in the Navy, you are going to need to be able to traverse slippery surfaces without falling on your arse. Otherwise, you'll be rolling around like Billy Bunter on every wave-lashed deck, won't you, Fat Boy?'

Chubby was clearly close to tears. His bottom lip was wobbling as he stood there gasping for breath. The other cadets all looked at the floor.

'Well, go on then,' Sneyd said, with considerable glee. 'We're all going for lunch. You are going to do the run again — this time, without falling on your arse.'

Chubby nodded and turned slowly. It was clearly all he could do to shuffle towards the gate with a pitiful jog.

'Detail and compassion,' Rom said, under his breath.

'What's that, Hutchinson?' Sneyd snapped.

Rom started to jog after Chubby. 'Just realised I also slipped over, so I'd better do it again too, sir,' he called over his shoulder.

Sneyd watched with his mouth open, guppy-like, as his beady eyes followed Rom's figure moving rapidly towards Chubby.

Then Thompson started to run after them. 'Me too, sir,' he called out.

A moment later a third cadet followed, then a fourth, and before Sneyd could utter another word, the whole group was running back out of the gate towards the distant Chattri Memorial.

'Detail and compassion, lads,' Rom called over his shoulder, when he saw his fellow cadets catching up behind. 'Detail and bloody compassion!'

*

Sneyd was gone when the cadets returned to HMS *King Alfred* a few hours later — all truly exhausted by their double cross-country run. But Rom knew that Sneyd would not forget this easily — there would be a black mark against his name in Sneyd's mind and he had quite prepared himself to replace Chubby as the object of Sneyd's malice.

Chubby himself had only got as far as the outskirts of Hove the second time around, and had collapsed against a brick wall. Rom, who had been running with him, man-handled him around the corner into an alleyway and told him to wait quietly and rest. He would do the run on his behalf and collect him on the way back down. Nobody would be any the wiser, he assured his exhausted friend.

The old Sikh had gone when Rom finally reached the monument for the second time that day, though his wise words were still ringing in Rom's ears as he paused on top of the hill to catch his breath again, fearing he might vomit. He managed to ride the wave of nausea by looking out at the distant blue horizon — just as his father had told him to do if he ever got seasick. After a moment's rest, he felt his stomach resettle and he turned to begin the long jog back down the hill.

Sneyd was as good as his word in one respect, at least — there was no lunch for any of the cadets that day, and in the afternoon, they were set the not inconsiderable challenge of stitching nametags into every item of their uniform. Rom, whose capacity with a needle and thread was non-existent, looked around enviously at those with shorter names, as he found himself having to stitch around countless slips containing the long words "Romulus Hutchinson".

'Why couldn't they just print Rom?' he grumbled.

Chubby, now recovered from his morning's exertions, chuckled, reached across and took the needle and thread from Rom's hands. 'Let me do the honours,' he smiled. 'I've already finished all of mine.'

Rom looked around Chubby's considerable bulk at the neat pile of clothes on his bunk, each folded pristinely and each featuring a neatly stitched-on nametag.

'My father is a tailor,' he added by way of explanation. 'And his father before him. As I will be, if I make it through this war. I've been sewing in the back of the family shop for as long as I can remember.'

'What a skill to have,' Rom said, willingly giving up his burden and patting Chubby on the shoulder. 'Thanks, Chubby. I owe you one.'

'Not at all, Rom. After all, I certainly owed you one for your support this morning. I swear, it would have killed me if I'd had to complete that run a second time. This is the very least I can do.'

Rom nodded and patted his jacket pocket in search of his cigarettes. He hoped that smoking might take the edge off his hunger. He offered one to Chubby, who declined cheerfully, the needle held between his front teeth as he reached for a pair of scissors.

'I wonder what new hell Sneyd is preparing for us by way of punishment for tomorrow morning?' Rom muttered as he strode across to the window, blew a cloud of smoke through the opening and watched as it was lifted on the sea breeze.

The following day the cadets were taking part in their usual navigation training, which consisted somewhat surreally of cycling around the cricket pitch with a compass, and stopping every few seconds to communicate with a fellow cadet on the other side of the field by using semaphore flags. Rom was following the instructions of Chubby, whose crisply waved flags had until that moment delivered him with precision to each coordinate. Sneyd was overseeing the operation, which was being carried out multiple times simultaneously by other cadets at even spacings across the pitch.

Rom was just beginning to feel a little smug about the ease with which he and Chubby had worked their way through the challenge, when he looked up to see Captain Pelly striding purposefully along the edge of the pitch. He stopped alongside Sneyd, the senior officer's eyes scanning the field and watching the manoeuvres of each cadet with keen interest. It was at this critical moment, as Rom paused to look over once again towards Chubby's semaphore flags, that he felt the bicycle judder beneath him. In the moment it took him to cast his eyes down towards the handlebars, the front wheel had dislodged with the peremptory ping of the fastening screw. As Rom fell unceremoniously face-forward over the handlebars towards the ground, the wheel itself rolled away until it too tumbled onto the grass.

By the time he had picked himself up and dusted himself down, Rom could feel the flush of blood colouring his cheeks. He looked across to Chubby, who had stopped his signals, but whose eyes were looking across at him in bewilderment. Behind him he could see Captain Pelly glaring in an uncharacteristic rage and even at that distance, he could sense the glint in Sneyd's eyes as a grin crossed his face. As Rom attempted to extricate himself from the broken bicycle chassis, he tripped and fell once again face-first towards the mud. He didn't need to look back up to hear Sneyd's guffawing, and the outraged Pelly calling, 'What the devil is he up to?'

The other cadets were now overtaking Chubby and Rom's advantage. Rom walked across and picked up the offending wheel before returning to the bicycle. He looked from wheel to chassis for a moment or two, scanning the ground to try to find the missing screw. Eventually he looked across apologetically at Chubby and shrugged his shoulders. He carried the chassis in one hand and the wheel in the other and returned to the edge of the pitch where a grinning Sneyd was waiting.

'You wouldn't know anything about this, would you, sir?' Rom asked angrily.

'Not such a young revolutionary now, are you, boy?' Sneyd sneered.

'It's hardly fair,' Rom muttered, as he tried to regain his composure.

'All is fair in love and war, eh, Hutchinson?' the training officer tittered.

Pelly marched across to the pair. 'What on earth is going on?' he bellowed.

'This young cadet failed to check his equipment properly before engaging in the exercise, sir,' Sneyd announced as he stood to attention.

Pelly looked from training officer to cadet with a frown. 'Bad business,' he muttered. 'Makes the whole outfit look ridiculous. Really, Sneyd, you must do a better job of preparing your men for an exercise.' Without another word, the captain marched back towards the building, leaving Sneyd frowning vengefully towards Rom and the broken bicycle.

'As you say, sir,' Rom said with a shrug. 'I suppose all is fair in love and war.'

CHAPTER THREE

The next morning Rom received two letters. The first was from his mother. His father's ship had set sail once again for the west coast of Africa and she was alone at home for the first time in her life. Her letter positively shook with the desolation of an empty nest. The second letter was from Remmie. He seated himself in a shaft of sunlight that was falling through the window and illuminating half of his bed.

Training Ship Vindicatrix
Old Arm
Sharpness Docks, Gloucestershire
31 October 1939

Dear Rom,

I hope all is going well with your training. Life here at Training Ship Vindicatrix is quite something. The rumour is that this ship was sunk in the last war and sat at the bottom of the ocean off Cape Horn before being raised and landlocked here as a training ship. I'm not sure how true that is, but it wouldn't surprise me — the place is a bit of a dump.

They're certainly keeping us occupied learning all kinds of nonsense that we'll probably never need once we're at sea — there is a lot of ropework, boat handling, signalling and general fiddling about with a compass, but the vast majority of our time seems to revolve around cleaning the old barky's decks. But it's all decent fun in its own way. I'm keeping my chin up. I can't wait to actually get on a real ship, though, and start to see a bit of the world beyond the River Severn.

The gaffer here does a decent job of trying to make life on board as close to actual sea service as possible, with watches kept night and day, time signalled on the ship's bell and even navigation lamps trimmed and lighted, though we never actually move anywhere. It's a bit like when we used to play make-believe as children. You have to use your imagination quite a bit.

The food in the mess is pretty good, which makes a big difference. Still, some of the lads are already pretty homesick, but most are loving it here. They're a nice bunch on the whole. There is one Cockney lad called Timpson who has us all in stitches with his wisecracks. There's a plan afoot for us to all head into Gloucester for a few jars when we get some shore leave. It would make a nice change to get to know the lads away from this queer old stage set of a ship.

I hope you are also having the time of your life down there on the south coast with all those posh lads. Don't forget to polish your medals.

Go steady, Rom.

Remmie

Rom smiled to himself as he read through the letter a second time, leaning back against the wall and lighting a cigarette as he tried to imagine his twin brother scrubbing the decks and fiddling with a compass. He put the letter down on his bed and walked across to the window. Down below he could see Sneyd once again prancing across the parade ground as if he was conducting the changing of the guard outside Buckingham Palace.

It sounded like Remmie was having some fun over on the Severn, while life at King Alfred was increasingly onerous under the constant beady gaze of Sneyd. Rom knew that having got himself on the wrong side of the greasy little sadist, there would be no escaping his tormentor until he was away from Hove. Just a few more weeks and he would be heading to Greenwich, he reassured himself. All he had to do was keep out of Sneyd's line of sight as much as he possibly could and try to avoid irritating him any further. Ultimately, he needed Sneyd on side enough to ensure he was able to pass out.

But he needn't have worried. As so often happened in this world, the solution Rom needed presented itself to him the moment he stopped looking for it.

Just like his brother, Rom had been looking forward to getting a bit of leave to go into town for a pint or two. When it came, he was among a group of half a dozen cadets exploring the pubs of Hove on a wet Thursday evening. Nobody seemed to notice that most of them were under the legal age to drink. After a few hours of drowning their sorrows, when the last orders bell rang, Rom was ready for his bed.

'No, no, my round,' Chubby announced, as Rom began to put on his overcoat.

'I've had enough, thanks, pal — you stay for one more. I can barely keep my eyes open.'

Chubby looked momentarily crestfallen, but shrugged and extended his offer once again to the group.

'I'll have one more drink with you, Chubby,' Johnson smiled. This brought a rumble of approving noises from everyone else around the table.

'Your good health, gentlemen,' Rom said with a smile as he finished the dregs in his glass, adjusted his hat, and waved to Chubby, who was already standing at the bar.

Rom stepped out of the convivial atmosphere of the pub and into the chill of the autumnal night air. The earlier rain had cleared, but there was a crispness to the breeze now that felt like the first real sign of winter. He walked across the dimly lit town towards HMS *King Alfred* and the down-at-heel hotel beyond, cutting through an area of municipal parkland to spare his tired legs the extra few hundred yards involved in keeping to the main roads.

The park was shrouded in darkness. He could barely see clearly enough to keep his feet on the path. He continued vaguely in the right direction, reassured by the sound of his boots crunching on the stones. In the stillness of this setting, with the metronome-like march of his own footsteps to calm him, he could feel his breathing easing and he yawned at the thought of making it back to his bunk. He stopped a moment and was reaching into his inside pocket for his packet of cigarettes when the stillness of the night was broken by an unexpected rustle coming from a nearby bush. A man's figure emerged from the undergrowth, silhouetted in the moonlight.

Rom caught his breath, a shudder of fear coursing through him at the unexpected appearance. But as the man brushed himself down and walked furtively towards the path, Rom recognised the silhouette as Sneyd. Rom took a moment to breathe out, calming his nerves in an instant, before calling out to the training officer. 'Are you quite all right, sir?'

Sneyd's face flicked round towards Rom in an instant. His normally beady eyes were wide with horror at the sight of the young cadet. Sneyd walked quickly across to Rom, patting down his greased hair as he approached. 'Not a word to anyone, Hutchinson, do you understand?'

'Sir?' Rom asked, puzzled. At that moment the bush rustled for a second time, and a young man emerged. He was in the distinctive sailor suit uniform of a Royal Navy able seaman, but appeared to be fastening his belt as he wandered towards the path. The young man glared at Rom as he passed quickly by before disappearing into the darkness.

Rom struck a match and took his time lighting his cigarette. The slightest hint of a grin emerged. 'Of course, sir,' he said, forcing a little cough to clear his throat. 'I can be the very soul of discretion.'

The officer nodded briskly, his face still crimson.

'That is,' Rom added matter-of-factly, 'as long as I can rely on your discretion when it comes to my assessment.' He paused. The silence between the two men seemed electrically charged, before Rom added a final, 'Sir.'

Sneyd simply gave another of his brisk nods, before turning on his heel and marching away into the night. Rom smiled to himself, took another long drag on his cigarette, and carried on walking at a more leisurely pace towards the gate.

Rom's training became remarkably straightforward after that. He was as good as his word and never mentioned Sneyd's secret predilections to another soul. Sneyd, in his turn, was like a different man. Never again did he give Rom or Chubby — or any of their fellow cadets — a hard time over anything. It was as if he had undergone a personality change overnight, much to the bewilderment of everyone at King Alfred. Rom smiled to himself as he heard the others discussing this sudden shift in temperament in their training officer, but he kept his lips tightly shut and even started to feel sorry for Sneyd. It was as if the venom he had so often inflicted on others had been Ingested into his own brooding soul.

Sneyd nodded tellingly as he shook Rom's hand following the cadets' passing out parade. *No doubt he's relieved to see me go*, Rom thought to himself. He wondered if Sneyd would return to his old vindictive ways the moment his group left and a new group of cadets arrived at Hove. Or had the hard edges been knocked off the older man for good by the shock of seeing one of his own cadets in the darkness of that park?

But Sneyd quickly faded from his thoughts when Rom passed out of Greenwich, ready to begin his new life at sea.

*

When he had written to his brother and his mother, Remmie had tried to keep his letters light-hearted. He wanted to give the impression that he was having a fine time down on the banks of the Severn. But it had been far from the truth.

The young merchant seamen cadets had been divided into two watches, and on alternate mornings one watch cleaned the decks while the other took part in physical exercises. Remmie wasn't sure which he hated more. Cleaning the ship included slopping out the sewage buckets that had been used during the night by his 150 fellow cadets. But the physical exercise involved running a couple of miles to the Severn Bridge and a couple of miles back, with a training officer running at the rear and whipping stragglers with a branch. Upon returning to the ship, panting for breath, there was a row of buckets waiting. The boys were lined up in two rows, and one line dipped their buckets into the canal and proceeded to throw the filthy water over his opposite number. But there was no laughter. The first line knew that they had the same humiliation coming, when the other line dipped their buckets into the canal.

Remmie found this sort of thing baffling. Why was it necessary to put them through these sorts of indignities? There was no alternative to pure discipline — a principle that Remmie could appreciate, given the importance of discipline at sea. But there were occasions when he wished he could be somewhere — anywhere — else, other than on the Training Vessel *Vindicatrix*.

One such occasion came on a freezing winter night. Talking after lights-out was a punishable offence, and when a training officer heard a whisper and called for the offending cadet to show himself, nobody was forthcoming.

'All right, lads, if that's how we're going to play it, all of you out,' the officer growled. All twenty of the cadets who had been sleeping in the space were marched onto the deck to scrub — or "holy stone" — the quarter deck on their knees for the next hour.

After five weeks of this kind of punishment, Remmie was relieved to see the end in sight. He had mastered the technicalities of 'boxing the compass', he had learned all his knots and splicing, he had memorised the contents and correct stowing of gear in a lifeboat, and he had proved his ability to row a boat across the docks to collect the day's bread supply from the bakery.

Remmie's brain had soaked up all of these new skills like a sponge, and he was confident that he knew what he needed to know to begin his life at sea. But that didn't prevent him feeling the fear in the pit of his stomach when he was summoned to the captain's cabin to be questioned. This face-to-face quick-fire test had scuppered many young trainees' hopes of escaping Sharpness Docks, and Remmie was keen to stay focused. He felt a bead of sweat trickling down his right temple as he answered the captain's random questions on everything he had learned in the previous five weeks.

The captain placed a piece of wood on his desk and told Remmie it was his boat, that the wind was coming from over his shoulder, then instructed him to give the sail and rudder orders to navigate the boat to the other side of the desk. At regular intervals, the captain would get to his feet and blow on Remmie's face from a different side of the desk, shouting, 'Change in wind direction!'

On the fifth tack, Remmie's mind raced, and he hesitated for a moment. The captain leaned over the desk, picked up the piece of wood and slammed it down, roaring, 'Think quickly, boy!'

Remmie took a slow, deep breath and regained his composure. He turned the vessel correctly and smiled as the piece of wood finally reached the harbour on the distant shore of the far side of the captain's desk.

'Good man,' the captain said fondly. 'Now, what would you do if your mast and sails blew away?'

'I would row, sir,' Remmie said, uncertain if it was the answer the captain had been hoping for. But the old man nodded contentedly.

'Well, that's you done, Hutchinson,' the captain said, reaching forward to shake his hand. 'You can have a few days of leave, then you can report to the *John Holt* office in Liverpool to be assigned your first ship on Monday morning.' He patted Remmie on the shoulder as he turned to leave. 'Enjoy it, lad,' he whispered. 'Don't forget to enjoy it.'

CHAPTER FOUR

There seemed to be no sign of any leave for Rom. He was directed towards an underground railway station across London, where in the docklands of the East End he was to meet his new captain for the first time. His time in Greenwich had been dull. A cold springy bed at night and during the day countless hours of studying and parading and stodgy meals of pie and mash. Christmas had been a spartan affair that had passed almost unnoticed. He was restless throughout his time there — desperate to get onboard an actual ship; desperate to see the sea and to feel adventure in the breeze. As 1940 dawned, he was more restless than ever and felt nothing but relief to finally pass out and to be stepping through the grimy backstreets of the capital, butterflies fluttering in his belly at the thought of catching his first glimpse of the G-Class destroyer to which he had been assigned, HMS *Grenade*.

Rom knew how lucky he was. To get a commission on a destroyer had been his dream — but he had equally been fully prepared to spend the next few years on a corvette, bouncing around the Atlantic with barely enough elbow room on the bridge to raise his binoculars to his eyes.

Grenade was in port being refitted and he was to meet the captain in a shed in the dockyards overlooking the ship. He asked for directions from a little, bespectacled man in the gatehouse, who looked up from his newspaper for just long enough to nod vaguely in the direction and mutter, 'Cabin 21.' Rom thanked the chap and pulled his bag back onto his shoulder, treading carefully between the ropes and chains that littered the dockside. He turned a sharp corner to find the vessel that would be his home for the next few months, ingloriously raised in a dry dock, almost hidden in the shadows of the neighbouring Victorian warehouses.

A wave of emotion broke through his chest. Even in her current inelegant position, her grey hull standing high and dry and sparks fanning out at various points from welding rods, she was unmistakably a thing of beauty. Her starboard bow was split into two clean levels with straight rails above which rose the bridge like a tentative frown, and a pair of reclining funnels behind with guns mounted both fore and aft. There was a section of scaffolding alongside her, where two men were repainting the pennant number on her bow — H86.

'Hutchinson?'

Rom turned towards where his name was being called by a man standing at the top of an exterior wooden staircase, leading from a two-storey cabin. Commander Richard Courtenay-Boyle RN was a tall, confident-looking man in his mid-forties. Flecks of grey showed in the sides of his hair beneath the line of his cap, distinguishing marks that suggested significant years of service at sea.

Rom straightened his back and strode towards him. He put down his bag and saluted. His new captain smiled warmly and returned the salute. 'Sub-Lieutenant Romulus Hutchinson, reporting for duty, sir.'

'Welcome,' Courtenay-Boyle beamed, giving Rom a friendly pat on the shoulder. 'It's always good to have new chaps onboard. You RNVR boys are always keen.' His eyes moved up and down Rom for a moment, assessing him. Then in one crisp movement, he turned towards the ship's enormous grey expanse. 'And here she is, HMS *Grenade* — a trusty vessel if ever you saw one. Though we've all had a few rather trying months, I don't mind telling you. Hopefully it'll be smoother sailing from here on in. Anyway, she's had a full refit, so the old girl will be all tarted up for your arrival.'

Rom gazed up at the ship. 'What happened, sir?'

Courtenay-Boyle looked momentarily nonplussed.

'You mentioned a trying few months.'

'Ah,' said the captain with a grin. 'One thing and another. You know how it is. When war broke out, we were still in Alexandria. We, along with the entire flotilla, were transferred to the Western Approaches Command in Plymouth. Then in November there was an accidental collision between *Grenade* and the flotilla leader, *Grenville*. So she was in for repairs until December. Then we were assigned contraband control duties in The Downs off the east Kent coast. Then *Grenville* struck a mine last month. We and *Griffin* rescued one hundred and seventeen men out of the water. No sooner had we got *Grenville*'s men back to London than I heard we were going in for more work.'

Rom nodded.

The captain looked back towards the ship and continued, 'A lot has changed in the last five years since she was launched. The Admiralty is trying to give her a fighting chance of keeping up with the new classes of destroyers.'

'Well, she looks fine to me, sir,' Rom heard himself gushing. He winced.

Courtenay-Boyle laughed. 'She'll do. She's nippy enough. She can look after herself too. Four quick-firing 4.7-inch Mark IX guns in single mounts.' He pointed at different places on the ship. 'We call them A, B, X, and Y.'

Rom's eyes worked across the ship swiftly as he tried to take everything in.

'All we need now is a bit more decent luck in her,' the captain said. 'Though the Admiralty assures me that's all part of the refit.'

'I hope so, sir,' Rom said.

'Absolutely. Now, listen, what do people call you? We can't use the name Romulus in the wardroom each evening.'

'Rom is fine, sir.'

'Rom it is. Good man.' Courtenay-Boyle slapped Rom's shoulder once again and turned to walk back up the steps. 'She'll be good to go very soon. Take a couple of days' leave and be back here for 0600 hours on Tuesday.' He gave a shooing motion. 'Go on, run free, my boy. The bright lights of London are that way.'

Rom briefly considered getting a room at the seamen's mission in the docks, but after taking one look at it, he decided he would much rather splash out on a hotel room. He found a place in a drab corner of Soho that was cheap. The elderly woman behind the counter handed him a room key and nodded towards the staircase.

'Fifth floor,' she muttered.

He dropped his bag in the room and went straight out to find somewhere to have a drink, but immediately became diverted by the city around him. Rom wandered first to Trafalgar Square, pausing to examine Nelson's Column like a tourist. He thought for a while about the great hero of Trafalgar. He wondered if Nelson had imagined all of this memorialising as he lay dying on the deck of the *Victory*.

He turned away from the square and his feet took him across St James's Park. There was an occasional man in uniform, like himself, and a few men in civvies — older chaps mostly. But the vast majority of people in the park were women and children. A couple of the children carried gas masks in boxes on strings as well as school satchels. But otherwise, there was little sign of war.

He reached the park gates, crossed the Mall and paused briefly in front of Buckingham Palace. The royal standard wasn't flying, so he guessed the king was elsewhere. He passed on through Green Park and stood for a moment, watching the double-decker buses negotiate their way along Piccadilly. He felt very young, yet at the same time unspeakably aged by the very prospect of going to war.

He thought about boarding the ship and leaving all of this behind in just a few short days. Death hovered in his mind as it had never done before. He walked towards Bond Street and imagined all of this bustle continuing without him. Did it matter, he wondered, that he must at some point cease completely? Did he resent it? Or was it not just a little consoling to believe that even if he died, all of this life on the streets of London would live on?

In an Oxford Street stationers' shop he bought writing paper then strolled back down Regent Street and negotiated the crowded pavements of Piccadilly Circus, before finally remembering why he had come out in the first place and slipping into a bar on the edge of Leicester Square.

It was quiet, with just a few other customers — including, he noticed, a few other young RNVR officers. He bought a pint of beer and settled himself at a table near the window. He checked the surface of the table for sticky patches, before taking out the writing paper and reaching into his pocket for his pen. He would send one last letter home to his mother, before boarding the ship.

He took a sip of his beer while he considered what to write. It was difficult to know quite what to say.

Dear Mother,

I have been given a couple of days' leave in London while my ship finishes a refit in the docks. She's a marvellous thing — a G-Class destroyer, just like the one Remmie and I saw once in the Mersey, before the war. I hope Remmie and Father are safe and well. Father must be halfway to Lagos by now and I suppose Remmie will be about to join ship too. I hope you will be all right, Mother, and will not worry too much about us lads as we ride the ocean waves.

Your loving son,
Rom

He read it through a couple of times, before folding it into an envelope, scribbling his home address and searching his wallet until he found a stamp. As he was rummaging, one of the young RNVR officers who had been standing at the bar approached him.

'I can stand you a pint if you're short, chum,' the man said.

Rom looked up at him and attempted to explain that he hadn't been looking in his wallet for loose change, but it all came out in a jumble of words, and before he knew it the friendly sub-lieutenant was back at the bar ordering two pints of beer.

'Mind if I join you?' he asked, as he placed one of the pints down before Rom.

'Not at all.' Rom offered a hand across the table. 'Hutchinson. Everyone calls me Rom.'

'Gordon,' the other man said softly. 'I noticed the mark of the Wavy Navy.' He pointed at the embroidered lines on the arm of Rom's uniform. 'Me too.'

'Yes,' Rom said. 'I'm just out of King Alfred. Waiting for my first ship to be refitted.'

'I came through King Alfred,' Gordon said. 'Passed out a few months back. I'm on my first shore leave. Only two days. It's jolly nice to stretch one's legs. I'm on a corvette.'

'I've been assigned to a G-Class destroyer, for my sins.'

'Lucky sod,' Gordon said. 'We watch those things racing past us and dream of having that much power. Or that much room.'

'She is a big beast.'

'You'll have your work cut out on the bridge of a destroyer, mind,' he said. 'You'd better enjoy your downtime while you can.' Gordon raised the remainder of his pint and made to head back to his shipmates at the bar.

'Thank you for the drink,' Rom said. 'I'll buy you one back next time we meet.'

'I'll hold you to that,' Gordon said. 'It's a small world out there.'

Gordon turned to go, but Rom raised a hand to stop him.

'Just a minute,' he said. 'What's it really like out there?'

Gordon frowned and glanced out at the bustle of the West End streets.

'Not out there,' Rom laughed. 'Out *there*. On the convoys.'

Gordon looked to the ground, took a deep breath, and with a considered smile reached across the table and patted Rom on the shoulder. 'You'll be fine, old boy. You'll be absolutely fine.'

Rom nodded and raised his glass as his new friend turned and walked back to the bar. Rom then finished off his pint in one satisfying gulp and headed back out into the daylight, in search of a post box. He found one just around the corner, in front of one of the big flashy cinemas. A chisel-jawed Clark Gable was glaring down at him from a poster. Somehow, dropping the letter into the post box made everything feel official. It was really happening. He really was going to sea. For a moment the boisterous West End crowds around him seemed to slow down. The rag-tag collection of soldiers, sailors and airmen walking towards Piccadilly were enjoying their leave, some with their arms drunkenly around each other's shoulders, some arm-in-arm with women wearing high heels and red lipstick. For a moment, they all morphed into the white-tipped waves of an angry ocean.

Rom stood alone and looked out at an endless expanse of sea — brutal and awesome.

Two days later, when Rom made his way back to the docks and the waiting ship, his nervousness had gone entirely. He just wanted to get on with it — to get out to sea and start doing the job he had spent so many weeks training to do, so many weeks thinking about, so many sleepless nights pondering.

The dry dock was strikingly empty when he reached it and the old man on the gate, who gave a nod of recognition as he looked up from his newspaper and pointed Rom to one of the farthermost quays a quarter of a mile away.

He shouldered his bag and strode off in the direction the old man had indicated. The sun had emerged from behind a cloud, and it felt warm on his back, like a good omen. He didn't need to walk far through the docklands before the familiar outline of HMS *Grenade* came into view — frowning and angular, like a prize boxer waiting to be announced into the ring. Rom smiled. *Grenade* was ready to sail, and so was he.

Remmie looked up at the ship that his father had briefly captained just a few months before. He had never imagined when he waited on the quayside for his father's homecoming that he would eventually serve on the very same ship. Its distinctive bright red funnel, tipped with a line of black, stood out in stark contrast to the freshly painted grey hull.

Remmie turned to find an older seaman standing beside him.

'I'm going to guess that you're the new deckhand?'

'Remmie Hutchinson,' he said, reaching out to shake the older man's hand.

'Ah, an illustrious name indeed. I thought I recognised your face. How's your father?'

'He's well, thank you.'

'I'm Able Seaman Tommy Scarisbrick. They call me Scaggs.'

'The grey isn't an undercoat?' Remmie asked, turning back to the ship.

'Sadly not. She's going to look this dour for the duration. They're even going to tone down the funnel colours, so I'm told.' Scaggs shrugged. 'But anything that means we're less of a sitting target for those bastard U-boats is a good thing by me.'

'I'll say,' Remmie agreed.

'You look nervous. First ship?'

Remmie nodded. 'Straight off the training ship.'

'You needn't be nervous. We're a friendly bunch on the *John Holt*, as I'm sure your father must have already told you.'

'It's the U-boats that worry me more than the crew,' Remmie said wryly.

'Well, they are less friendly, that's true enough,' Scaggs admitted with a chuckle. 'If this war goes anything like the last one, we'll be needing to watch our backs constantly. The Krauts have form for some pretty merciless behaviour when it comes to torpedoing merchant ships — and liners, for that matter. Remember the *Lusitania*?'

Remmie shook his head.

'No, you're too young of course,' Scaggs said. 'But you don't need to be worrying about that sort of thing. We have the

Royal Navy boys to worry about all that. All we have to do is keep going — getting stuff in and out. Simple as that.'

Captain Cecil Gordon Hime was a distinguished-looking character, who gave the impression of being far older than his years. He was unexpectedly standing on deck at the top of the gangplank, causing Remmie to drop his bag in surprise and give a flustered salute.

'Cadet Remus Hutchinson, reporting for duty, sir.'

'Ah, the new boy,' Hime said, looking Remmie up and down with a studied frown. 'What kind of a name is Remus?'

'People call me Remmie, sir.'

'I will call you Hutchinson,' Hime muttered sternly. He spoke with a soft-edged Birkenhead accent, and he reminded Remmie of his own father. 'It's your first ship?'

Remmie nodded.

'Ah, then you'll fall in love with her.' Hime's voice softened. 'We all fall in love with our first ship. I certainly remember my first ship. She was a thing of wonder. Not like these modern steamers. This one is five thousand tons of ugliness. But she does her job and she does it well. Do you know why that is, Hutchinson?'

'No, sir,' Remmie's voice quivered nervously.

'She does her job well, because we all do our jobs well. No room for slacking on this ship, understood?'

'Understood, sir.'

Hime nodded in a considered way, and gestured towards the fo'c'sle. 'Go and make yourself known to the chief mate, George Daniels, and he'll show you your cabin and so on.'

'Yes, sir.' Remmie saluted again, picked up his bag and turned to walk away. As he did so, the captain called his name once again.

'You're Bill Hutchinson's lad, aren't you?'

'Yes, sir.'

Hime nodded and played with the cuffs of his uniform. 'Don't think for one moment it makes you special, son, will you?'

CHAPTER FIVE

Two hundred miles away, Rom couldn't believe his eyes as he turned onto the quay. There, standing in the shadow of the destroyer, a familiar rotund outline caught his attention. It couldn't be, could it? The figure turned towards him.

'Rom! Don't tell me you've been assigned to this old girl too?'

A smile broke out across Rom's face. 'Chubby, dear boy! I certainly have. We're going to be working together!'

'Delighted.' Chubby gave Rom a friendly pat on the shoulder and turned to pick up his bag from the ground. 'In that case, I suppose we had better make our presence known.'

They turned at the sound of a pair of boots confidently striding towards them along the quayside.

'Excellent!' Courtenay-Boyle bellowed. 'I see you chaps have met.'

Rom and Chubby stood to attention and saluted. As they were doing so, another officer strolled across to join the group.

'Carter — these are the two new subs,' the captain said, before turning to formally introduce the man. 'Andrew Carter, your first lieutenant.'

The new recruits saluted once again.

'Never mind all that,' Carter said, with a dismissive wave of the hand. 'Save it for the captain.'

'You can save it for the Admiral as far as I'm concerned,' Courtenay-Boyle laughed. 'We try to run a friendly bridge on *Grenade*.'

Carter reached out to shake the hands of both men.

'Good to meet you, sir,' Rom said. 'I've been so looking forward to this day.'

Carter smiled.

'It felt as if we were in training for a lifetime,' Chubby wheezed.

Carter and Courtenay-Boyle both laughed. 'You Wavy Navy boys don't know you're born,' Carter said. 'How many weeks were you at King Alfred?'

'Twelve, sir,' Chubby said.

'Twelve weeks!' Carter laughed again. 'As long as all that? I've had blisters longer than that.'

'Not to worry,' Courtenay-Boyle said, clapping his hands together and rubbing them in a gesture of determination. 'Your real learning starts from the moment you walk up that gangplank.'

Rom and Chubby exchanged a glance.

Courtenay-Boyle nodded. 'Come on then, subs, let's be getting you both aboard. She's looking really rather wonderful after her refit. I don't think you chaps will be at all disappointed in your first vessel.'

Carter stepped back to allow the captain to lead the way up the gangplank, which bounced with each of Courtenay-Boyle's enthusiastic bounds. 'Come on, come on!' he bellowed. 'There is work to be done, lads.'

Once on board, Courtenay-Boyle said that he would leave them with Carter and strode off purposefully towards a group of sailors who were gathered around one of the rear guns. Carter gave a comic 'follow me' motion with a single finger raised in the air, and Rom and Chubby obediently followed behind the first lieutenant. They walked beneath a lifeboat, winched up in a cradle above their heads, and climbed a few metal steps that took them on to the bridge. The only crewman present was the quartermaster, a wiry-looking man with a dour expression and a broad Glaswegian accent.

'Chaps, let me introduce you to Wheels,' Carter said.

'Petty Officer Robert Vincent,' announced the quartermaster as he shook the young sub-lieutenants' hands. 'But everyone calls me Wheels.' He turned to Carter. 'If you will excuse me, sir, I was just on my way to give Viner a hand with the new radio equipment.'

Carter nodded and Wheels left the bridge.

'So, a quick history lesson before we get started on the really technical stuff,' Carter said. '*Grenade* is now home to one hundred and forty-six souls, including yourselves. She was laid down in thirty-four, launched in thirty-five, and commissioned in thirty-six. Like Wheels there, she is Glaswegian in origin. But unlike Wheels, she is a nippy thing and you can normally understand what she's saying to you. She can do 36 knots on a good day. She displaces 1,370 tons with a standard load. As I'm sure the captain has already told you, she is a thing of beauty and we love her dearly.' He paused to flash a grin at the new recruits. 'She was assigned to the First Destroyer Flotilla of the Mediterranean Fleet upon commissioning and was given a post-completion overhaul in Malta in thirty-seven, which incidentally is when I joined her,' Carter added with a flourish. 'She had another refit at Chatham in the summer of thirty-eight and was then briefly transferred to the Red Sea in October of that year. We were in Alexandria when war broke out and were brought straight home — the entire flotilla came back and came under the Western Approaches Command in Plymouth. All clear so far?'

'The captain mentioned you've had a bit of a tough time of things?' Rom ventured.

Carter laughed. 'You could say that. We worked on contraband duties for a few months in the Downs. Then the flotilla leader, HMS *Grenville* had the misfortune to strike a mine. Between our sister ship, *Griffin*, and ourselves, we managed to pull one hundred and seventeen men out of the water. But she went down quickly, and we lost seventy-seven of her crew. Poor buggers. Shook us all up a bit, I don't mind telling you. We knew those chaps pretty well. Anyway...' Carter paused. 'That just about brings us up to date, I think. She's spent the last month in dock, and we have some swish new kit to play with. Any questions?'

'When do we sail, sir?' Chubby asked.

'We cast off half an hour before high tide, so at roughly about four o'clock. Why don't you chaps get yourself settled in for an hour? Come on, I'll show you your cabin.'

Rom looked around the confines of the cabin he would be sharing with Chubby. There was no porthole, and the space offered just about enough room for him to take the single step between the cramped wooden bunk bed and the small wooden desk. There was an empty shelf, designed for books. Chubby opted for the lower bunk and Rom swung his bag up onto the top bunk.

'So what do you reckon, Chubby?'

'Everyone seems jolly friendly.'

Rom nodded.

'I had rather expected the captain to be terrifying,' Chubby said. 'You'd think it should go with the role. But he seems jolly decent. And Carter seems nice. Just think on it, Rom,' he added wistfully. 'In a couple of hours, we will be up there on the bridge as *Grenade* begins her refit sea trials. I almost felt as if I'd never actually get to sea somehow. If it had been down to that bastard Sneyd, I don't suppose I ever would have done.'

Rom, who was changing into a clean shirt, laughed. 'That's true enough, I suppose.'

'No, listen, old chap, I've never had the chance to properly thank you for everything you did for me back at King Alfred. I know I'm a bit of a duffer, and I certainly wouldn't be here today if it hadn't been for all your help. It really is very much appreciated.'

'The pleasure is mine entirely, Chubby,' Rom said. 'I can't think of anybody I would rather be setting off with on this particular adventure.'

Later that afternoon, as they joined the bridge and began to put into practice everything they had learnt back at King Alfred and Greenwich, Rom felt a swelling pride within his chest. The sun was low in the sky, picking out the edges of the great city's hulking dockland warehouses, the great twin-shaft steam engines were humming and throbbing somewhere far below them, and the bustle of the crew pulling in the tethering ropes was in stark contrast to the calm stillness of the captain, who stood with one elbow resting on the edge of the open air bridge, his keen eyes flicking back and forth with every movement on the quayside.

'Very good. Let's ease her out, Wheels,' he muttered to the quartermaster, who acknowledged the command with a crisp, 'Aye aye, sir.' Once again, Rom felt a fluttering in the very pit of his stomach as the great ship began to move out into the river. It was as if he had stepped straight into one of the adventure stories he used to read as a child.

Courtenay-Boyle took a position at the centre of the bridge. He gave Rom a quick glance, but turned his eyes back towards the bow as he said dryly, 'Are you planning on keeping that grin on your face for the entire day, Hutchinson?'

Rom blushed. 'No, sir, sorry, sir.'

Courtenay-Boyle laughed and gave him a cheerful pat on the shoulder. 'You never need to apologise for being happy, sub, not on my watch.'

The smile was swiftly wiped off Rom's face on his second day as the ship properly began its refit sea trials off the Kent coast. Of all the things Rom had worried about, seasickness had never crossed his mind as being a serious concern.

Storm clouds rolled in menacingly on the horizon, but the sea itself had barely been affected by the weather when Rom first had to excuse himself from the bridge to vomit into the nearest toilet. He came back to the bridge looking green and sheepish.

'Keep your eyes on the horizon,' Courtenay-Boyle advised. 'It'll pass.'

Carter was equally sympathetic. 'We all went through it in our first few weeks. Your body will get used to the swell eventually. Still,' he added, looking again at the rolling black clouds that barrelled towards them from the horizon. 'It looks as if you may have a bit of a baptism of fire in the next few hours.'

Courtenay-Boyle nodded. 'Go back to your cabin for a few hours and get some sleep while you can. Carter's right. It's going to be a bit choppy tonight and if you're feeling a little rough already, it's sensible to make yourself as comfortable as you can.'

'Thank you, sir,' Rom said, feeling a little pathetic as he turned to leave the bridge.

*

The senior officers had known what they were talking about. The next couple of days were hellish — with both Rom and Chubby lying on their bunks and groaning, taking it in turns to make a mad dash to the toilet to throw up. The sea was merciless, rolling and tumbling, leaving them hollowed out, next to useless on the bridge and incapable of rest in their cabin. Finally, on the third day, the weather eased and both young recruits noticed a lightening of their symptoms. They returned to full duties apologetically.

Although a fellow sub-lieutenant, so technically an equal, as a Royal Navy man, Colin Gallagher did nothing to hide his distaste for the two new RNVR recruits. He spoke with a broad Belfast accent and had a shock of red hair and pale eyebrows that seemed to be in a constant frown. His nose, freckled like a schoolboy's, wrinkled at the sight of the RNVR markings on Rom and Chubby's uniforms.

'Layabouts,' Gallagher muttered, as they returned to the bridge. 'Did you get a blind seamstress then, lads?' he asked, pointing at their sleeves. 'Sure, she's had a fine crack at keeping those lines straight, but hasn't done too grand a job.'

He was the only one who laughed at his own joke — laughter without an accompanying smile.

'See, when this war is over, and you runts go back to being bank managers or accountants, or whatever shit it is you do on civvy street, we regulars will still be here on the bridge defending our nation.'

Rom shrugged. 'Whatever you say, pal.'

Gallagher edged his face unnaturally close, so that Rom could smell him and feel the Irishman's breath on his own cheek. 'Well, I do say, you see,' Gallagher muttered. 'You boys had better know your place on this bridge. We may both have a single ring on our uniforms, but don't be under any illusion, sunshine. My single ring is worth more than your single ring. Understood?'

Not so long ago, Rom's temper would have sparked by now. He had never liked bullies and had one natural reaction to them — hit first and hit hard. But every ounce of common sense he had told him that landing his fist on the nose of a fellow officer on the bridge of his new ship would not be a smart move. So, he kept calm, breathing rhythmically and keeping his eyes diverted from his tormentor's surly face.

But Gallagher moved closer still. 'And another thing...' he began, but was immediately interrupted by a violent eruption of vomit that splurged from Rom's mouth so swiftly that even Rom was taken by surprise. Both men attempted to take a step backwards, but it only served to spray the sick more widely across Gallagher's uniform — from his epaulets to his shiny shoes, splattering the single embroidered golden ring that was so much more valuable than the one on Rom's sleeve.

For a moment, Gallagher stood gasping and panting, as if he was unable to move from the spot. Rom stood stock-still too, gazing in disbelief at the bilious liquid that had sprayed across his fellow sub-lieutenant from his own mouth. The horrific tableau was finally broken when Gallagher screeched, 'You bastard!' and stormed off the bridge.

Rom turned to Chubby, who was grinning at him.

'Well, that will be Sub-Lieutenant Gallagher leaving the bridge, presumably to go and polish his precious single ring,' Chubby said dryly.

Rom made his way down into the pilothouse. Wheels stifled a wheezy laugh when he saw him. 'You'd better watch out, sir,' the Scotsman warned. 'That Gallagher is not a man to be messed with.'

'Well, I hardly did it on purpose, Wheels,' Rom said, wiping the edges of his mouth. 'I didn't even feel it coming. It's this blasted sea.'

The quartermaster took a sharp breath, while keeping his focus on the navigation of the vessel. 'You'll no be wanting to have the sea hearing you cursing her either, sir. You may call me superstitious, but you'll see she can be a vengeful spirit.'

Rom gave a weary sigh and felt Chubby's hand patting his shoulder.

'Why don't you go and get yourself cleaned up, Rom?' he said kindly. 'You'll feel much better then, and I'm sure Gallagher will be more open to an apology once you both have clean uniforms on.'

'Do you really think he deserves one?' Rom asked.

'Probably not, but it might be politically astute to do so, old chap.'

Rom knew that Chubby was right. He had to put right this relationship with the sour-faced Irishman. The bridge was too small a place for petty feuding. So once he had cleaned himself up, he knocked on Gallagher's cabin door and took a deep breath.

'You've some nerve knocking here,' Gallagher spat as he opened the door.

'I wanted to apologise,' Rom said, raising his face so Gallagher met his eyes square on. 'I had no control over that — it wasn't deliberate, I can assure you.'

'Your apology is not accepted, you little runt,' Gallagher said scornfully. 'If I was the master, I would refuse to take scum like you.'

Rom raised his eyebrows. 'Thankfully, that's a scenario that is never likely to happen,' he said and walked back to his own cabin.

*

An hour later, there was a knock at Rom's cabin door. He opened it in his vest and pants, fully expecting it to be Gallagher looking to continue the contest. But to Rom's surprise — and evident embarrassment — it was the captain himself.

'Get your shirt, Hutchinson, and join me on the bridge in two minutes,' Courtenay-Boyle muttered sternly.

'Yes, sir,' Rom said.

Moments later, he was standing to attention before the captain on the bridge. Gallagher was also there, breathing loudly through his nose, as if struggling to not speak. It was clear he was desperate to make his case against Rom at the earliest opportunity.

'I don't want to hear it, Gallagher,' said Courtenay-Boyle, anticipating the Irishman's intention. 'You too, Hutchinson. You've both had plenty to say on this bridge today, from all I've heard. Now it's my turn to speak. First things first, this is a Greyhound-class destroyer of His Majesty's Royal Navy, not the Mother's Union kitchen. This is not the place for your petty squabbles. So it ends here and now. Understood?'

Both men nodded — Gallagher somewhat more reluctantly than his RNVR opponent.

'Now shake hands,' Courtenay-Boyle added.

Rom held out his hand to Gallagher, who eyed it suspiciously.

'Well, go on then, Gallagher. I won't tell you twice,' Courtenay-Boyle barked.

Gallagher took Rom's hand, finally consenting to the shake, but with his eyes fixed on Rom's as if they were lining up the sights of a gun.

'Good,' Courtenay-Boyle said. 'Now you can get back to your downtime.'

Gallagher stormed off the bridge without another word. Rom paused at the top of the steps. He took a breath, as if about to speak, but the captain waved him away.

'Go on, Hutchinson, get some rest,' he said.

Although a little aggrieved to have been considered an equal party in the unpleasantness, Rom was relieved that the conflict had been brought to so swift and decisive a conclusion. Gallagher was an idiot, he told himself, but even he wasn't stupid enough to defy the captain by continuing the feud. They would never be best buddies, Rom knew, but he could live with that.

Rom went to the wardroom that evening with an open mind, but it was clear from the moment he entered that Gallagher wasn't about to strike up a conversation with him — or anyone. The Irishman sat in a corner, brooding over his pipe. Chubby raised his eyebrows at Rom and tried to make small talk. But a moment later, Gallagher got up from his chair and left the room.

'He'll get over it eventually,' Chubby said.

'He'll have to.' Rom shrugged. 'How did the captain find out about it?'

'From Wheels, I imagine,' Chubby replied, offering Rom a cigarette. 'Don't worry about it, old boy.'

'I am worried about it, though,' Rom said, blowing a cloud of blue smoke into the air.

'Why?'

'Gallagher's the type to hold a grudge. I can tell.'

The day-to-day business of being a junior officer on the bridge of a Royal Navy destroyer seemed to come naturally to Rom.

He settled into the rhythm of it all — the watches, the roles. Within a week, he felt as if he had served for decades, fitting like a puzzle piece into the reassuringly clipped formality of the bridge.

With the refit sea trials completed, the ship headed back to London. But she had barely entered the mouth of the Thames when disaster struck. The RMS *Orion* was a lumbering brute of a ship — recently converted from a liner to serve as a troopship for the duration of the war. She had just completed an xhaustting passage halfway across the globe from Australia, and it was clear that her captain was in a rush to get her up alongside and set foot back on the streets of London. The 23,000-ton liner had steamed along behind them impatiently as if *Grenade* had developed an ugly shadow for the past hour.

'I'm going to go down for a shave,' Courtenay-Boyle muttered, stroking his cheek. 'I need to look smart. I'm going ashore for a dinner this evening.'

Carter nodded, while Chubby and Rom exchanged a silent grin at the thought of the old man tarting himself up.

'Can you take the bridge for half an hour, Carter?'

'Aye aye, sir.' Carter stepped across to the edge of the bridge and frowned at the bow of the liner. As the waterway began to narrow from an estuary to a river, the presence of the ship edging ever closer to their portside was clearly irritating the first lieutenant.

'Impatient bastards, aren't they?' he said to Gallagher, who nodded.

Carter gripped the shining brass handle of the engine order telegraph and shifted it to "Slow". 'We'll go at our pace, not theirs,' Carter said. But his grin twisted into a grimace as his hand reached down to cradle his stomach. 'Terrible indigestion,' he muttered. The first lieutenant shuffled about and after a few moments handed command of the bridge to Gallagher. 'I'll be two minutes,' Carter said as he walked down the metal staircase, his hand still resting on the side of his stomach.

Gallagher, left alone with Chubby and Rom, saw his chance to speak freely for the first time since their very public dressing down from the captain.

'Well, I hope you're happy with yourself,' Gallagher grumbled.

'What's eating you now?' Rom muttered. But before Gallagher had the chance to say another word, the portside window filled with the mammoth outline of the *Orion*.

'Watch out!' Rom cried, but Gallagher had barely had the chance to turn his head when the bow of the great liner struck. It reverberated through the whole ship with a sickening scraping sound, which was immediately joined by the booming call of *Orion*'s horn. But it was far too late for any warnings. Rom heard the crunch as the rail of the destroyer's deck was prised away from the bow of the troopship by the momentum as the ships rebounded off each other.

'You'll be sent packing for this!' Gallagher hissed.

Within a moment the captain was back on the bridge, swiftly followed by an ashen-faced Carter.

'What the hell happened, Carter?' Courtenay-Boyle bellowed.

'Stomach problems, sir,' Carter said weakly. 'I had to hand over the bridge to Gallagher.'

Courtenay-Boyle dashed to the portside of the bridge to survey the damage. Beyond his shoulder, Rom could see a group of sailors looking down from the deck of the *Orion* at the point of impact.

'It was his fault!' Gallagher yelled, pointing a shaking finger across the bridge towards Rom.

'Don't start that again, Gallagher,' Courtenay-Boyle growled. 'You had the bridge, not Hutchinson.'

'You don't understand,' Gallagher gabbled. 'He lunged at me. He tried to punch me the moment the first lieutenant left.'

'I did absolutely nothing of the sort,' Rom defended himself, but he felt a weight in the pit of his stomach — a sense that it was Gallagher's word against his own. Then he heard a discreet little cough from the back of the bridge. He had forgotten that Chubby was even present.

'Hutchinson did nothing of the sort, sir,' Chubby said. Rom could see the terror in his fellow cadet's face as Gallagher's fierce eyes darted between him and the captain. Chubby steeled himself to speak once again. 'If anything,' he added, with a wobble in his voice, 'it was Sub-Lieutenant Gallagher doing the attacking. He was so busy verbally abusing Hutchinson, he had completely taken his focus off the *Orion* to the portside.'

Gallagher turned towards the captain and opened his mouth to speak, but he was swiftly interrupted.

'Get off my bridge!' Courtenay-Boyle dismissed Gallagher. 'Carter, get down there and give me a damage report immediately. Viner,' he bellowed down to the young telegraphist, 'signal the captain of the *Orion* and request a damage report from her too.'

Although he knew he was entirely innocent of any wrongdoing, Rom felt humiliated by the debacle. All he could think was how enormously grateful he was to Chubby for standing up against Gallagher in the way he did. He knew that had taken a lot of guts, but it had undoubtedly saved his skin.

Gallagher seemed to get away with the whole thing. The captain went through the motions of conducting a detailed investigation for the next ten days, while *Grenade* was patched up, before moving on to Harwich, where she underwent more thorough repairs. But in the end, with his temper eased by the passing of time, Courtenay-Boyle simply put it down to one of those nautical misunderstandings that occasionally happened amid the chaos of war. But Rom knew that the animosity between Gallagher and himself now could never pass. It left a sour taste in his mouth, and he knew it was only a matter of time before Gallagher lashed out at him again — or worse still at his loyal young friend. Now he knew that Gallagher would stop at nothing to get Rom thrown out of the service — even openly lying about his conduct — Rom told himself that he would need to tread very carefully indeed.

CHAPTER SIX

Following a long ten days at Harwich, with repairs completed, *Grenade* was sent back out into the North Sea, and then ordered to head north to join the Home Fleet at Scapa Flow. Rom stood on deck and looked out at the bleak slate-grey waves, stretching out to the horizon. He imagined the war-torn European continent somewhere beyond, out of sight over the shimmering line of blue that marked the visible extent of the curvature of the earth. He hoped that he might be able to keep his head low long enough for things to settle down on board. One enemy was enough for him, especially when that was represented by the full might of the Third Reich.

But the destroyer had barely travelled beyond The Wash when another storm started brewing. It was a barely noticeable swell at first, but the motion hit Chubby straight away, and he made a dash from the bridge to the toilet to vomit. Rom, who seemed to have found his sea legs at last, proved much more resilient on this occasion. The queasiness simply didn't come, and as the storm conditions worsened and the officers found themselves being increasingly thrown into a stumble by the lashings of the vicious North Sea, Rom actually found himself enjoying it. The heavy storm clouds rolled overhead like carved ebony, and every third or fourth wave found its mark and crashed across the bow in a great explosion of white froth. The wind was whipping up too, whistling around the funnel and clattering the metal steps and ladders.

Courtenay-Boyle controlled the bridge with a determined calmness, occasionally muttering words of support and reassurance. 'Easy does it, Wheels,' he said to the quartermaster, who was at the helm.

Gallagher gave a little cough. 'I'm sorry, sir,' he said. 'I'm feeling a little rough. Permission to leave the bridge. I think I'm going to be sick.'

Courtenay-Boyle looked Gallagher up and down suspiciously. 'Go on then,' he muttered. 'I'm sure we can do without you for now.' Once Gallagher had left, Courtenay-Boyle turned to the quartermaster. 'My goodness,' he said. 'I think this seasickness must be catching. It seems to be working its way around all the subs.'

Wheels smiled an acknowledgement, but kept his focus on negotiating the angry sea. There was a flash of lightning ahead and moments later a deep rumble of thunder.

'We're right in the heart of it, I'd warrant, sir,' he said with his peculiarly dour Scottish lilt.

'It's just a little bit of weather,' Courtenay-Boyle chuckled.

In the very next moment, an even brighter flash of lightning illuminated the entire bridge. It hit with an ear-splitting, electrical crack. All the officers looked towards the starboard side of *Grenade*, from where the lightning seemed to strike. A moment later, the crack was echoed by a rattle and thudding sound that was unmistakably something coming loose and crashing against the deck.

'Damage report, Hutchinson,' Courtenay-Boyle ordered. 'Take a look and let me know what the hell is going on out there.'

'Aye aye, sir.' Rom nodded and stepped out onto the ladder to face the lashing wind and sideways rain. He felt the rainwater immediately drench his jacket and his feet slipped warily on the wet deck as he stepped off the bottom rung of the metal steps. The crashing of the waves against the bow from behind gave an ominous pounding noise that echoed around him despite the howling wind.

'Jesus Christ,' he cursed, as he held on to his cap with one hand and walked with great difficulty into the wind. Almost immediately, he caught sight of one of the great lifeboats looming halfway along the deck, slumped like an injured animal, leaning to one side. The fixings had come away altogether at the stern, causing the lifeboat to almost stand up on end. 'Dear God!' Rom cried into the wind as he walked on towards it as quickly as he could manage.

He had only gone a few more steps when he spotted the shape stretched out on the deck. He caught a glimpse of a navy-blue jacket illuminated by another flash of lightning, as if the falling boat had pinned a pile of uniforms against the steel deck. But with a few more steps, Rom quickly realised he was not looking at a pile of washing. The shape pinned against the deck was human. As he moved closer, he saw that it was clearly Gallagher. The shock of ginger hair lay capless and motionless on the slippery deck, where the lashing rainwater was landing in a thick circle of blood.

For a moment Rom's feet became rigidly fixed to the deck. 'Jesus Christ!' He finally found the capacity to move again and lunged forward to try to lift the lifeboat from Gallagher's body. Its great wooden bulk had him pinned across the chest. Rom struggled to get any kind of purchase on the wet wood of the boat; it repeatedly slipped from his hands, far too heavy for him to shift. He looked down at Gallagher's face — the curled lips of the mouth that he had last seen sneering at him as he left the bridge moments earlier, now gaped open and motionless. His eyes stared up towards the heavens from where the lightning had come in that fateful moment.

Rom knew in an instant that Gallagher was dead. Unable to shift the boat at all, he ran back towards the bridge, slipping and sliding all the way, falling and landing heavily, flat on his face at one stage. He swept back on to the bridge, panting, sodden, dishevelled and with blood pouring from his nose.

'It's Gallagher!' Rom cried. All the officers turned to look at him. 'The lifeboat,' he gasped, struggling to speak. 'The lifeboat is on top of him!'

Courtenay-Boyle's first step swiftly turned into a dash. 'You've got the bridge, Carter!' he bellowed. 'Hutchinson, Thompson, come with me.'

At the first horrifying sight of the lifeboat's upturned bow rocking in the wind, as though buckling over with remorse, the captain called back to Thompson, 'Gather a dozen men at the double. This thing is going to take some lifting.'

Thompson returned with a group of sailors who together managed to prise the lifeboat up long enough for Gallagher's body to be slid out.

Gallagher had vomited a lot of blood in his final moments, but with the weight of the boat finally removed from his chest, he seemed to resemble himself once again. Yet he wasn't there anymore, Rom thought, as he looked down at the body. He was transfixed by the enormity of what had happened. It was the first time he had seen a dead man and his hand began to shake uncontrollably.

'Get him bagged up and take him down below,' Courtenay-Boyle said to the group of young ratings who had helped to remove the boat from the body, before adding, 'Poor bugger,' with a little more emotion in his voice.

Back on the bridge, the officers stood in silence for what seemed like a very long time, watching the waves crashing across the bow and swaying sombrely with each rise and fall of the ship. It was Courtenay-Boyle who eventually broke the silence.

'We'll not bury him at sea, not this close to land,' he said to nobody in particular. 'Viner, raise the Grenville and inform them we have lost a soul onboard in the storm. Tell them we intend to make an unplanned call into Kingston-upon-Hull with the body. From there he can be taken across the country and put on a ferry back to his family in Belfast.'

'Yes, sir,' Viner nodded and began to relay the message to the captain of the flotilla leader, HMS *Grenville*. The exchange was brief.

'What did he say?' Courtenay-Boyle asked.

'He said, "Worst luck" and "God speed".'

Courtenay-Boyle nodded. 'It will knock us back by a day, perhaps. We can rendezvous with them at Scapa Flow.' He rubbed his hands together, still trying to get the feeling into his fingers after the icy soaking they had endured out on the deck. 'Relay our intentions to Plymouth, would you?'

'Aye aye, sir.'

The crew was subdued for the entire passage up the east coast and on into the welcome shelter of the Humber. The storm had passed and the sun was shining. The docks of Hull were busy with fishing boats, frantically unloading their catches, and the whole city seemed to have an aroma of wet fish hanging in the air. Gallagher's body was carried off the ship in a long canvas bag, two sailors struggling with the weight of him. Rom stood on deck, leaning on the rail, and watching the macabre spectacle. Courtenay-Boyle had stepped ashore first and was having a subdued conversation with two soldiers who were preparing to put the body into the back of an Army ambulance. The captain held his cap under his arm and bowed his head to the bagged-up remains of Gallagher as the rear doors of the ambulance were closed on him. Rom watched as the ambulance pulled away along the precarious quayside, swerving from side to side to negotiate the jumble of nets and crates that littered the route.

Rom took a deep breath and looked up towards the city centre with the green copper domes of a municipal building glinting in the sunlight. He imagined Gallagher being transferred into the care of an undertaker and a wooden coffin, before setting off to cross the Pennines and take his last voyage across the Irish Sea to his final resting place in some sleepy corner of Belfast. He pictured Gallagher's family gathered around the graveside, sprinkling a little soil from a silver platter. Earth to earth, ashes to ashes. He had never liked the man. Indeed, there had been few people in his life that Rom had disliked more — even Sneyd back at King Alfred had somehow had more to like than sour-faced, mean-spirited Gallagher. But still he felt a sort of horror at his passing. For all his distaste for the man, he would never have wished such a thing on him.

'You all right, old chap?' Chubby asked as he approached along the deck. 'Seeing old Gallagher off once and for all?'

Rom nodded. 'Poor bugger,' he said. 'What were the chances of that happening at the exact moment he was passing across the deck?'

'Such things are an act of God.' Chubby nodded sagely. 'Maybe it was His vengeance for Gallagher being such a complete and utter pain in the arse since we boarded the ship.'

Rom laughed, the tension of the past few days breaking in an instant. 'You can't say that.'

'Well, it's true enough.' Chubby shrugged. 'Anyway, Carter has said we can have an evening's shore leave. We're here until midday tomorrow, while the engineers come aboard and fix the winch on that lifeboat.'

Rom raised his eyebrows.

'So,' Chubby added, 'if you fancy finding your land legs for the evening, I'm sure we can find a hostelry or two in Kingston-upon-Hull. I like a good northern pint of bitter.'

Rom didn't need asking twice. Within the hour he and Chubby were wandering along the cobbled streets of the old town. They had to steer a careful course to avoid the slippery remnants of fishing hauls that littered the quay. Further along, a group of dockers were busily unloading the crated cargo from a small old tramp steamer moored at the end of the quay, swearing and cursing with every new load.

They found a pub just around the corner on the quayside — a red-brick, wedge-shaped building, with a creaking sign that had "The Minerva, est. 1829" hand-painted on it alongside a rudimentary illustration of an owl. They climbed the steps beneath an unlit glass lantern and were hit by a rich smell of tobacco and stale ale as they made their way inside and through the smoke-filled bar. A group of locals turned to watch them for a moment — they looked like a ragtag collection of dockers and fishermen, alongside a few men in dark brown suits, sipping on solid-looking pints of stout. After a moment, all interest in the two young naval officers seemed to pass, and the room full of men returned to their grumbling conversations, their pints and their roll-up cigarettes. Since Rom and Chubby were in their uniforms, the barman didn't question their ages.

They carried their dripping pints from the bar to a vacant table near the window, where they looked out at the Humber with the thin grey line of Lincolnshire on the far side of the estuary.

'Well, here's to our first adventure on *Grenade*,' Chubby said, raising his glass. Rom raised his own and took a long draught of the beer. 'Do you know, I think I might just be getting on top of the seasickness too.'

'That's good,' Rom said. 'We're going to be a man down now on the bridge, so there will be less opportunity to spend hours on your bunk clutching your stomach.'

'It was Wheels who told me the trick in the end. He gave me a stick of ginger and told me to chew on it, like a cigar, if I was feeling a bit queasy,' Chubby said. 'Anyway, it seems to work a treat.'

'Whatever it takes.' Rom shrugged. 'I just found my stomach got used to it after a while. I hardly feel the swell now.'

'Not like poor Gallagher,' Chubby added with a grimace.

'No, he certainly felt the swell. God rest his soul.'

The two men sat for a moment in silence, considering their pints. Rom looked up at Chubby. He had become noticeably thinner in recent weeks. The weight had fallen off him. Not surprising, given how much time he had spent vomiting. He could almost see a defined jawline, and his eyes seemed bigger and more expressive — wiser, somehow.

'Anyway, perhaps it will be plain sailing from here on in, with Gallagher out of our hair,' Chubby said at last.

'Perhaps,' Rom agreed cautiously. 'We can only hope for the best.' He raised his pint once again towards his friend, who returned the gesture and settled back into the solid wooden bench for a long evening.

One hundred and thirty miles to the west, Remmie was on board the SS *John Holt*, as the ship returned to the Mersey at the conclusion of his first voyage to Lagos. The past few weeks had been a revelation — both for good and ill. Remmie had almost immediately felt as if he had found his calling, working the decks of the busy tramp steamer. He had felt right at home, with the friendly crew seeming like an extended family. Perhaps it was because his father had captained this very ship, but she felt extraordinarily familiar to him.

For much of the voyage out he had been almost euphoric — the experience of seeing the ocean in all its glory and grandeur for the first time was overpowering. With no seasickness at all, he had launched himself enthusiastically into simple manual labour and felt for the first time in his young life that he was properly living. The weeks at sea, surrounded by tropical blueness made his stomach flutter with happiness as he worked.

Africa — the little of it he had seen — had also been something of a revelation. Lagos itself was a sprawling, unforgiving city, much of it consisting of low-level slums perched along the banks of a swampy lagoon. But the people were welcoming. Remmie felt like an explorer, as if he were the first Englishman to set foot there, despite the trappings of empire visible all around.

He only had two nights in port, while the ship was being loaded, but the captain gave the nod for a dozen of the crew to spend an evening in the city, under the strict proviso that they refrained from getting too drunk or too intimate with the locals.

Part of Remmie was utterly terrified by the prospect of stepping off the ship and spending an evening in this unfamiliar land. Africa was a dark continent in his imagination — a place that for him existed only in books. But here he was, thousands of miles from his father and mother and twin brother, stepping ashore into an unknown world. He was relieved to be surrounded by his older and more worldly crew mates, who kept a careful eye on him as they made their way into the old town and found a bar bustling with a heady mix of locals and Europeans. A band was playing on a small stage with unfamiliar instruments, their music heavy with repetitive drumming, and there were dozens of young couples dancing energetically. It was like nothing Remmie had ever seen in the dance halls back home. Their foreheads glistened with sweat as they moved to the rhythms of the music in the sticky night.

He could barely take his eyes off the dancers as he and his crewmates were shown to a table by the window and trays filled with glasses of cold beer were delivered. 'Cheers, boys,' said the chief engineer, Stanley Clensy — the most senior member of the crew present, who had taken on a paternal sort of role for the evening. He grinned as Remmie knocked back the cold beer, his smile glinting around the gap in his teeth. 'How are you enjoying life aboard the *John Holt* then, Remmie lad?' he asked in his gravelly Liverpudlian accent.

Remmie smiled. 'I love it, Chief. It's everything I'd hoped it would be.'

Clensy smiled back and nodded. 'That's what I like to hear,' he said, pointing the cigarette he had been hand-rolling. He put it in his mouth, lit it and took in a deep lungful of smoke, which he retained for a long moment, before turning towards the open window and releasing it into the steaming African night. 'There's nothing like it,' he added before taking another puff of the cigarette. 'Life aboard a solid merchantman like the *John Holt* is just the ticket for a lad of your age, eager to see the world and experience a thing or two.'

Remmie nodded. 'Exactly,' he said enthusiastically.

Clensy laughed hoarsely and took another mouthful of beer. It was only then that Remmie noticed the pair of eyes watching him from across the table. The beady-eyed frown was coming from Eric Taylor, one of the stokers, who had something of a reputation as a brawler.

Later in the evening, the crew dissipated around the room. Some were chatting to the locals, some propping up the bar, and in at least one case, dancing with a group of whooping women who seemed to find the Englishman's evident inebriation hilarious. Remmie was not yet so far gone, but he was getting there, and the world had taken on an echoey, hazy film. It was then that he noticed Taylor taking a seat beside him, the sweat glistening on his muscular, tattoo-covered arms.

'You enjoying yourself then, youngster?' Taylor asked, without smiling. Remmie nodded. 'I saw you socialising with the Chief,' the stoker added, frowning down at the sticky wooden table that was crowded with a couple of dozen empty beer glasses.

'Yes, he seemed nice enough,' Remmie replied with a shrug.

'Listen, pal.' Taylor's voice became harder but simultaneously quieter as he moved closer. 'You better not think you're something special because of who your father is.'

Remmie's face twisted with anguish. Is this what his crewmates thought of him? Did they see him as the entitled son of a captain of the line?

'No, not at all. I'm just a normal lad, like anyone else,' he insisted, slurring his words a little as he spoke. He looked down to see the fist that Taylor had made, almost hidden in the shadow of the table. It looked brutal with its strong fingers gripped tightly together, drawing out solid-looking knuckles, each marked with a tattooed letter. The letters spelled out BELOW on the left hand and DECKS on the right.

'No, you're not, pal. You won't be one of the lads for a long time. You're the lowest of the low on this ship — don't be forgetting that,' Taylor growled, then moved back towards the bar, pausing briefly to lean in again and hiss, 'Remember your place, son. The lowest of the low.'

It was the only animosity that RemmIe had experienced from anyone during the whole voyage and it unsettled him, sobering him instantly and making him feel as though he wanted to return to the safety of the ship. He turned to Mitchell, a fellow deckhand who had joined the ship on the same day as him. He was seated a few yards away, moving his shoulders in time with the music.

'I'm going to head back to the ship!' Remmie shouted across to him. 'I've had enough for one night.'

Mitchell gave a nod and a thumbs up, so Remmie shuffled towards the exit alone. Outside the streets were deserted, and the crickets made a loud rasping noise from their hiding places in the occasional stretches of scrubland. Remmie walked on, moving gradually between the circles of light projected by the few-and-far-between streetlamps like islands in a sea of darkness. As he neared the edge of the docks, he heard footsteps moving quickly behind him. He turned to see a figure, silhouetted against the light from the last lamp he had walked beneath. It was a large figure, broad-shouldered and more than six feet in height.

Remmie turned back towards the docks and increased his pace. But within moments, the stranger had approached him.

'My friend, my friend,' the African man said, his eyes darting around as he spoke. He slapped Remmie's shoulder with his large hand.

'What do you want?' Remmie asked nervously.

'Every English sailor is my very best friend,' the man grinned. 'What can I treat you to during your time in our great city? Whiskey? Opium? Perhaps a liaison with one of our ladies of Lagos?'

'No, thank you very much,' Remmie said, shrugging his shoulder away from the man's hand. The man was wearing some sort of traditional attire, unfamiliar to Remmie — a vibrant green smock-like garment and a small, circular hat, which perched on his bald head like a lid on a teapot.

'You must not be unfriendly,' the man said, with mock offence. 'You know, I was once a stranger here myself. I am not from Lagos. I'm Yoruba. My people are from Benin. But I've been here a long time now — long enough to show you, my friend, all the very best places for fun in the city. Now, what kind of a lady do you like? A big girl? A small girl?'

'I've no interest in being introduced to a lady, thank you,' Remmie said as firmly as he could, and once again he attempted to walk away from the man.

He was stopped by the big hand taking hold of his shoulder once again, only this time, the grip was firmer. He turned and saw that the smile had vanished from the man's face.

'You're not being friendly at all,' the man remonstrated, suddenly angry. 'In fact, white boy, you are being most impolite. Now, here —' the anger dissipated mid-sentence, and the grin reappeared on the man's face as he took hold of Remmie's wrist — 'here is a very fine watch indeed.'

He forced Remmie's wrist up towards his face, so he could study the watch with its twin clockfaces. 'A most unusual timepiece, most unusual,' he muttered. He let go of Remmie's wrist. 'How much do you want for that watch?'

'It's not for sale,' Remmie said.

'Hey, hey, everything in this world is for sale. It's all about naming the right price,' the man said. 'Give me that watch.'

'No.'

'Here, give it to me. I just want to take a look.'

Remmie shook his head.

'Come on, white boy, give me the watch.' He now loomed over Remmie like a shadow. 'Give it to me now,' he insisted, this time with a hint of his earlier venom back in his voice.

Remmie looked back and forth along the dark street. He was quite alone and was starting to feel like a cornered animal. He reluctantly removed the watch from his wrist. 'It's not for sale,' he said feebly, as he handed it over. 'It was a gift from my father and mother. But you can take a quick look if you like.'

The man snatched the watch from Remmie, and his wide smile erupted once more. 'Now you're being friendly,' he said with a sort of mock relief. 'I'm going to try this watch on.' He strapped it to his wrist — fiddling for what seemed like an eternity to fix the clasp into a previously unused hole in the leather, his wrist being much larger than Remmie's.

'Be careful, please. It was a gift,' Remmie said.

'I am being careful,' the man hissed, momentarily angry once again. Then his grin re-emerged. 'How much do you want for this watch?'

'Like I said,' Remmie insisted. 'The watch is not for sale. Give it back to me.'

The man lifted his wrist high in the air as Remmie reached for it. Within a moment, the attempt to retrieve the watch from the man's wrist evolved into a scuffle, and Remmie found himself being wrestled to the floor. As he went to find his feet once more, the African man struck out with a heavy fist that knocked Remmie straight back down into the dust.

For a moment he knew nothing except pain and a dizzying, spinning sensation. Shaking the ache from his jaw, he looked up to see the man running at full speed away from him and being quickly enveloped by the darkness. Another moment and he heard a wail from the man, as he was being dragged back along the street in the grip of another. Remmie shook his head again to clear his vision, and as he did so he recognised the equally intimidating silhouette of Taylor. His fists, marked with the tattooed words "BELOW" and "DECKS" had a firm grip on the African man's neck as he flung him down beside Remmie.

Mitchell and a few of the other members of the crew appeared from behind Taylor.

'Give him back that watch now or you're a dead man,' Taylor growled.

The would-be thief hurried to unfasten the strap, before casting it back towards Remmie as quickly as he possibly could. 'I don't want any trouble,' he pleaded.

'Then you'd better hop it,' Taylor hissed.

The man didn't need a second invitation. He ran away into the night as fast as his legs could carry him. Taylor reached out a hand, the one marked "BELOW", and pulled Remmie back to his feet.

'Thank you, pal,' Remmie said, wiping the blood from his nose, before reaching down to put the watch strap back on his wrist. 'I owe you one.'

Taylor shrugged. 'You might be the lowest of the low onboard that ship, but out here, there are plenty lower.' He laughed a gravelly sort of laugh, and the group of men walked back towards the docks together.

CHAPTER SEVEN

Grenade glided down the Humber, leaving the bustle of the city of Hull behind. The estuary itself was a stony grey, with a flat, unexceptional landscape of muted greens on either side. The waters seemed peculiarly calm; Rom had become accustomed to the stormy conditions of the North Sea. He paced the bridge after his first watch of the day was completed, simply enjoying being part of the life of the ship. The atmosphere seemed to have lightened since Gallagher's body had been removed. It was a terrible thing to think, Rom knew, but he couldn't help but feel an overwhelming sense of relief that the Irishman was gone. He stepped outside and approached a young rating who was busy servicing the Lewis gun that provided somewhat inadequate anti-aircraft cover for the upper decks.

'It's Bill Ridgewell, isn't it?'

The sailor put down the parts of the gun on the deck, wiped the grease from his hands and stood to attention. 'That's right, sir,' he said. 'Able Seaman Bill Ridgewell.'

'At ease, Ridgewell. I was only saying hello.'

The junior rating's shoulders relaxed. 'You're one of the new subs, sir. You joined us at London.'

Rom smiled. 'That's right. Sub-Lieutenant Rom Hutchinson.' He held out his hand and the junior sailor shook it warily. It wasn't the usual greeting onboard ship.

'You're new to the service then, sir?' Ridgewell asked, but his tone was not unfriendly.

Rom laughed. 'You can tell, I suppose. Yes, the whole thing is new to me. I'm only just out of King Alfred.'

'You got over the seasickness yet?' Ridgewell grinned.

'Just about.'

'The trick is to keep your eyes on the horizon, if you're feeling rough.'

'So I've heard,' Rom said. 'Somebody also mentioned chewing ginger.'

'I've not heard that one, sir. There doesn't tend to be a great deal of ginger to hand on a destroyer.'

'You been on *Grenade* long?' Rom asked.

'I joined up in thirty-eight, sir. I sailed out to Egypt on a troopship and joined *Grenade* at Port Said. It was easy going at first, of course. Lots of cleaning the decks and keeping the place tidy.'

'I hope you enjoyed the downtime, while you could.'

Ridgewell smiled. 'It was a good experience, sir. In and out of ports down there, showing the flag. In August of thirty-nine, the flotilla was sent to our war station in the Red Sea. So we knew something was going to happen. But we were asleep on the deck when war was declared. Our first order was to paint all the brightworks.'

Rom frowned at him in puzzlement.

'You know, sir, the brasses,' Ridgewell went on. 'Didn't want the sun reflecting off any part of the ship once we were on a war footing. Anyway, we were relieved. You can't imagine how much time we had spent polishing them previously. It was one less job each day. Still...' Ridgewell shrugged. 'There were lots of new jobs to keep us occupied.'

'I'll bet.'

The two men looked out to see the solid outline of the Spurn Point lighthouse nearing on the portside. It seemed to be standing sentinel at the mouth of the Humber.

'It was the funniest thing,' Ridgewell said. 'Anyone told you yet about how we nearly attacked a lighthouse?'

Rom shook his head. 'However did that happen?'

'Christmas Day last year we were patrolling in the Irish Sea,' Ridgewell recalled, leaning against the rail as he thought back to the events of the previous winter. 'We had a patrol out with a force-ten gale blowing. The waves must have been fifty or sixty feet high. You'd see the screws one minute, then you'd see the bows the next. Anyway, we were on alert, looking for a German battleship. We called it the *Scharn*. But it was really called the *Scharnhorst*. Bit of a mouthful for us Brits. You can understand why we had to shorten the name, sir.'

Rom nodded. 'So what happened?'

'Well, she had just sunk the HMS *Rawalpindi* — a merchant cruiser. The German battleship was supposed to be on her way down the Irish Sea, and we were supposed to go and see if we could find her. What we would have done to her, I don't know.'

Rom gave another nod.

'Anyway, we suddenly went to action stations,' Ridgewell continued. 'We'd just had our Christmas Dinner. We were eating tinned pears and cream. Beautiful. Lovely, they were. But we left our pears and rushed onto the upper deck. I had to go to the lookout, almost being drowned by the spray. Somebody said, "There it is!" The skipper had a look at it and agreed it was the battleship. We challenged it with a signal lamp. There was no response. So the skipper said, "Right, we're going to torpedo her." The torpedo crews closed up and were about to fire the bloody thing when somebody shouted out, "Aboard! Aboard! Aboard!" The bloody thing was flashing us. It was a lighthouse, off the coast of Ireland. Christ knows what would have happened if we'd torpedoed it!'

Ridgewell leaned back and laughed heartily. Rom couldn't resist laughing along.

'That certainly wouldn't have gone down well with our Irish friends,' he agreed.

Ridgewell reached down and returned to cleaning the workings of the Lewis gun.

'I'll let you carry on then, Ridgewell,' Rom said.

'It was a pleasure to meet you, sir.'

'You too, Ridgewell.' Rom smiled and made his way back down to the main deck.

The passage up to Scotland was remarkably unexceptional. No storms. No sign of the enemy. Just mile after mile of grey rolling sea. A few hours refuelling in Aberdeen, and *Grenade* continued on up the increasingly rugged coast until the mainland was left behind altogether, and soon the stubby green islands of the Orkneys emerged over the horizon.

Rom stood on the bridge and glanced down at his watch. It was two o'clock. They would reach Scapa Flow within the hour. He took the watch off his wrist and spent a moment idly winding it. There was comfort in holding it. The watch's presence on his wrist reminded him of home and his mother and father as he'd last seen them, standing on the doorstep of the family home in Liverpool. But it also reminded him of his brother, out there somewhere on the ocean looking at the twin of this timepiece. *I'll bet he is somewhere a damned sight warmer than this*, he thought to himself with a half-smile.

'What are you muttering to yourself about?' Courtenay-Boyle asked him.

'Nothing, sir,' Rom said with a little cough to bring himself back to the job at hand. He replaced the watch on his wrist and returned to the charts that were in front of him.

The captain looked over his shoulder. 'I reckon we'll be there within the hour,' he said. 'Have you ever been to Scapa Flow before, Hutchinson?'

Rom shook his head. 'I'd barely ventured out of Lancashire until a few months ago.'

'It's a remarkable place,' Courtenay-Boyle said, smiling briefly at Rom's admission. 'Incredibly sheltered. You have the main island to one side — the place that the Orcadians call the Mainland, rather confusingly. But then you also have a series of other islands surrounding Scapa Flow — Graemsay, Burray, South Ronaldsay and…' He leaned in to look more closely at the chart. 'Hoy. You must have heard of the Old Man of Hoy?'

Rom shook his head. 'I've never met anybody from the Orkneys, sir.'

Courtenay-Boyle laughed. 'You do have an awful lot to learn, Hutchinson, don't you?' He patted the youngster on the shoulder. 'Well, you're in the right place for it.'

'Yes, sir.'

'Anyway, I've had word that the admiral will be paying us a visit as soon as we're on our mooring. So we all need to be on our best behaviour, shined and polished to within an inch of our lives.'

'Yes, sir, of course.'

'He has this God-awful habit of appearing before you've had time to tie up,' the captain added. 'The first opportunity to spend an hour or two exploring the drinks cabinet in a new wardroom, and you can guarantee that the old bugger won't miss it.' He gave a little conspiratorial laugh, before adding, 'That's between you, me and the gatepost, of course, Hutchinson.'

'Of course, sir, naturally.'

'Anyway, Hutchinson, at least forewarned is forearmed.'

*

A little under an hour later and *Grenade* was taking up her mooring in the middle of Scapa Flow, surrounded by an eclectic mixture of other Royal Navy ships, ranging from an enormous aircraft carrier to a dozen or more neat little sloops and corvettes, all evenly spaced at points across the almost landlocked stretch of water.

As Courtenay-Boyle had predicted, the admiral arrived, ferried across from the aircraft carrier on a little boat with a cluster of young officers from his staff. He was whistled aboard and the bridge stood to attention as he carried out his inspection.

'At ease, gentlemen.' The admiral waved away any formality with a brief lifting of his hand. 'Good Lord, you're all looking very well,' he added, with a degree of informality that Rom had not prepared himself for. 'You must be one of the new subs,' he went on, turning to Rom.

'Yes, sir. Sub-Lieutenant Romulus Hutchinson, sir.'

'Good Lord,' the admiral muttered.

'He shortens it to Rom,' the captain said.

'I should jolly well think so.' The admiral's attention turned back to Courtenay-Boyle, much to Rom's relief. 'There seems to be more Italians on the Orkneys than Scotsmen these days,' the senior officer grumbled. 'POWs, of course. They're about to set them all to work on Churchill's idea of linking the islands up with a causeway to stop the bloody U-boats getting in here and running amok. You can't criticise Churchill's ambition, but God only knows how they're going to actually manage to get a load of Italian prisoners to get off their backsides and put in the amount of back-breaking work that such an undertaking is going to involve.' The admiral laughed heartily at the idea of it.

'Extraordinary, sir,' the captain said.

'Now, Courtenay-Boyle, why don't you show me around your ship? How well stocked is your wardroom?'

Later in the evening, Rom stepped out onto the deck to have a moment to himself with a cigarette. But before he had even closed the door behind him, he was taken aback by an extraordinary sight. The night sky was illuminated with gargantuan sheets of colour, billowing like curtains in a breeze — vibrant reds, purples and greens.

'Aurora Borealis,' a voice said from the darkness. Rom turned to see a young lieutenant leaning against the rail, also smoking a cigarette. He was a member of the admiral's staff. 'The Northern Lights,' the officer added. 'I'd never seen them until I came up here.'

'They're incredible,' Rom gasped, his neck craning as he tried to take in the epic display that was unfolding above them.

'Tommy Treble.' The young lieutenant offered his hand in the darkness.

'Rom Hutchinson, sir.'

Treble waved away the formality. 'You can drop the "sir" while we're having a cigarette together, Rom. How are you finding life up here in the bleak north?'

'Not too bad,' Rom said, cupping his palm around the end of his cigarette to shield it from the biting breeze, as the spark from his lighter became a little orange globe in the hollow of his hand. He lit the tip and drew in a lungful of smoke, lifting his head and releasing a wispy cloud towards the dancing colours of the sky.

'It can take a bit of getting used to,' Treble said. 'Feels like the back of beyond, but it's surprisingly sociable, given all the different crews stationed here at any one time.'

'What are those ships at the mouth of the sound? They look as if they've been scuttled.'

Treble turned to face the same direction as Rom. 'They have,' he laughed. 'They are blockships — filled with concrete, a clumsy attempt to scupper the U-boats' chances of getting in here again and wreaking absolute havoc.'

'Again?' Rom was alarmed. 'You mean you've had U-boats in here before?'

'It's a challenging place to get a submarine into, but it must always be bloody tempting — knowing they could take out the bulk of the home fleet within minutes. We had a raid last year. Most of the fleet was out, thank God. But the *Royal Oak* was sunk.'

'Of course, the *Royal Oak* — I remember seeing that in the papers. She sank here?'

Treble nodded grimly, indicating an area to the west of them with his cigarette. 'A mile or so from here — it was a ghastly night.'

'You were here?'

'Here? Yes, of course,' Treble said. 'I was a junior officer on the *Royal Oak*. We didn't know what had hit us — quite literally. After the first strike, the consensus onboard was that it must have been a CO_2 bottle going off in the hold. We just never imagined a sub might have got in here. The captain had been asleep in his cabin. He came on deck with us, but even then, no orders were given to get the men to action stations. The bow compartments were small and sealed off by watertight bulkheads. He thought we'd struck a drifting mine, but we'd be all right. Then all hell broke loose. She hit us with another torpedo amidships. It took out the broadcasting system, so we couldn't give any orders, not even "abandon ship". Then the cordite store took light. We had fire raging through the vents and a hole in the hull that you could have driven a double-decker bus through.'

'Jesus…' Rom muttered.

'It was horrendous, Rom, just horrendous. Most of the crew were belowdecks. Some of them actually went deeper into the ship, assuming that we must be under air attack. They hoped to gain cover from the deck armour overhead. Others fought to get up the ladders to escape. As the ship heeled over to an angle of forty-five degrees, two of the armoured hatches at the top of the escape ladders suddenly slid shut, slicing two men in half and dropping the lower halves of their bodies back into the bowels of the ship, where their severed legs knocked some of the men lower down off the ladders and sent them tumbling to their deaths. Those of us who did get off before she sank faced icy waters with hardly any life jackets. They had not yet been issued. Somehow, I managed to get to the shore and drag myself onto the rocks. I was one of the lucky ones. Of the crew of one thousand, two hundred and thirty-four, no fewer than eight hundred and thirty-five were killed that night. I helped a group of chaps get out of the water who were already succumbing to hypothermia, so I was given a shiny new medal, a promotion to lieutenant, and a cushy job on the admiral's staff. The irony is, it means I now spend most of my time right here, where it all happened.'

Treble shook his head as if the gesture might loosen some of his memories and allow them to slip away from his mind. 'I still see it so clearly. I was on the rocks by the time the ship slipped below the waves. There were hundreds of men in the water. Those that couldn't swim were splashing around in sheer panic. Those that could were trying to get to the shore, singing "Daisy" to try to keep out the cold. "Daisy, daisy, give me your answer do…"' Treble sang under his breath and looked back out across the dark waters. 'One sailor made it to the rocks, but was burned so badly that the flesh ran off his hands and face like water,' he went on, raising his hands up before his eyes. 'He was holding them in front of him like claws and saying to me, "Sir, sir, what can I do? What can I do?" Then he slumped to his knees before me, as if he was about to pray, but he fell down dead and rolled backwards into the sea. There was nothing I could do.'

Rom held another lungful of smoke for a beat, before releasing it slowly towards the sea and turning back to Treble. 'How do you ever get over something like that?'

'You don't,' the lieutenant snapped, before calming himself and softening his tone. 'I'm sorry. But you don't get over it. I don't expect I ever will. It lives within you, becomes part of who you are. I relive it most nights in my sleep.' Treble finished his cigarette and allowed a weak smile to flutter across his lips as he turned to Rom. 'But I shouldn't complain,' he added. 'As I say, it's landed me a cushy job for the duration, as far as I can make out.'

Rom finished his own cigarette. 'I'd say you deserve it,' he said, with a warm smile.

Treble placed a hand on Rom's shoulder. 'Thank you, Rom,' he said quietly. 'I appreciate that. Goodnight.'

Rom turned to watch the young lieutenant as he walked silently across the deck towards the nearest door. 'Goodnight, sir.'

CHAPTER EIGHT

A few days later word reached the wardroom of *Grenade* of a death among the admiral's own staff. Lieutenant Tommy Treble, who had recounted so vividly to Rom his experiences during the sinking of the *Royal Oak*, had been found in his cabin hanging by his belt from a bulkhead beam. He hadn't left a note. But Rom could imagine the guilt he must have felt as one of the few survivors of such a tragedy. Word was that the admiral was terribly cut-up about the loss of the young officer. He had written to Treble's parents back home in Leicestershire, and after some careful consideration, had chosen not to hide the true nature of his death to the family, as he might have done under normal circumstances.

Rom listened to his fellow officers talk about Treble's suicide in a sombre but abstract sort of way, but he felt too winded by the news to join in with the conversation. Rom's mind flickered back to that night on the deck, when he had smoked and chatted with Treble as the Northern Lights had cast their otherworldly glow across the sky. He managed to make it back to his cabin before he wept.

Two days later, in the cold early morning light, *Grenade* slipped anchor and moved silently away from Scapa Flow, as the crew prepared to join the escort for Convoy ON25 — Rom's first experience of being part of the protective ring of steel around a merchant convoy.

From the moment *Grenade* met the forming-up convoy outside Kirkwall, it became clear to Rom just what an awesome responsibility the naval ships were taking on. The convoy consisted of a total of forty-three ships, ten of which had joined from Kirkwall. Nine of the ships were British, sixteen Norwegian, nine Swedish, four Danish, four Finnish and one Estonian. Two of the ships were detached — part of the convoy, but not ultimately bound for Norway.

Both the escort commander, on HMS *Vivien*, and the convoy commodore, on the *Caledonia*, became intimidating figures, despite Rom having met and rather liked the commander during one of the earlier wardroom soirees at Scapa Flow. It was these men who would respectively take command of the convoy escort and the merchant convoy itself. With the hardy V-class destroyer a dart-like silhouette against the grey sea towards the head of the convoy, the commander, in particular, took on a God-like status. Even Courtenay-Boyle seemed to defer to him in the nervous delivery of his clipped messages on the shortwave radio voice set at the aft of the pilothouse.

HMS *Woolston* and HMS *Wolsey* had joined them from Rosyth, while HMS *Manchester*, HMS *Southampton*, HMS *Calcutta*, HMS *Breda*, HMS *Javelin*, HMS *Juno*, HMS *Janus* and HMS *Eclipse* all joined the escort. To Rom, *Grenade* felt part of a powerful unit, a defensive shield that took its position on either side of the three mighty columns of shipping that seemed to spread for miles, despite their tight formation, both behind *Grenade*, where she steamed along on the starboard side of the convoy, and ahead, towards distant Norway, where the outlines of HMS *Vivien* and *Breda* could just about be made out leading the way.

There was a real sense of entering the unknown. German U-boats were said to be operating throughout great swathes of the North Sea, apparently undeterred by the Royal Navy's superior numbers. There had been talk for months of constructing a Northern Barrage stretching between northern

Scotland and Norway — a recreation of the North Sea Mine Barrage of the previous war, which it was hoped could prove to be an effective obstacle to prevent U-boats accessing the Atlantic from the North Sea. But the reality was that so far, few mines had yet been laid, and the German wolf packs were still free to roam beneath the waves of the North Sea almost as freely as they could out in the open Atlantic.

The shadow of the Nazi threat had been rising up from the European mainland and creeping towards the neutral nations of Scandinavia for weeks, with aggression by the German U-boats towards British shipping within Norwegian waters seen as a direct threat against Norway itself. The Norwegian government had mobilised parts of the Norwegian Army and all but two of the Royal Norwegian Navy's warships. The Norwegian Army Air Service and the Royal Norwegian Navy Air Service were also called up to protect Norwegian neutrality from violations by the warring countries. It was clear to all that a full invasion was imminent, and the Allied priority had been to devise a way of protecting northern Norway, with its vital coverage of shipping routes to the Baltic.

The next day, the radio operator brought a message to the captain, scribbled as a note on a scrap of paper. The officers on the bridge understood that this deviation from relaying messages vocally indicated either the importance or secret nature of the communication — or potentially both. Courtenay-Boyle screwed up the piece of paper in his fist, and his expression tightened angrily. He didn't keep the contents of the message from his fellow officers for long.

'We are being turned around,' he muttered. 'The bloody Germans have launched an invasion of Norway. We need to take these poor blighters back to the relative safety of Kirkwall for the time being.'

Rom shared the captain's sense of deflation. It was his first convoy of the war, and it had reached just 55 nautical miles north-east of the Shetlands before having to abort the mission of getting the ships safely into Norwegian harbours. To add to Rom's frustration, shortly after the bulk of the convoy had turned back for the Orkneys, HMS *Vivien* had obtained a good potential U-boat contact on its ASDIC system and together with HMS *Woolston*, had left the convoy behind to go hunting.

By first light the next morning, *Grenade* was back at Kirkwall.

'Don't take it too badly, Hutchinson,' the captain said, patting Rom on the shoulder as the ship was being refuelled. 'We all feel a bit flat, especially given what's happening in Oslo. But have no fear, you'll get your chance to take the fight to the krauts. We all will. You just need to be patient.'

Rom nodded glumly. 'It's just a little frustrating, sir. Especially with a U-boat out there for the taking.'

'It's the way the convoy works.' Courtenay-Boyle shrugged. 'She can't be left defenceless without an escort while we all engage every contact that's made.'

'Did they get it, do you know?'

'They put it down as a probable kill,' Courtenay-Boyle said. 'They attacked with a full pattern of depth charges and sighted oil after the first wave, so fingers crossed that's one less of them out there anyway.'

Rom smiled. 'Good for them.'

Courtenay-Boyle gave him another pat on the shoulder. 'We'll get our chance to engage sooner or later, Hutchinson, have no fear.' He walked away, leaving Rom to enjoy the golden Orcadian sunrise.

In fact, the respite did not last long. The following day, *Grenade* was heading back out into the vast grey expanse of the North Sea. The ship and the destroyer HMS *Encounter* were charged with escorting the oil tanker SS *British Lady* to Flakstadøya in the Lofoten Islands, where a refuelling and repair base was being set up to support British naval operations in northern Norway.

Rom had never before heard of the Lofoten Islands, and as the days progressed and the three ships journeyed on higher and higher into the Arctic, he began to understand why. The Lofoten Islands were so far north, there was almost no land beyond them. As he worked on the chart table, Rom became aware that they had ventured further north than Iceland. It was like being on the edge of the world.

He had expected ice and snow, icebergs and polar bears, but was met by relatively spring-like weather — colder and greyer than Scotland, but nevertheless it didn't feel like arctic conditions. A few months earlier in the year and it would have been a very different experience at this latitude.

Even the enemy proved benign for the time being. There was no sign of any threat from either below the waves or above them. The voyage passed in snapshots of the great hulking tanker cutting a swathe through the friendless waves and the solid, professional presence of *Encounter* acting as a second shield on the tanker's starboard side. On the bridge of *Grenade*, Rom was feeling increasingly at home. The general sense of anxiety he had felt in his first few weeks eased and he enjoyed being part of the great machine that made the ship function. With four hours on and eight hours off, he even had plenty of downtime, so there were opportunities to do more than just sleep in his cabin. He and Chubby talked wistfully about their former lives as if they belonged to another century, although it had only been a few months since Rom had left Liverpool behind.

He thought about his mother alone in the family home and increasingly his mind strayed to Charlotte. There was a constant background hum of guilt. He had done what he thought was the right thing by her, setting her free rather than tying her to a childhood sweetheart that may never return. But now he began to sense that perhaps ending their relationship so swiftly had been brutal and far from kind. Was she even thinking about him? Perhaps she had moved on? Perhaps she had found another sweetheart? It was an uncomfortable thought to ponder out here in this vast wilderness of grey sea and sky.

The Lofoten Islands provided a long-overdue flash of green in this monotonous landscape; a dramatic steep-sided mountain overshadowed a small fishing village of red- and white-painted wooden houses. With the tanker safely unloading its valuable cargo at a newly constructed jetty, Rom walked up and down on the rain-soaked decks, looking out at the mist-enshrouded community that suddenly found itself as the unlikely focal point of a global war.

'Poor buggers,' Rom muttered to Chubby as he looked out at the village below.

'It gives me the shivers,' Chubby said. 'After all, it's Norway today, but what's to say that tomorrow it won't be England shaking to the march of the Wehrmacht's goosestep?'

There was no easy response to that thought. Rom took a long drag on his cigarette and thought once again of Charlotte as he had last seen her on that day at Crosby Beach, the wind catching her hair.

Rom had expected *Grenade* to be sent straight back down to Scapa Flow to await her next orders, but the orders to return did not arrive. For the rest of the month *Grenade* escorted the battleship *Warspite* and the aircraft carrier *Ark Royal* on manoeuvres in Norwegian waters, designed in part to project a timely reminder of the Royal Navy's dominance at sea, partly to reassure the local communities, but more importantly to set a line in the sand — to make it clear to the Germans that northern Norway would remain under Allied control. It was, Rom knew, a vital strategic lynchpin in maintaining the security of the merchant traffic up into the Barents Sea to maintain safe access to the northern ports of the Soviet Union.

So the spring months passed in interminable patrols of these arctic waters. There was a brief moment of excitement when a rumour took hold that the Germans were occupying Bear Island, a barren rock in the middle of the Barents Sea, with plans to build a meteorological station there. *Grenade* was sent as part of a small flotilla to rid this tiny scrap of Norwegian sovereign land of the invading Nazis. All ready to turn their guns against the tiny island and blow the German occupiers to pieces, the mission experienced a swift anti-climax when upon arriving at the rock they found a down-at-heel whaling station, a few surprised but cheerful and hardy locals and countless pairs of nesting guillemots, but no sign of the Third Reich.

On the Norwegian mainland however, things were certainly hotting up. With British and French troops fighting the Germans around Namsos in the first significant land encounter between the two sides since the last war, there was a growing sense that preventing the Germans from taking control of the whole of the neutral country was becoming almost impossible.

It was as if time slowed down as *Grenade* entered the latest fjord. This high-sided inlet at first seemed indistinct from any of the thousands of fjords the crew had seen on the journey down the coast of Norway from the high arctic in the previous few weeks. But this one was different. Somewhere along this waterway, Allied troops were fighting the Germans amid this harsh, rugged terrain. Rom was on the bridge with Carter as the officer of the watch and the quartermaster, who was slowly manoeuvring the ship towards the lofty opening.

A group of H-class destroyers had been fighting aggressive battles with the Germans for control of the fjord for some time, and the impact of the battles became clear when *Grenade* arrived at a small sheltered inlet, which had been turned into a makeshift repairs yard, where battle-scarred ships were being patched up to make them seaworthy enough to take on the crossing of the North Sea for full repairs back in England.

'Dear God, it looks like all hell has broken loose,' Rom muttered to Carter, who stood beside him. The two officers gazed in horrified awe at the great gashes made in the fo'c'sle of one of the H-class destroyers that had taken a torpedo. Courtenay-Boyle joined them on the bridge.

'It looks like these boys have had a tough time of things,' he said, with a nonchalance that reflected his extensive experience at sea. It took more than a few mangled ships to shock him. 'I'll take her in, Carter. Get some rest.'

'Of course, sir, thank you.' Carter saluted rather formally as he left the bridge.

'I couldn't sleep,' Courtenay-Boyle said to nobody in particular.

'We could hear some heavy artillery half an hour ago, coming from further inland, sir,' Rom said. 'That's probably what woke you up.'

'No, that didn't trouble me.' Courtenay-Boyle went to speak again, as if he was about to confide in Rom, but he appeared to catch himself and think better of it. 'Never mind,' he muttered. 'We're here now anyway.'

The captain gave a series of clipped instructions to the quartermaster below that brought the ship in alongside a Tribal-class destroyer, HMS *Eskimo*. She was in a worse state than the other wounded ships, with both her fo'c'sle and mess decks a mangled mass of twisted metal around the gash left by the torpedo's explosion.

'They were lucky to be able to get her back to here,' Courtenay-Boyle said to Rom.

'Yes, sir.'

'If that had happened out at sea, she'd be consigned to the seabed by now.'

It was a grim sight — as if the whole ship had been sawn in two, revealing the inner levels and cabins, just like in the kind of blown-diagrams of ships that Rom and Chubby had studied back at HMS *King Alfred*. A few of the surviving crew members were standing around, gazing down blankly into the void that had been left behind.

'She certainly won't be getting patched up and sent back to England,' Rom said.

'She's absolutely buggered,' Courtenay-Boyle agreed. 'Look at the way the upper deck has folded down like a house of cards.'

Rom sensed the arrival of people behind him. He turned to see the ship's doctor and sick bay assistant wearing their heavy winter coats and looking grim-faced.

'I'm sorry to ask you to do this, Hutchinson, but I'm going to need you to lend a hand with a rather delicate operation.'

'Of course, any way I can be of assistance.'

'Good man,' Courtenay-Boyle said, patting Rom's shoulder in a way that brought a nervous flutter to his stomach.

It wasn't until Rom had stepped off the gangplank with the two medics that he asked what exactly the purpose of their visit was. The doctor sighed impatiently and thrust the fabric bundle that he was carrying into Rom's arms.

'Hold the body bags, Sub,' he muttered. 'We're here to remove the corpses as best we can from that smashed up fo'c'sle.'

Rom felt his mouth go dry in an instant and a shudder fluttered up the back of his neck.

'It's not going to be a pretty sight in there,' the doctor warned, his bushy grey eyebrows drawing together in a frown. 'But we need to treat what remains of these men with respect and give them as much dignity as we can.'

'Of course,' Rom said, tightening his grip on the pile of body bags.

He followed the doctor and the sick bay assistant onto the mangled remains of the ship. They climbed down into a dark void that now stood where the mess decks should have been. Some of the surviving crew members stood and watched them, shock carved into their features.

Once inside, the doctor lit a torch and handed it to Rom. 'Make yourself useful,' he said. 'Hold on to this.'

The light from the torch shone into the darkness to reveal a mess of mangled steelwork. At first, Rom was struck by an oddly pungent smell, like burnt sausages.

'Where are they?' Rom asked.

'Pretty much everywhere,' the doctor said, his face contorting in horror.

Rom followed his gaze and gradually began to see what the doctor had seen. The jumbled mass of metalwork was peppered with what looked like large, torn-up pieces of raw meat. But on closer inspection, it became sickeningly obvious to Rom that what he was looking at was the assorted mortal remains of a couple of dozen crew members.

The hands were the parts that looked most human, screwed up into fists and dotted around the place. The feet too were recognisable, some still in their boots. Any parts of the torso, arms or legs seemed to have been almost entirely obliterated, but it was the sight of the heads that seared into Rom's brain so violently that he knew in an instant this would be an experience he would never fully recover from.

'I would like to say a prayer, before we move anything,' the sick bay attendant said in a soft voice that sounded as if it was always on the edge of breaking.

'Of course.' The doctor nodded, and the three men stood to attention and bowed their heads, while the attendant spoke the words of the Lord's Prayer into the metallic darkness.

There was no real way of separating the remains back into collections of individuals' body parts. The three men worked in silence, making sure there was one head and a reasonable number of limbs in each body bag. They then sewed them up and rigged up a pulley system to lift them out of the darkness and back towards the light.

Another group of ratings came off *Grenade* to carry the body bags back along the quayside and up onto the deck of the intact destroyer. The doctor, sick bay assistant and Rom stood panting on the quayside, each of them working hard to regain their composure before returning to the ship.

'It had to be done,' the doctor said. 'Better for us to do it, than to expect the men who served with them to have to do it.'

Rom nodded wearily.

Later that afternoon, *Grenade* was taken out of the fjord. She made her way a few miles out to sea, before Courtenay-Boyle took his small leatherbound Anglican prayer book out onto the quarterdeck, where a few dozen members of the crew had formed up beside the bodies, now shrouded grandly beneath carefully folded Union Flags. The engine was cut for the few moments of the service, draping the entire ship in an eerie silence as it drifted at the whim of the waves.

'Our comrades from HMS *Eskimo* are crossing the bar this day,' Courtenay-Boyle began, with an informality and warmth that surprised Rom. He then read out the names of all the men. It was a long list, with the captain pausing between each name, as if to offer each soul to the wind. 'We therefore commit their bodies to the deep, in sure and certain hope of the resurrection of the body, when the sea shall give up her dead,' he said, closing the little leather book. 'May they rest in peace.'

At an imperceptible signal from the captain, the bearer parties lifted each catafalque in turn, retaining the flag and allowing the body bag beneath to slip swiftly down into the waves.

Courtenay-Boyle bowed his head for a moment, before looking up. 'Thank you, gentlemen,' he said softly. 'Carry on about your business.' He turned sharply on his heel and made his way back to the bridge as the engines fired back to life deep beneath them.

Rom and a few of the other officers followed the captain back to the bridge, where he was already giving a clipped command to Wheels, who was at the helm. The ship moved sombrely back towards the mouth of the fjord, leaving the dead dropping down toward the seabed far below.

Moored back at the inlet, a group of men from *Grenade* were sent out onto a captured German supply ship, from which they returned with crates filled with provisions — tins of cherries, tobacco and packs of rich German chocolate. The spoils were divided among the crew, but an extra helping of tobacco and chocolate were given by the captain to Rom, the doctor and the sick bay attendant.

That evening, as Rom came off his watch at midnight, he returned to his cabin and sat quietly on the edge of his bunk, so as not to disturb Chubby who, on a different watch, was already fast asleep. He ate a few squares of the German chocolate and tried to think about nothing at all, slowly slipping into a dream.

The light was streaming in through his bedroom window. He must have left the curtains open in his haste to fall into the comfort of his childhood bed once again after so many hours of travelling. Rom's eyes scanned the room as he slowly came to, taking in the familiar warmth of his things — his complete collection of all three *Hornblower* novels, the little wooden globe that his father had given him and his brother for their twelfth birthday, and across the room, Remmie's empty bed, looking uncharacteristically neat and unslept in.

Suddenly his life at sea seemed a long way away. He looked at the clock; it was approaching midday. His mother must have left him to sleep in. He sat up with a groan and stretched the tired muscles in his shoulders that had been strained by carrying his heavy bag. He felt around with his bare feet for his slippers, then retied the string on his pyjamas and unhooked the dressing gown from the back of the bedroom door. As he did so, he heard a sudden knock on the front door. A moment later, once he had put the dressing gown on and tied the cord, the knock came again. Where was his mother? Why wasn't she answering the door?

Rom walked downstairs swiftly, paused to flatten his unkempt hair with the palm of his hand, and opened the front door. To his astonishment, he was met by the familiar face of the king himself, dressed in full naval uniform and holding his cap casually against his hip.

Rom was rooted to the spot, transfixed by the sight of the King of England standing on his doorstep. After a very long moment, he remembered his manners.

'Sub-Lieutenant Romulus Hutchinson, sir,' he said, making as if to salute, but stopping himself upon realising he wasn't wearing a cap. He looked down at his dressing gown and pyjamas. 'Excuse my appearance, sir,' he stammered. 'I'm on leave. I had no idea, you see.'

The king waved his apology away magnanimously.

'Is there...' Rom paused. 'Rather, I mean to say, can I be of assistance to Your Majesty?'

'I rather wondered if I might be able to come in and trouble you for a cup of tea?' asked the king.

'Of course,' Rom said, tripping over his words while opening the door wider and stepping aside to let his sovereign liege into the hall.

'Thanks ever so much, Hutchinson,' the king said. 'No fear, I don't make a habit of calling on every serviceman on leave, you know, much as I'd like to.' He laughed a little. 'I was just passing on my way to visit a naval unit in Liverpool. But then I thought, you know what I need? I really need a cup of tea. I imagined there was probably somebody at home who might oblige.'

Rom dashed into the kitchen and began frantically looking for a teacup. The usual cupboard was completely bare. He looked behind the door of every unit in the kitchen. He looked on the draining board and in the sink. There were no cups anywhere. He felt a rising sense of panic.

Rom ran into the back room and searched in there. Still no cups. The king had called on him for one purpose, and he was proving wholly incapable of serving him.

'The king wants tea,' he said over and over again under his breath, his panic rising now to nightmarish levels. He ran back to the kitchen and put the kettle on the hob. The kettle started whistling as the king's familiar silhouette appeared. Rom looked down once again at his pyjamas and dressing gown, only to discover that they had inexplicably disappeared and he found himself standing completely naked before the King of England. The whistling of the kettle grew into a scream as he reached down to shield his modesty with his hands.

Rom sat bolt upright in bed and discovered that the scream was coming not from the kettle, but from his own mouth. His skin was sticky with nervous perspiration, but he was relieved to recognise the dark interior of the cabin he and Chubby shared and to feel the reassuring pitch and roll of the heaving sea beneath the ship.

'I say, old boy, everything all right?' Chubby's voice came from the other bunk. He sounded gruff and bleary-eyed.

'Yes, sorry, I'm fine,' Rom replied rapidly, before pausing to catch his breath. 'I was having the most ridiculous dream about trying to find a cup to serve the king some tea.'

Chubby adjusted himself into a seated position. 'You know what Mr Freud would have said. It's your subconscious trying to tell you something.'

'No doubt,' Rom said, rubbing his eyes wearily with his knuckles. 'I'm sure it's telling me that I'm wholly failing to serve King and Country adequately. To be honest, I'm surprised I didn't dream about collecting body parts all night. I suppose you have to be thankful for small mercies.' He paused. 'I don't know, Chubby. Didn't you think there would be more of an opportunity to take Jerry on? It feels like we're always on the sidelines somehow.'

'The sidelines sound like the safest place to be, if you ask me,' Chubby said. 'I wouldn't worry too much, old boy. There'll be plenty of time for all the derring-do and getting yourself killed business. "The greatest victory is that which requires no battle." So said Sun Tzu in *The Art of War*.'

'You do far too much reading,' Rom said, rising to his feet and tousling Chubby's already unkempt mop of hair.

'Even in the midst of chaos, there is opportunity,' Chubby said sagely, picking up a leatherbound book and waving it in Rom's direction. 'That's Sun Tzu too. Clever chap, considering.'

The following day, while they were still safely alongside in the inlet, Paymaster Lieutenant Geoffrey Stanning, who had served as the logistics officer on the H-class destroyer HMS *Hardy*, visited *Grenade*. *Hardy* had been sunk at Narvik just weeks before. Stanning, who was waiting to join a troopship home, walked with a pronounced limp as he joined *Grenade* for drinks in the wardroom. *Grenade*'s crew had been saddened by the news of the sinking of the *Hardy*, and especially the death of their master, Captain Warburton-Lee, who had been a regular visitor to *Grenade*'s wardroom during happier times back at Scapa Flow.

'We were all bloody cut-up about it,' Courtenay-Boyle told Stanning, with a sympathetic hand resting on the logistics officer's shoulder. 'But you'll be joining *Grenade* for a couple of weeks, so you can hitch a ride back to Blighty. We have a little bit of work to do down at Namsos getting our boys out, but then we'll be taking them and you, and the other injured from

Hardy, back across the North Sea for some proper R and R. At least, that's the current plan.'

'Thank you, sir. Delighted to hear it. We have had a hell of a time,' Stanning said, as Carter, Chubby and Rom leaned in closer, keen to hear of the ship's last moments.

'We had already made two runs at Narvik that day,' Stanning explained. 'But then we were engaged by three surviving German ships. The enemy got across the flotilla's path, and quickly knocked out our forward guns. Further shots with high-explosive shells destroyed much of the pilothouse, set the superstructure on fire and killed or seriously wounded nearly all the officers on the bridge. The captain was past helping, as was the ship's coxswain in the wheelhouse. I realised I was the only bloody officer in a fit state to assume direct command of the ship. The first lieutenant wasn't anywhere to be seen. He was right down aft, though for all I knew he was dead too. Well, as a paymaster, I'm more of an accountant than a conning officer. My ship-handling training had been bloody brief, I can tell you.'

The men laughed supportively as Stanning paused to take a sip of his gin.

'I'd taken a damned bullet in the foot, so I wasn't in a fine way myself. But I could see that the ship was careering out of control towards the shore. I got no answer from the voicepipe to the wheelhouse, so I did what any one of us would do — I climbed the ladder and took control of the helm myself, to the best of my ability.'

'Extraordinary,' Rom muttered.

'Yes, you did a damned fine job, Stanning,' Courtenay-Boyle said.

'So, what happened?' Chubby asked.

'I got her under control and after a brief time two ratings found me in the wheelhouse and took over, thank God. I returned to the bridge to receive damage reports. *Hardy* was still heading straight for the German destroyers passing across her path, and I determined that the best thing we could do was to ram one of the buggers, in keeping with the last order of the captain, you see. "Keep on engaging the enemy," he had said as he lay dying.'

'You rammed her then?' Carter asked.

'I tried to,' Stanning recalled, his eyes distant. 'But as we closed in on the German destroyer, further shells struck home and knocked out one of the boiler rooms, and the engine room began to flood. That's when I knew that the only course of action open to us was to turn the ship towards shore and beach her. So, with *Hardy* now well ablaze and the rear gun still firing, we coasted onto the shore and heeled over. At this point the first lieutenant, who had been at his action station in the stern, reached the bridge and took over the evacuation. It was a hell of a day, I can tell you.'

The officers of *Grenade*, who were all still leaning in towards their guest, taking in every word of his recollection with bated breath, stood silent for a long moment. Eventually, Courtenay-Boyle shook his head. 'I suppose I'd better get you another bloody drink,' he said.

CHAPTER NINE

HMS *Warspite* arrived back at the mouth of the fjord like a great benevolent giant. She was returning after playing a key role in the Battle of Narvik earlier in the month. More than twice the size of *Grenade*, she loomed over her. The Queen Elizabeth-class battleship was also considerably more battle-tested — having launched in 1913, she had been completed at the height of the last war in time to serve in the Battle of Jutland. But within a few hours, even she was dwarfed, as HMS *Ark Royal*, the epically proportioned aircraft carrier, glided towards them from the horizon, all 22,000 tons of her. With the flight deck overhanging the stern, there was no mistaking her silhouette, and within half an hour she had taken up position as a truly imposing presence on the seascape, complete with neat rows of Swordfish aircraft ready for action.

Grenade met this imposing new flotilla and led them out for manoeuvres along the coast. Rom had grown used to being on the bridge in the largest ship around, so to be joined by two such giants of the oceans was a bewildering, Gulliverian experience. But the initial flutter of nerves soon passed, and buoyed by the reassuring presence of Courtenay-Boyle, who seemed entirely unfazed by the ships they now sailed beside, the men settled into a series of familiar patrols.

But just hours later, *Warspite* left the group and lined up her four mighty 15-inch twin guns. After a brief and eerie pause, her bombardment of Narvik began. The town was now entirely under German control, and it was as much as the Royal Navy could now do to fire at it from a distance, while keeping a careful watch for U-boats, which were known to be operating in the area.

The following day, *Grenade* received orders to peel off from the Narvik action to support the evacuation of British and French troops from Namsos, further south. Within hours they joined another flotilla of British and French destroyers, under the command of Lord Louis Mountbatten. As he was a second cousin of the king, the officers on *Grenade* looked upon their new flotilla leader with a slightly starstruck awe. Even Courtenay-Boyle showed signs of nervousness, fiddling with the buttons on his cuffs when he reported to Mountbatten for the first time on the voice set. But moments later, he walked back across the pilothouse and stood beside Rom and Carter, muttering, 'Actually, he seems rather normal.'

They sailed into a thick soup of fog as they neared Namsos — conditions that had held locally for days, forcing Mountbatten to repeatedly delay the evacuation of Allied troops. Meeting the other British destroyers, they took their place in the misty flotilla and waited for the weather to turn in their favour, monitoring the ASDIC unit constantly for signs of lurking U-boats.

At midnight, Courtenay-Boyle yawned and turned to Rom, who had just come on watch. 'You have the conn, Mr Hutchinson,' he said, without any particular emphasis.

'I have the conn, sir?' Rom double-checked. He had never yet been made conning officer, the officer in control of the ship. He felt a rising panic at the awesome responsibility that was being placed on his shoulders. It may have been a quiet moment in terms of any obvious enemy threat, but despite the still heavy fog, he was about to officially take control of the bridge for the first time.

'Yes, you have to step up and get some experience at some time.'

'Of course, sir. I have the conn, sir.'

'Good man,' the captain smiled, turning to make his way down to his cabin to catch a few hours' sleep. 'Do raise me if there are any problems,' he added.

'Yes, sir,' Rom said, saluting and turning back to the helm. Not quite at anchor, they were on the maritime equivalent of treading water, occasionally turning in large figures of eight, bringing them sometimes closer to and sometimes more distant from the other destroyers in the flotilla. Rom was under orders to maintain this pattern, keeping a constant lookout for signs of any enemy threat against the flotilla.

'Well, Wheels,' he said to the quartermaster, who was on the helm, 'steer course two six seven, steady as she goes.'

'Steady on two six seven, sir,' Wheels responded mechanically.

Rom took a deep breath and watched the fog roll around the ship as she moved silently through the cold night. The sea had an eerily still glint, like onyx. He could hardly believe that the ship was in his hands. The safety of more than three hundred men rested on his shoulders. Some were working around the ship or eating in the mess, while others slept soundlessly in their bunks. He made a conscious decision to simply carry on with his work without giving the potential risks too much thought. But just twenty minutes in, the ASDIC rating came through on the voicepipe.

'We have a contact, sir,' the voice said hesitantly. 'It's only faint at the moment, but there's something there.'

'Could it be a U-boat?' Rom asked nervously.

'Yes, sir, it could be.'

Should he wake the captain after just twenty minutes' sleep for what could well be a false alarm?

'How far distant?' Rom asked.

'Three miles or so, sir. Course zero four zero.'

'Keep me informed if it gets more definite.'

'Yes, sir.'

Rom turned his orders back towards the wheelhouse. 'Steer a course zero four zero. Possible U-boat contact.'

A minute passed, then two minutes. The fog seemed to be lifting a little. He returned to the voicepipe. 'Any clearer?'

'Yes, sir, it is definitely looking more like a U-boat.'

'Very well,' Rom muttered. 'Messenger!' he called out, and a young rating emerged from the shadows at the back of the pilothouse. 'Please wake the captain and tell him we have a probable U-boat contact.'

'Yes, sir,' the youngster said, and was gone in a moment.

The speed at which Courtenay-Boyle managed to return to the bridge told Rom that the captain had not been asleep and probably had not even taken his shoes off.

'Well done, Hutchinson,' he said calmly. 'I'll take the conn.'

'You have the conn, sir.' Rom worked hard to keep his voice calm as the relief surged through him. He stepped back, ready to set about his more familiar work.

The captain spoke once again into the voicepipe to the ASDIC rating below. He then radioed the flotilla leader. 'We have a contact, sir, three miles distant. We are going after it.'

'Understood,' Rom could hear the clipped voice at the end of the line respond jovially. 'Happy hunting, *Grenade*.'

'Should I move the ship to action stations, sir?' Rom asked tentatively.

'Good God, no, not yet, lad!' The captain laughed. 'Let the poor buggers sleep on for a while yet.'

'Yes, sir.' Rom felt his cheeks reddening.

'I'll let you know when, Hutchinson. For now, act as talker, would you? Save me moving back and forth to that thing.'

'Yes, sir.' Rom nodded and walked swiftly to take up the voicepipe. He listened carefully to the voice of the ASDIC rating and relayed everything he said to the captain. 'The contact is bearing zero eight seven, sir.'

'She's turning,' Courtenay-Boyle grumbled, before relaying a change of direction to Wheels.

'Contact steady, one mile distant.' There was a momentary pause, before Rom added, 'ASDIC reports she's turned again, sir, and is heading straight towards us.'

'I don't believe she's aware we're here just yet,' Courtenay-Boyle mused. He turned to address the chief armourer. 'Lake, prepare the depth charges. Hutchinson, sound action stations.'

The klaxon sounded harshly throughout the vessel. As the ship's crew was brought to their action stations, the atmosphere on the bridge became noticeably tense.

'Range eleven hundred yards, sir,' Rom said.

Courtenay-Boyle walked across and took a look for himself at the ASDIC repeater. 'Slow her down to six knots — I don't want to draw attention to ourselves.'

'Yes, sir,' barked Carter, who had joined them on the bridge.

'Range five hundred yards, course steady.'

'Let's be ready, gentlemen,' Courtenay-Boyle muttered. 'They have absolutely no idea we are closing in on them.'

Rom frowned as he listened to the ASDIC rating's next message. 'ASDIC reports, sir, that the contact has broken up.'

'Broken up?' Courtenay-Boyle barked back.

'It has split and is heading in numerous directions.'

There was a silence on the bridge.

'ASDIC reports contact lost, sir.'

The tension on the bridge seemed to be at breaking point.

'ASDIC confirms contact was most likely a school of fish, sir,' Rom repeated after a moment.

'Stand down action stations,' Courtenay-Boyle said, rubbing his eyes wearily. 'Let the men who aren't on watch get themselves back to bed.'

Grenade was back with the rest of the flotilla by the early hours of the morning. The fog that had clung to the crest of every wave for days was beginning to lift, and the Norwegian coast appeared as a jagged black line to the east, with the lights of a few wooden houses at Utvorda glowing like stars in an otherwise darkened sky. At four o'clock in the morning, Rom's watch came to an end, and he gave Chubby a weary pat on the shoulder as his friend replaced him as the junior officer on the bridge.

Chubby yawned theatrically. 'Broken sleep,' he grumbled. 'I hope you are more successful in getting your head down, old boy.'

'It's looking like the operation will be underway at first light to start getting our boys onboard. Namsos is just a few miles up the fjord.'

'I heard from Carter that they're pretty well surrounded by the Germans,' Chubby grimaced. 'They'll be glad to get on board.'

'Yes, it sounds like it's not a moment too soon.'

'Well, go on, get your head down while you can.'

But Rom couldn't sleep. The cabin was swaying grotesquely as the ship slowly circled, barely moving more than a few hundred yards for the next two hours. A couple of times, Rom thought the seasickness he had done so well to avoid since the first week aboard was set to make a spectacular return. But he managed to overcome the wave that coursed through the pit of his stomach. Perched on the side of his bunk, he took long, deep breaths, and found his mind returning inexplicably to the Sikh gentleman back at the Chattri Memorial all those weeks before. What was it he had said? Detail and compassion? Those would certainly be the joint requirements for the coming hours if they were to successfully evacuate 10,000 troops before it was too late.

Rom could hear more Allied ships mustering around *Grenade* in preparation for the mission. He grabbed his jacket and walked back out of the cabin, along the corridor and onto the nearest deck to take a look. Far from lifting, it seemed that the fog was descending once again. HMS *Kelly* was treading water a few hundred yards away. The K-class destroyer was a few years younger than *Grenade* and somehow it showed. But it was Mountbatten's ship, and maybe the imperceptible glow that she exuded was more to do with the glamorous royal touch — a subconscious sense that she must somehow be better than *Grenade*. Perhaps a little more polished, at least.

News filtered through to the officers on the bridge of *Grenade* that the decision had been made to go ahead with the evacuation.

'The fog's not entirely lifted, but realistically, they believe it's today or never, given the Germans' increasing dominance around the outskirts of the town,' Courtenay-Boyle explained. 'The good news is that our boys from the RAF have been busy bombing the bastards. They have put Stavanger airport out of action, which will help to give us some air supremacy locally, given the *Ark Royal*'s presence. HMS *Glorious* also arrived overnight, with more aircraft and fully rested pilots. So we're in decent shape to go in. The King's Own Yorkshire Light Infantry is occupying a position close to the main quay.

They've fought their way through all the way from Dombås. It must be more than two hundred miles of extremely rough terrain, with the Germans biting at their heels. They are going to be thoroughly exhausted, so we need to be ready to welcome them warmly. Make sure the sick bay is fully prepared and arrange some temporary bedding wherever you can.'

'Yes, sir,' Carter said. 'MacGregor is going to lead a party to prepare for our guests.'

'Good, good.' Courtenay-Boyle nodded. He walked across to the chart table and pulled out a map of the coastline. Rom, Carter and the rest of the officers on watch gathered around him.

'Two cruisers and four destroyers will wait off the Kya Lighthouse while the three French transports, the *York*, and five destroyers, including ourselves, will be heading straight in, arriving off Namsos itself about 22:30 hours tonight. God knows there is very little in the way of night in this part of the world, so we need to be in and out as quickly as possible.' The captain looked up and carefully considered the officers on the bridge before him. 'I don't want to spend a moment longer than is necessary in the fjord, do you understand? It's like sailing straight into a rat trap.'

'Yes, sir,' the officers answered as one.

'Two transports will be loaded at the stone quay.' He motioned towards a point on the map. 'The other two big ships will be loaded from destroyers and trawlers.'

The day passed quickly in a flourish of preparation. Rom's watch meant he slept from midday until four o'clock in the afternoon. He slept soundly and woke with a start, realising with a flutter of nerves that the operation would be launched within hours. At eight o'clock he was back on the bridge.

The small flotilla moved soundlessly into the mouth of the fjord at 22:30, with *Grenade* following *Afridi* around the twists and turns of the waterway, steep green mountains rising ominously on either side of them in the moonlight. They passed the twisted remains of HMS *Bittern*, sunk just days before, when merciless waves of dive bombers had finally got the better of her anti-aircraft gunners and a single bomb had made contact with her depth charge supply and obliterated the entire quarterdeck. A shiver ran through Rom as he looked down upon it. It resembled a whale carcass that had washed ashore.

After a final turn around a headland, Namsos came unmistakably into view — a vibrant orange glow ahead amidst the darkness of the woodland on either side. *Half the town must be burning*, Rom thought, taking a deep breath as the captain gave his reassuringly calm commands to the wheelhouse without a hint of nervousness in his voice.

Grenade was the third ship to make it to the dilapidated wooden jetty, and the soldiers were lined up neatly in their hundreds, ready to board. Rom joined the captain out on the wing of the bridge and looked down at the battle-weary men in the darkness. Judging by their uniforms, they were not all King's Own Yorkshire Light Infantry, as Rom had expected. Rather they were a mishmash of regiments and ranks, and nationalities — there were escorts from the Norwegian Army wearing pale, overall-like skiwear, open at the neck with regular uniforms beneath and funny little peaked caps that reminded Rom of school caps.

'There are French troops, too,' Courtenay-Boyle said, pointing to a group of men further along the line. The gangplank was down, and the men were moving in an orderly fashion onto *Grenade*, apparently impervious to the booms and crashes of explosives that were lighting up the sky a few miles away on the edge of the town.

'They must be relieved to be getting aboard,' Rom said.

Within just a few minutes, the gangplank was being raised, and *Grenade* slipped away from the quay and ferried the men swiftly back down the fjord, where the cruiser HMS *York* and the troopship *El Mansour* were lying off, waiting to welcome them. At an isolated stone quay close to the mouth of the fjord, *Grenade* moored briefly and the men transferred onto the waiting ships. Stanning and the other injured officers and men from the *Hardy* went with them — Mountbatten having decided it would be best for the *Hardy*'s survivors to get home as swiftly as possible, rather than staying aboard *Grenade*. Stanning paused at the quayside, looked up at the captain, who was once again standing out on the wing with Rom, and saluted. Courtenay-Boyle returned the salute.

Moments later, *Grenade* pulled away from the quay and turned back towards Namsos. After three runs back and forth to the mouth of the fjord, the dawn was rising in the west as one of the other destroyers, *Afridi*, took the British rearguard on board, with the gun crews of *Grenade* covering this final manoeuvre. Rom looked at his watch. It was only 2:20am, but already the sun was casting a watery light on the quayside, its rays rising rapidly behind the wooded hills.

This final group of hardy soldiers had waited behind to explode the Bangsund bridge at midnight, leaving them with ten miles to cover to the embarkation area. Moments after *Afridi* had taken the last of the British troops on board and raised her gangplank, the Germans started shelling the massed motor transport left behind on the quay. *Afridi* turned rapidly and with *Grenade* escorting close behind, the two destroyers made a swift escape out of the lightening fjord.

'Just in the nick of time, I'd say,' Courtenay-Boyle said.

Rom smiled and returned to his duties with another deep breath. Finally, he felt as if he had played a small part in this war that would be worth writing home about.

'Well done, chaps,' the captain added quietly. 'Excellent work from everybody. That was a tremendous effort.'

The mouth of the fjord opened up ahead of them, with the expanse of sea offering a welcome sight for all the officers of the watch after so many hours cramped between the two lofty sides of the fjord. Rom took a moment to process his relief at achieving a successful retreat, but the next words from the captain told him his feelings might be misjudged.

'Your heart goes out to the poor bloody Norwegians left behind,' Courtenay-Boyle muttered. 'They're waking up alone with the enemy in charge. Their national sovereignty has gone, just like that.' He clicked his fingers theatrically and the jubilant mood on the bridge was hushed in an instant.

'Yes, God help them,' Carter said at last, breaking the silence.

'God help them indeed,' Courtenay-Boyle agreed.

The men looked ahead at *Afridi* and beyond her, at the French destroyer *Bison*, forming up into a convoy escort for the troopships setting out on a south-west course towards the British Isles somewhere over the far horizon. At that moment, there was a cry from the lookout above. The captain stuck his head out onto the port wing.

'What is it?'

'Dive bombers heading in from the north-east, sir!'

'Wheels, full right rudder and set a zigzagging course,'

'Aye aye, sir!' the quartermaster bellowed from the wheelhouse.

The captain dashed to the aft of the pilothouse, picked up the voicepipe and ordered the communications officer to radio all ships in the flotilla a warning of dive bombers approaching. But by the time Courtenay-Boyle had got his words out, the two Junkers 87 aircraft were fully visible ahead, screaming mercilessly as they plummeted down at a dizzying fifty-degree angle, concentrating their payloads towards the front magazine of the French destroyer. The bombs seemed to hang in the air for a brief moment, before making contact with the deck of *Bison* in a booming ball of flame.

'They've struck *Bison*!' the lookout shouted down needlessly.

All the officers on the bridge were gazing in horror towards the stricken vessel.

The Junkers aircraft, which had regained altitude rapidly with a steep climb on the port side of *Bison*, seemed to give their wings a jubilant waggle as they turned back towards the land before *Grenade*'s anti-aircraft guns even managed to rattle off a single round.

'Message from Com escort,' Carter called over from the voicepipe. 'We're to join *Afridi*, *Imperial* and *Griffin* in the rescue operation. The crew of *Bison* are abandoning ship. She's badly damaged.'

Sure enough, in the precious few minutes it took for *Afridi* and *Grenade* to catch her up, *Bison* had already started lurching and some of the French sailors had managed to lower lifeboats and were pulling away from the destroyer. *Afridi* slowed to meet the lifeboats, while Courtenay-Boyle directed *Grenade* to line up alongside the lurching *Bison*, and a party was sent up to the forward deck to help the French who were all too keen to make the perilous leap away from *Bison*, which was now well alight. *Imperial* and *Griffin* caught up with *Bison* and set about supporting *Grenade* and *Afridi* in their rescue efforts.

Rom and Chubby, who had been sent down from the bridge to help manage the rescue operation from the forward deck, ran from one Frenchman to the next to offer blankets and a guiding arm of support. Some were badly burned, and stretchers were produced to carry the worst casualties straight down to the sick bay, where the doctor had been alerted.

In just minutes, *Bison* was abandoned, the captain being the last to make the perilous jump across onto the deck of *Grenade*. Rom would later find out that more than one hundred and thirty men had been killed in the initial blast, but the speed at which the three Allied destroyers were on hand to facilitate such a rapid rescue operation meant the casualty numbers had been kept to an absolute minimum.

As *Grenade* finally pulled away from the stricken French ship, *Bison* slumped unceremoniously down towards the sea, and in moments the waves were crashing across her fo'c'sle. The French captain stood on the deck of *Grenade* and watched as his ship went down.

The solemnity of the moment was broken by the returning JU87 aircraft, joined now by a pair of JU88s mirroring the attack from the opposite side of the sky. This time, as they dived towards the flotilla, it was clear that it was *Afridi* that was in their sights. *Afridi*'s own gunners turned towards the aircraft, as did the gunners on *Grenade*. But the nippy little bombers seemed to easily evade the lines of anti-aircraft fire, and released their bombs apparently effortlessly towards *Afridi*. The bombs from the JU88s followed in quick succession. One connected with *Afridi*'s port side, just forward of the bridge, while another struck the boiler room and immediately started a ravaging fire at the after end of the mess decks.

The flotilla watched in impotent rage as *Afridi* met her fate within moments. She went down bow-first, leaving the remaining destroyer crews shell-shocked as they floated in this now suddenly peaceful stretch of open sea, 150 nautical miles west-north-west of Vega Island.

Grenade circled back to pick up any survivors she could, but many men went down with *Afridi*.

Two of the Stukas turned and reapproached from the west. Courtenay-Boyle must have sensed the threat, because from where he was, working to help the survivors of *Bison* on the forward deck, Rom felt the ship lurch beneath him as the quartermaster turned right full rudder and increased the speed to zigzag away from the scene.

The two JU87s were already diving again towards *Grenade*. This time, only one bomb was released. It exploded on the edge of the deck, taking out the forward gun, the crew of which had been turning to face the enemy.

'They've taken out a gun!' Rom called out to Chubby, as he dashed back up towards the bridge.

By the time he reached the pilothouse, *Grenade* was steaming out into the open sea, and the dive bombers must have thought better of risking another approach. They disappeared into the ashen skies.

Remmie was also embarking on a new experience. As the *John Holt* steamed away from the quayside at Gladstone Dock, the familiar waterfront of Liverpool opened up in her wake. Remmie took a moment to look up from his work painting the bulkheads, and let the crisp breeze blowing in from the Irish Sea ruffle his hair. He looked on towards the mouth of the Mersey, with the familiar outline of New Brighton Pier appearing to the portside. With its ragtag collection of fairground rides and penny slot machines, and its landing stage for the ferry at the end, it provoked a burst of nostalgia in Remmie. He could almost taste the sticks of rock he knew from his childhood visits to the resort. Today the pier looked empty and devoid of life.

But a little beyond it, in Liverpool Bay, a small flotilla of three dozen merchant vessels was lining up in columns, overlooked by a sturdy escort of three Royal Navy corvettes and one destroyer. It would be Remmie's first experience of sailing as part of an Atlantic convoy, but increasingly this kind of formal protection was the only realistic way of taking on the North Atlantic relatively safely. With the U-boat fleets growing in strength by the day, a ship's safety even when part of such a mighty convoy was by no means guaranteed. Many merchant vessels were being torpedoed and sunk each month, and news of such disasters striking ships familiar to Remmie was becoming increasingly commonplace. The *John Holt* would remain under the protection of the convoy as far as the Azores, before peeling off to head south — taking on the second half of the voyage to the Gulf of Guinea alone.

He had heard so much about convoys from the other crews, Remmie was thrilled to be part of such an enormous demonstration of British pluck and sheer organisational brilliance. He turned back to his paintbrush and continued making cheerful strokes, while the *John Holt* edged into her place in the convoy that was forming up. He could see the commodore's ship flashing a signal to the bridge with what he assumed to be instructions about the formation. He heard the clatter of the *John Holt*'s signal lamp as it flashed back.

The destroyer manoeuvred nimbly around them, with its captain — who Remmie knew would also be the commander of the escort — surveying them through a pair of binoculars. The sight of the destroyer so close at hand, frenetic in all its bustling glory, made Remmie immediately think of his brother, serving out there somewhere on a destroyer much like this one.

But his thoughts for his twin were cut short by another sharp reminder of how his family's fates lay in the hands of Neptune. The voice of one of his fellow deckhands, Jimmy Matterson, reached him across the deck. 'It's your Da, Remmie!'

Remmie followed Matterson's pointing finger out towards the west, and sure enough, steaming towards the mouth of the Mersey was the familiar outline of the *Robert Holt*. He knew his father would be on the bridge, ready to meet the pilot, and he couldn't resist offering a wave — a futile gesture, given the 1,000 yards between them. The sister ships gave each other a sororal toot of their horns as they swept past each other, the doubling of their combined speed making the encounter fleeting. As the *Robert Holt* moved off out of view around the Wirral coastline, Remmie somehow felt more alone than he had done just a few minutes before.

CHAPTER TEN

After transferring the survivors from *Bison* to a hospital ship, *Grenade* was given permission to depart briefly from the flotilla to conduct another burial at sea. *Grenade*'s five gunners who had been lost in the action slipped beneath the waves alongside the dozen men from *Bison* who had not long survived their injuries after making it on board *Grenade*. The men reticently sang a few unaccompanied verses of 'Eternal Father, Strong to Save'. Their words were quickly swept up by the wind and scattered out across the waves.

Courtenay-Boyle walked back to the bridge holding his leatherbound prayer book, his expression one of deep sorrow, but his voice betrayed no emotion as he returned to the pilothouse and in his familiar clipped voice gave the next steering order to Wheels.

The damage to *Grenade* herself was quickly patched up, although A-gun would be out of action for the remainder of the voyage. Rom walked across and spoke with Bill Ridgewell, the able seaman he had met servicing his Lewis gun just days before. Ridgewell was ashen-faced as he looked out towards the open sea.

'You all right?' Rom asked.

'The bloody thing jammed,' Ridgewell said. 'It jammed right up.'

'What jammed?'

'The blasted Lewis gun. After all that work to maintain it for weeks, when the bloody thing was needed, it just jammed up. I couldn't do another thing once it jammed, sir.'

Rom patted Ridgewell on the shoulder. 'Don't worry, man, you did what you could. We all did what we could.'

'I know, but I had the Lewis gun, sir, and I couldn't fire back. I feel terrible about it, sir, really I do.'

'You mustn't concern yourself, Ridgewell,' Rom said, his voice gentle. 'Nobody could have done any more than you did. Sometimes it's just all down to luck. You have to play with the hand you're dealt. You did your duty to the very best of your ability.'

'Thank you, sir,' Ridgewell said. His eyes turned back towards the horizon, but Rom could see his bottom lip shaking as he spoke. 'That's very kind of you, sir.'

The atmosphere was subdued throughout the ship as she returned to join the flotilla making its way back across towards Harwich. For the first few hours, *Grenade* steamed along on the starboard flank of the troopships, serving as part of the protective screen against potential U-boat attacks. Night was drawing in as the voice set crackled into life. It was a message from the flotilla leader. Courtenay-Boyle's face creased into a frown as he listened.

'We're being sent hunting once again, gentlemen,' he announced, once he had replaced the receiver. Picking up the voicepipe, he called down to the ASDIC rating on duty. '*Kelly* has picked up a contact a mile to the west, bearing zero five zero. See if you can pick it up; she's certain it's a U-boat.' He turned his attention from the voicepipe to the wheelhouse, ordering a sudden change in direction towards the incoming threat.

'ASDIC has her, sir!' Carter shouted across from the voicepipe a moment later. 'She is turning right in front of us, eight hundred yards distant.'

'She's not spotted us.'

'Looks to be the case, sir.'

'Prepare the depth charge teams, Mr Lake,' Courtenay-Boyle ordered. Rom sensed something almost weary about the captain's tone.

'Aye aye, sir,' the chief armourer said.

'She has turned again, sir,' Carter interrupted. 'She's going to move straight below us on this course.'

'She really doesn't know we're here, does she?' Courtenay-Boyle's enthusiasm for the battle was clearly on the rise.

'Two hundred yards distant, steady as she goes, sir,' Carter called again. 'ASDIC reports she seems fairly deep.'

'Reduce speed to twelve knots. On my signal, Mr Lake, set for a deep pattern.'

'Deep pattern, aye aye, sir.'

'Fifty yards.' Carter sounded breathless. 'She's going to pass right beneath us.'

Rom looked from the first lieutenant to the captain to the chief armourer, his heart in his mouth.

'Fire, Mr Lake,' Courtenay-Boyle said calmly.

'Fire one!' Lake called down the voicepipe.

The barrel-shaped depth charges clattered over the side of the ship, and a moment later the sea lit up with a deep boom — as if lightning was forming below the surface all around the destroyer.

'ASDIC reports contact is turning,' Carter said, then more loudly, with a hint of excitement creeping into his voice, 'ASDIC reports contact is rising rapidly.'

Rom was at Courtenay-Boyle's righthand side as the submarine burst through the grey waves to the portside of the ship, before almost immediately diving once again.

'I think we've damaged her,' Courtenay-Boyle said. 'Lake, have your gunners ready for her if she resurfaces. Does ASDIC still have a contact, Carter?'

'ASDIC reports contact is stationary.'

'Bring her round again, Wheels,' Courtenay-Boyle said.

'They're back on the surface, Captain!' Chubby shrieked from down in the pilothouse. 'They're bobbing around like a cork out there.'

'They're completely out of trim,' Courtenay-Boyle agreed. 'We must have knocked out their ballast tanks. They seem incapable of diving.'

'Looks like we'll need to take prisoners, sir,' Rom said. 'The hatch on their conning tower has opened.'

Completely forgetting his bridge discipline in the excitement of the moment, Chubby scampered across the pilothouse and dashed out on to the outside port wing to get a better view. 'They have their hands up!' he shouted jubilantly up towards the captain on the bridge, but at the same moment a loud clatter came from the U-boat's 20mm anti-aircraft gun. A hail of bullets peppered the wing of *Grenade*'s bridge, lifting Chubby and jerking his body around in a grotesque jig as his blood sprayed back against the portside windows of the pilothouse. As the firing ceased, his body was released from its macabre dance, and he fell heavily back into the pilothouse, crumpling like an empty sack.

Rom gazed in horror at the remains of his fellow cadet.

'Mr Lake,' Courtenay-Boyle said calmly, 'give them all you've got. Fire at will.'

'Fire at will,' Lake repeated down the voicepipe.

A moment later the armoury crews let rip with machine guns. Within seconds the stream of bullets tore through the two submariners who had been manning the anti-aircraft deck gun. In another moment, two of the big 4.7-inch guns burst to life and pummelled the U-boat, sending the crew members who had emerged tumbling from the conning tower. The vessel barrel-rolled like a dying whale, before letting out an enormous death groan, twisting in the water. She slipped down vertically beneath the waves, and within another moment she was plummeting out of sight towards the depths, leaving behind nothing but an expanding pool of oily bubbles.

There was a long silence on the bridge. Nobody moved, until Courtenay-Boyle finally spoke. 'Call for the doctor to come up to the pilothouse, please, Mr Carter.'

'Aye aye, sir.'

Rom climbed down to the pilothouse, his hands shaking. He stepped around the body and slumped himself against the cold metal of the superstructure, unblinking in his stunned fury as he watched the medical team arrive and transfer Chubby's remains into a body bag. Courtenay-Boyle and Carter continued with the business of directing the manoeuvres of the 1,300-ton destroyer; a job that could not be put aside on account of grief or shock. The captain took to the voice set and reported the destruction of the U-boat to the flotilla leader on HMS *Kelly*.

Courtenay-Boyle handed control of the bridge over to Carter and moved wearily down the steps. He glanced towards Rom, who couldn't stop trembling as he watched the scene. It was as if he was somehow separate from it, like a viewer in the auditorium of a cinema. It took the doctor and three sickbay attendants to carry the body bag out of the pilothouse and lower it down on to the deck.

'Go and get some rest, Hutchinson,' Courtenay-Boyle said.

'I'm still on watch,' Rom said with a jolt, as if he had momentarily forgotten he was supposed to be working.

'No, you need to take some time alone in your cabin. It's been a damned shock for us all, but I know you two were good pals.'

'Yes, sir,' Rom said and, collecting himself, he stepped out of the pilothouse. He stood for a while on the deck and gazed out towards the flotsam that remained of the submarine, which was now being left far behind in their wake. It was almost impossible for him to take on board what he had just witnessed — the killing of his friend, but more shocking yet, the unsentimental way in which the running of the bridge had gone on with barely a second glance at the corpse. He fully understood that there was a bigger picture that needed to be taken into account, but he was dumbfounded by the lack of an emotional reaction.

Rom wondered if Courtenay-Boyle had perhaps just developed a capacity to delay his response. Would he crumple, perhaps, the moment he closed the door of his cabin? Rom lit a cigarette, cupping his hands around his silver lighter to prevent it from being blown out by the bitter wind coming up off the North Sea. He took a long, slow draw on the cigarette and released the lungful of smoke over the side of the rail. He thought carefully about the captain's ability to cope so rigidly with the horror of having a sub-lieutenant gunned down in front of him.

'Detail and compassion,' he said aloud, talking only to the wind and the waves that stretched out ahead of him, but remembering the Sikh man at the Chattri Memorial. Is this what he had meant? The capacity to focus on detail first and compassion second?

Later that day the officers and men formed up once again on the quarterdeck. A single catafalque was waiting, shrouded in a

Union Flag. Courtenay-Boyle's now familiar words from the prayer book echoed against the bulkheads and Rom felt a heavy weight pulling at the pit of his stomach as he watched what was left of Chubby Smith slide discreetly towards the hungry waves.

CHAPTER ELEVEN

A few days later, *Grenade* moored up at Harwich where she was to await repairs to her forward gun. Courtenay-Boyle had given Rom six days' leave and he caught a train and settled in for the long journey back up to Liverpool. He had to disembark in London and travel across the capital using the underground, before meeting the train that would head north. He found he was sharing a carriage with an elderly vicar, who wasted no time in striking up a conversation as the locomotive ahead of them groaned and hissed its way out towards the northern suburbs.

'You've been at sea?' the clergyman asked, noticing Rom's uniform.

'Yes, sir,' Rom nodded. 'Evacuating the poor blighters from Norway.'

'Bad business,' the vicar said. 'Did your ship see much action?'

Rom nodded and turned his face towards the window. 'We got men out. We sunk a U-boat. And we lost a good man — a good friend — in the process.'

The vicar nodded. 'It's so hard to lose our friends, especially in war. But you must be strong, my boy. You have lost a friend, but it sounds very much as though he gave his life saving many others.'

Rom shook his head. 'In fact, it was a senseless blunder. He should never have been out on the wing like that with a U-boat on the surface. He was a damned fool.'

The vicar raised a calming hand. 'You needn't tell me the details if it's painful. But it's right and proper that you should remember your friend with compassion.'

Rom looked back at the vicar with alarm. 'Why do you say that? Detail and compassion.'

The vicar looked at him blankly. 'What do you mean, my boy?'

'Never mind,' Rom said, and turned back towards the window. 'If you'll excuse me, I need to get some sleep.'

'Of course, you must be so tired. Get some rest.'

Rom was welcomed home by his mother, who laughed and wept simultaneously when he turned up unannounced on the doorstep. His father and brother were both at sea and the house seemed strangely quiet. He watched the dust motes circling in a shaft of sunlight as he waited patiently for his mother to boil the kettle for tea.

'Has it been strange, being here on your own?' he called out towards the kitchen.

'Yes, it has — I'm so used to having you boys about. It's been eerily quiet. When do you have to go back?'

'I'll have to be back down in Harwich on Sunday. She sails Monday morning.'

'Such a flying visit.'

'I know,' Rom said. 'I'll just be glad to sleep in my own bed for a few nights.'

Eileen returned with a tea tray.

'Biscuits too — you're spoiling me, Mother.'

She put her cold hand to his stubbly cheek. 'Well, I'll need to feed you up while you're home, won't I?'

Rom laughed. 'The food's not so bad on *Grenade*. Good old-fashioned stodge, mostly.'

She poured the tea and looked at him cautiously. Rom imagined she was about to ask if he had seen much action, as the vicar on the train had done. But then she clearly thought better of it, and offered the plate of biscuits.

'They're rationing biscuits, so I've been holding on to this packet,' she said. 'I didn't like to open them just for myself. It seemed a waste.'

Rom bit the biscuit. 'Well, we'd better enjoy them while we can, I suppose.'

'Sugar, meat, cheese — it's all on ration now, you know,' she went on. 'It has me up the wall, with all the coupons. I give my sugar coupons to young Mrs Firmstone next door. With little ones around, she can make better use of it. I don't need it. I've even got used to not having it in my tea.'

Rom took a sip and scrunched up his face a little. 'Oh yes, it's not quite the same, is it?'

Eileen smiled benevolently. 'Well,' she said, turning her eyes to the back garden where the apple tree was in blossom, 'nothing's the same anymore, is it? We all have to make our little sacrifices.'

Rom nodded. 'That's true enough, Mother.'

The two of them sat for a moment and listened to the ticking of the clock.

'So have you seen much of anybody?' Rom asked, breaking the silence.

'Charlotte, you mean?'

'No,' Rom flushed. 'Not particularly. Why, have you seen much of her?'

'It was wrong of you to give that girl the heave-ho just because you were going off to sea.'

'I thought it was for the best,' Rom said quietly. 'You know, in case anything happened.'

'Things always happen in life. There's no accounting for that, Rom. You can't let what might happen stop you from living.'

Rom nodded. 'Maybe I'll look her up while I'm home. See how she's faring.'

Eileen smiled and patted his shoulder. 'Yes, you do that. More tea?'

Rom handed her his empty cup. 'That would be lovely.'

Eileen picked up the teapot from the tray. By the time she had turned back towards him, Rom had crumpled over and was sobbing.

'Oh, Rom,' she said soothingly, quickly replacing the teapot on the tray and putting an arm around him. 'What is it?'

'My friend was killed right in front of me,' he gasped, giving a loud cough as he tried to gain control over his emotions. 'I'm sorry,' he added. 'It's been a difficult few weeks.'

'You poor dear,' she said quietly. 'What happened out there?'

Rom took a deep breath and lifted his shoulders back as he wiped away the tears with his fists. 'It's all right. I'm fine now,' he said. 'It's the shock of being home, I think.'

'Of course it is, dear.' His mother nodded understandingly. 'You must not know whether you're coming or going.'

The next morning Rom put on his dressing gown and wandered down to the kitchen.

'I half expected that the king might have turned up for a cup of tea,' he said to his mother, as he put the kettle on the hob.

'Oh, Rom,' his mother chuckled. 'You do come out with such nonsense. What are you going to do today?'

'Just relax and get my strength back, I suppose. I might go for a walk later.'

'Good idea. Now, I'm assuming you'll be wanting the full fry-up for breakfast? Bacon, eggs, sausage, fried bread, mushrooms and fried tomatoes?'

'I thought you were under the thumb of the ration book?'

Eileen smiled. 'A good mother will always find ways round such things for special occasions. Now, don't you be worrying about any of that. Just sit yourself down at the kitchen table. I'll make the tea,' she added, shooing him away from the hob.

'I do hope you're not getting yourself into trouble,' Rom muttered as he took his seat, 'just for the sake of doubling my fighting weight in a week.'

'Nonsense,' Eileen tutted. 'One egg or two?'

'One will be fine, thank you, Mother.'

An hour later, with the breakfast dishes piled high in the sink, Eileen encouraged Rom to go for a walk.

'I can't have you under my feet all day. There's work to be done.'

The streets of the leafy suburb felt peculiarly familiar, as if nothing here had changed at all, while Rom's life had been so thoroughly transformed. It was an unsettling feeling. He found himself wandering around looking at these surreally familiar sights in search of a sense of normality, but somehow finding none. He stood and looked up at the old school building, the playground shrouded by the silence of the weekend. He walked to the local library, where he had until very recently been a regular borrower. He was hit by the familiar musty smell of the books, the clunk-click noise of the librarian's stamp. There was a comfort to being there, with dusty shafts of light slanting in from the high, narrow windows that circled the space above the bookshelves.

He picked up a familiar novel — one of the *Hornblower* series. The dust jacket was the same as the one he had at home, but the library's copy was a little more frayed around the edges. He glanced through it, then returned it to the shelf and wandered back out into the street.

Rom walked to the local park and sat for a while on a bench, enjoying the feel of the sun on his face and the sound of the ducks in the pond flapping and fussing. Then he knew where he must go if he was really going to be able to take some time to think about the trials and tribulations of Norway. He walked down onto the fine, powdery sand of Crosby beach. The sea stretched out before him, glistening in the spring heatwave. The wiry grass in the dunes quietly shushed the calling gulls that circled above. There was a saline smell wafting across the waves of the estuary and a merchant ship was heading out around the coast. It seemed to be riding high on the gently rolling sea, having just unburdened itself of its entire load in Liverpool's docks.

Rom walked on a little to the quieter end of the beach, where the sands were broad and open, as the tide had retreated, stretching out into a vast void of watery light and wet, rippled sand. His first thought, as he saw the feminine silhouette appear ahead of him in the haze, was that his imagination was at play; that he was replaying in his mind that final moment of goodbye when he had last turned from Charlotte towards the sea. But as he walked closer, he realised it was a woman standing with her back to him, taking in the sweeping vista. A few steps closer still, and he knew it was her — he had never seen another woman with hair that flamed and danced in the breeze quite like Charlotte's.

'I do hope you've not been standing here this whole time,' he said, having silently walked to within a few yards of her. She turned with a start, her forehead creasing as she raised a hand to sweep the hair from her eyes and gaze back at Rom. 'You've not been standing here since we last spoke, have you?'

'You needn't flatter yourself,' she said eventually, before softening her tone. 'How are you, Rom?'

'Surviving, thanks. How about yourself?'

Her eyes glistened and her lips moved silently before she eventually spoke again. 'I thought I'd never see you again.'

'I wasn't sure myself,' he replied with a shrug, walking closer to Charlotte. They stood side by side and both took in the view out across the waves. 'I'm only home for a few days' leave. It's so strange to be back.'

'You've grown accustomed to life aboard ship then?'

Rom nodded. 'We've been serving in Norway for the last few weeks. Getting our boys out, as the Germans swept up through the country. It was a bad business.'

'I was thinking about you,' Charlotte said quietly.

Rom turned to her, but didn't say anything for a few moments. 'I've thought a lot about you too,' he said at last, and turned back towards the sea.

'My sister has been trying to get me to see some farmer chap — a friend of her boyfriend. But he lives miles away, out near Ormskirk, and only comes into town to go to the grain merchant. So it was hardly convenient.'

'Did you like him?'

Now it was Charlotte's turn to shrug. 'I hardly knew him. He wasn't my type at all. But he was pleasant enough to chat to. It was him who put the idea into my head about joining the Land Army.'

'You're joining the Land Army?' Rom laughed a little. 'It hardly sounds like your cup of tea.'

'Well, nothing's decided yet.' Charlotte shrugged. 'I'll have to do something for the war effort, won't I? It'll be the Land Army or the WRNS.'

'I suppose we're all having to do our bit. I think you should opt for the Wrens, but then I'm biased. Though the blue uniform would do much more with your complexion than the brown of the Land Army.'

Charlotte slapped his shoulder playfully. 'Women don't just spend all their time thinking about how they look in their clothes, you know,' she said. 'Although the blue uniform would be more flattering.'

'Are you still working in the corner shop?'

'Oh yes,' she said. 'I couldn't leave Mrs Johnson in the lurch at a time like this.'

'She's lucky to have you,' Rom said with a smile.

Charlotte turned to study his face. 'Is she?'

For a moment, it felt like they were about to embrace, but they didn't. Their hands flickered, as if they might reach out and grab each other at any moment, but then they were awkwardly returned to their sides.

'Well, it was good to see you, Charlotte,' Rom said weakly.

'You too,' Charlotte whispered, reaching up to move her long hair back from her eyes once again and turning her face into the wind.

Rom started to walk away, but Charlotte made a little sound to call him back. 'Will you write to me, Rom? We should at least keep in touch.'

Rom nodded. 'Yes, I'm sorry. I will. Will you write to me?'

'If you tell me where to send my letters.'

'I will.' He paused a moment, as if he was about to speak again, but then waved it away with a nervous laugh. 'It really was so nice to see you.'

Rom didn't leave Charlotte waiting long for a letter. By the time she had got home from the beach, he had pushed a hastily scribbled note through her front door:

Charlotte, do you fancy the pictures tomorrow night? Come and knock on my door at seven o'clock, if you do, and we can get a drink somewhere before the eight o'clock film. It would be good to see you again, before I rejoin the ship.

Rom

The next evening, Rom was dressed in his finest civvies and fiddling with his tie in the hall mirror, when Charlotte knocked on the door as the clock was still striking seven. Rom opened the door and laughed.

'You always were a stickler for being on time.'

'Are you not wearing your Navy uniform?'

'Did you want me to wear my uniform?'

'I just imagined you might.'

'I can go and change, if you like,' Rom said.

'Don't be silly, of course not. You look nice.'

'Thanks.' Rom nodded.

'And I suppose I look like the dog's dinner,' Charlotte said after a brief pause.

'No,' Rom laughed. 'I mean, you look lovely too.'

The film, *Waterloo Bridge*, starred Vivien Leigh. She played a ballerina who met an army officer, played by Robert Taylor, by chance, on Waterloo Bridge in London. He was preparing to return to the front when their love blossomed in a whirlwind romance. They parted, promising eternal devotion to each other, but a few weeks later, Vivien Leigh's character found the officer's name among a list of the dead in a newspaper. Her life spiralled and she ended up working as a prostitute in the direst depths of despair while longing for her lost love.

Rom and Charlotte didn't speak for a few minutes as they walked out of the cinema, hand in hand. It was Rom who eventually broke the silence. 'Well, it wasn't the ideal choice of film, was it?' he said. 'I had no idea. I'm sorry.'

Charlotte smiled at Rom in the muted lamplight. 'It's all right. It was just a film.'

'Yes, quite.' Rom walked Charlotte home. She reached up to kiss his cheek as he delivered her to her doorstep. He sensed the curtains twitching in the windows.

'My mother's still up,' she said.

'I'll be getting the train back down to Harwich tomorrow,' Rom said.

'Take care of yourself, won't you?'

Rom nodded. 'You too, Charlotte.'

'You will write, when you can, won't you?'

'I will. I promise.'

Charlotte glanced at the window and the curtain jostled back into place. She leaned forward swiftly and kissed Rom's lips. 'I'll be waiting for it every day,' she said, before adding, 'the letter, I mean.'

'Next time, I'll take you to see something a bit jollier, I promise.' Rom felt her hand squeezing his.

'Do take care of yourself,' she said again.

He squeezed her hand in return before letting it go and then immediately feeling its absence. He stepped away into the darkness, with a quiet, 'Goodnight.'

CHAPTER TWELVE

It was a long, slow train journey back to the South East, but Rom had plenty to think about. He crossed the capital wearily and made it to the Harwich train with moments to spare. Images flashed before his eyes as he watched the scenery outside the window change gradually from city to countryside. He thought about his mother, alone once again at home. He thought about his brother and father out there somewhere at sea. He thought about Chubby's death and how he would be alone in his cabin now when he got back to the ship. And he thought about Charlotte. Was he doing the right thing, in starting to contact her again? Or should he have trusted his first judgement — that the right thing to do was to release her to live a life without being weighed down by the anxiety of courting a man who is at sea with German U-boats using him for target practice?

Harwich was a depressing, grimy sort of place — as far east as you could travel across Essex before dropping off into the North Sea. It was dominated by a boxy little church that had a small steeple on top of a small tower, as if its builders hadn't quite been able to make up their minds. Then there were ranks of terraced houses and grumbling, sour-faced locals. Rom couldn't get back aboard *Grenade* quickly enough, and was relieved to find her back on the wharf with her new forward gun neatly in place and her decks sparkling.

'Welcome back, Hutchinson,' Carter said as he met him at the top of the gangplank. 'She's all ready to set sail at first light tomorrow morning. You should sleep as soon as you can.

You're back on duty at 0400 and we'll be casting off at 0500 hours.'

'Thank you, sir.'

'Oh, another thing,' Carter added as Rom was about to pass by. 'We've taken all of Smith's things from the cabin. His personal effects will be sent home to his mother. I know she will be devastated. He was a decent boy.'

'Yes, sir, he was.'

'You'll be in there on your own for now, but don't get too used to the space. We have some new subs due to join us in a few weeks' time, fresh out of King Alfred.'

'Right you are, sir.'

'You're looking much better, by the way, Hutchinson,' Carter added. 'It always hits hard — the first one.'

'The first what, sir?'

'The first time you lose a shipmate to this damned war.'

'He wasn't the first, sir, but he was my friend.'

'Absolutely. Get some sleep.'

He did sleep. After the long journey across the country in those stifling, rickety trains, he could have slept for a week. By the time he had dragged himself from his bunk, pulled on his uniform, combed his hair and made it to the bridge, the ship once again had the buzz of a living thing, bustling with activity as the crew prepared to set sail.

'You probably heard, Hutchinson, the Germans have entered the Low Countries,' Courtenay-Boyle said, by way of a greeting. 'So we will be keeping fairly close to the French coast. Word is that our boys will be needing to come home with their tails between their legs rather sooner than we had anticipated, I'm afraid.'

'Are things looking that bad, sir?'

'I'm afraid they are, Hutchinson.'

Within an hour, *Grenade* was pulling out of Harwich and slipping steadily into the uncharacteristically calm waters of the North Sea. Rom looked at the distinctive double-face of his watch. 0500 hours precisely.

At the very same moment, Remmie was 2,721 nautical miles away, watching the sun-baked port of Lagos diminish into aquamarine sea. He looked at his own watch, with its twin time zones both showing 5am. The fact that Lagos shared the same time zone as Liverpool somehow made him feel more at home. He was thinking of his twin brother. What would Rom be doing now? In his mind's eye, he had his destroyer pictured at the heart of a great naval battle, all gun smoke and dive bombers.

From behind him the noise of a man vomiting came from the open windows of the sick bay. Taylor, the stoker, had been taken ill whilst in port. The local Nigerian doctor had at first suspected dengue fever, but later downgraded his diagnosis to dysentery.

'He's not a well, chappie,' the doctor had said. 'But he'll probably be all right to sail back with the *John Holt*, as long as he takes it easy and keeps his fluids up.'

Captain Hime had asked Remmie to keep an eye on Taylor during the voyage, knowing that the two men had become somewhat unlikely pals in recent weeks. It was a responsibility that, in truth, Remmie did not relish. He was squeamish and didn't make a natural nurse. But he visited him in the sick bay every couple of hours, bringing fresh water and food at mealtimes — though Taylor had not been able to keep anything down for days.

'How are you feeling, Taylor?' Remmie asked as he stepped into the dim light of the sick bay, standing for a moment as his eyes adjusted from the bright sunshine of the deck.

'I feel like shit,' Taylor mumbled. 'I've just puked again. The other end is just as bad. I don't know which way to turn, if you know what I mean.' He grinned weakly.

'Are you drinking plenty of water?' Remmie asked, putting a flask of water down beside the springy bed, and picking up a half empty one and giving it a shake.

'It just makes me feel sicker.'

'I know, but it's important for you to drink,' Remmie said. 'You know what the doc said.'

'Aye, whatever you say, Nurse Hutchinson. Now, I'm going to try to get some shut-eye, if that's all right with you?'

Remmie laughed and headed back towards the deck.

Within days the coast of Africa had once again become a distant memory, as the *John Holt* passed through a featureless ocean, enroute to a rendezvous with an Atlantic convoy, close to the Azores. The convoy would provide some protection for the little ship on the second half of the voyage, where it was much more likely to come under threat from German U-boat activity.

When he wasn't throwing himself into the seemingly endless manual chores — from swabbing the decks to painting the bulkheads — Remmie spent much of his time returning to the sick bay to check up on Taylor. He seemed to be sleeping for most of the day, muttering in his sleep and talking nonsense when Remmie attempted to rouse him.

'I think he's getting worse, sir,' he said to Chief Officer George Daniels as he emerged from the sick bay and found the officer standing on the deck outside, tapping an empty pipe on his palm.

'Is he delirious?'

'He's certainly getting that way. He's running a hell of a temperature.'

'Is he drinking water?'

'He does when I nag him.'

'Good man, Hutchinson,' Daniels said. 'Make sure he keeps drinking water and as soon as we get into Liverpool, we'll get him straight up to the School of Tropical Medicine. The docs there will get him sorted in no time.'

'But we're still ten days from Liverpool, sir.'

Daniels shrugged. 'True, but there's not much else we can do for him at the moment, lad. Keep his chin up.'

'Yes, sir,' Remmie said.

By the next day, Remmie had his own medical troubles to concern him. A section of his right shoulder, which had been unaccountably itchy for some days, started to blister up into boil-like mounds and the itch became increasingly painful.

'It looks like I've burnt it, but it's got to be more than that,' he said to Taylor, as he sat beside him in the dim light. Taylor was more lucid than he had been the previous day, and showed some interest in his nurse's affliction, despite being too weak to lift his head from the pillow.

'Take off your shirt. Let me have a look,' he muttered.

Remmie did as he was told, revealing the angry boils that were blossoming across his shoulder. The stoker laughed a little from his sweat-soaked bed.

'There's no mystery in that,' he said quietly. 'You have got yourself a case of mango fly infestation.'

Remmie was horrified. 'I've got what?'

'Don't worry.' Taylor laughed again. 'It's not that uncommon to pick up this kind of thing in sub-Saharan Africa. Were you bronzing?'

'Bronzing?'

'When we were in port, did you take off your shirt and sunbathe on the deck?'

'I did a bit,' Remmie said, worry etched across his brow. 'Should you not do that?'

'It's a bit of a risky business, sunbathing that close to the equator. What would you have done if you'd got burnt?'

'It was only fifteen minutes or so, in my downtime.'

'That's when they get you, though, lad — the mango flies. They burrow into your skin and lay their eggs.'

'But I didn't feel a thing.'

'You don't, until the larvae start growing.'

'Jesus. What do I do?'

'Tell the chief engineer. He's been working in this part of the world for years. He sorted me out, when the little buggers got me.'

Remmie left Taylor in the relative peace of the sick bay, and rushed down into the noisy, steaming hell of the engine room. He found Chief Engineer Stanley Clensy tapping at a dial, the purpose of which was beyond Remmie's understanding.

'What are you doing down here, lad?' he said, shouting to make himself heard.

'Taylor said you'd know what to do,' Remmie said, pulling the top of his shirt open to reveal the blistered shoulder.

Clensy nodded. 'Mango fly larvae.'

'Yes, that's what Taylor said.'

Clensy flicked his head, prompting Remmie to follow him up to the deck. He grabbed a pot of petroleum jelly from a locker filled with oils and tools.

Once outside, Remmie could hear the chief engineer speaking clearly. 'How is Taylor?' he asked, putting the pot down at his foot and reaching into his pocket for a cigarette. He cupped his hand to shield it from the breeze coming in from the portside of the ship.

'He's up and down. Sometimes he seems perfectly coherent, then at other times he's talking gibberish and running a high temperature.'

Clensy nodded and put the cigarette packet back in his pocket without offering one to the young deckhand. 'It can be really bad, dysentery. It's not just a dose of the shits, you know. It can kill you. That's why you shouldn't eat any meals anywhere other than in the mess. The stupid bastard was eating all kinds back in Lagos. Sit down on the deck, with your back against the bulkhead.'

Remmie did as he was told.

'Take off your shirt and turn your shoulder towards me,' Clensy added, taking a draw on the cigarette and pulling a fleck of tobacco from his tongue.

'What are you going to do, Chief?'

'Never mind about that,' he said, opening the pot of petroleum jelly and lathering it across Remmie's shoulder. 'It draws them out. They can't breathe through the grease, so they have to come out.'

'What would happen if I just left them?' Remmie asked hopefully.

'You'd have adult flies crawling out of your flesh before we got back to Liverpool. It'd do nothing for your chances with the girls.' Clensy gave a gravelly laugh as he reached into his pocket and produced a small wooden toothpick. At first, Remmie thought the chief was going to use it to pick the tobacco from between his teeth from the roll-up. But then he saw he had other plans for it.

'They're coming out already,' Clensy said under his breath. He seemed to be concentrating as he did something intricate with the little wooden tool. Remmie was glad he couldn't see his own shoulder blades. 'I'm just rolling them up on the toothpick,' the chief explained, with the cigarette hanging limply in his mouth. 'If you pull too tight, you leave half a larva under your skin and that would cause all kinds of infection.'

'Jesus Christ,' Remmie said through gritted teeth, feeling the painful pulling sensation.

'Don't worry, lad, nearly there,' Clensy said. A moment later, he revealed the toothpick and showed Remmie a slithering group of grotesque larvae, which he flicked onto the deck. 'Now, hold still. This bit will hurt,' the chief said, swiftly putting the toothpick back into his pocket and reaching up to his mouth. Remmie tensed with frightened anticipation as Clensy grabbed the lit cigarette between the thumb and index finger of his right hand and pushed it into the hole in his shoulder blade from which the larvae had just been plucked.

'Jesus, Chief, you might have given me a bit of warning!'

The chief engineer calmly put the cigarette back between his lips and took another draw. 'I'm not sure a bit of warning would have really helped,' he said with a smile, revealing his distinctive gappy teeth. He tousled Remmie's hair playfully. 'Go on then, lad, get your shirt back on. It should heal itself up now. Sorry about that, but the cigarette burn helps to stop it getting infected.'

Remmie nodded as he replaced his shirt gingerly. 'I guessed that was the idea and it wasn't just for larks. Thanks, Chief. It's a good job you knew what to do or I'd have been crawling by the time I got back to Blighty.'

*

A relieved Remmie returned to the sick bay, rubbing at his stinging shoulder blade.

'He did it, Taylor!' he announced jubilantly as he went into the shaded room, but the shape beneath the sheets did not stir. For a long moment, Remmie was convinced that Taylor had died. He took a step closer and watched. Then he stepped closer again and was overcome with relief when he caught sight of the rise and fall of Taylor's chest.

'How are you feeling, Taylor?' he asked tentatively, but received no response. Remmie reached across and placed his hand on Taylor's forehead. He was hot and clammy. He moved his hand to the stoker's broad, muscular shoulder and tried to shake him awake.

'You still with us, Taylor?' he quipped, but Taylor was consumed by a sleep so deep and senseless, it was clear that there would be no rousing him. Remmie sat beside the bed for a while, becoming alert each time Taylor muttered and grumbled incoherently beneath his breath. But he knew that this was just the babble of the man's delirium.

'Come on, Taylor,' Remmie muttered. 'You're putting the fear of God in me, pal.'

He sat a while longer at Taylor's bedside, feeling the rise and fall of the great ocean beneath them and wishing that Taylor was back in Liverpool now, safe in the care of a hospital ward. He had a long way and the most dangerous half of the voyage still to travel. If he wasn't able to rouse him and encourage him to keep taking sips of water, Remmie worried that Taylor would be facing a burial at sea long before the mouth of the Mersey appeared ahead of their bows.

Remmie visited Captain Hime on the bridge. He hovered tentatively at the door to the pilothouse for a moment, fearful of interrupting the old man in his work. But the captain seemed to sense his presence without even turning his head.

'How is the patient, Hutchinson?'

'I think he's getting worse, sir,' Remmie said. 'I can't even wake him now.'

Captain Hime nodded. 'You're doing a fine job, Hutchinson. We know you're doing all you can for him. It's in God's hands now — whether Taylor makes it home.' He turned to look at Remmie for the first time. 'The way things are getting out here, it's in God's hands whether any of us make it home. His and the protective wing of our convoy escort, should we manage to rendezvous with them today.'

'Yes, sir.'

'Go and do what you can for Taylor, Hutchinson. And say a prayer for the ship as well as your shipmate, while you tend to him.'

'Is there no chance of making another port sooner, Captain?'

The shock of silver hair beneath Captain Hime's cap shook definitively from side to side. 'I'm afraid not, Hutchinson,' he said, turning back to the charts that were laid out before him. 'We can't afford to miss our rendezvous with the convoy and once we're with them, we won't be able to leave the relative safety of the convoy until we're back in the Irish Sea. I'm afraid I have to prioritise the lives of the many over the few.'

'Yes, sir,' Remmie whispered. He understood the captain's dilemma. 'Thank you, sir,' he added, turning back out towards the quarterdeck. 'I'll do what I can for Taylor.'

'Good man, Hutchinson,' Captain Hime called after him as he closed the door and stepped out into the buffeting Atlantic wind.

Remmie wasn't a religious young man. But when he returned to the sick bay, he did what the captain had suggested and sat beside Taylor's festering body and prayed to whatever God might be listening. As he listened to Taylor's shallow, rasping breaths, praying felt like a final act of desperation.

The ship groaned beneath them, as up on the bridge the captain had given the order to turn to starboard. The nature of the swell changed perceptibly as the ship's course was altered. He looked anxiously down at his watch. *We must be turning to meet the convoy*, Remmie reasoned. It was going to be a very long day.

CHAPTER THIRTEEN

HMS *Grenade* was leaving Harwich behind. The town was now just a grey line of buildings with the yellow twist of Dovercourt Beach below. Felixstowe, with its solid eighteenth-century fort perched at its southern tip, was now also melting into the landscape as the destroyer cut its way out towards the featureless sea. The weather was turning squally, blending the horizon like a watercolour painting, so it was impossible to tell quite where the sea ended and the sky started. Rom stood at the chart table beside Courtenay-Boyle while he prepared his route. After a few hours' sleep, it felt remarkably homely to be back in the pilothouse at the heart of the action. It gave Rom a real sense of belonging, to be setting about his chores on the bridge, playing his small part in the working of this great machine of war.

Out there somewhere beneath the distant waves, there doubtless were wolf packs of U-boats biding their time and waiting for their next victims to fall into their clutches. Beyond this lurking threat, the continent was stretching out, somewhere over the horizon, the great unstoppable force of the German army sweeping across and reaching its tentacles ever closer to the increasingly isolated island nation that Rom and *Grenade* were once again leaving behind in their wake. As these great tentacles of evil swelled and stretched and grabbed at people's liberties, the beleaguered British soldiers would be funnelling towards the French coast, where they would either be rescued by their naval comrades, or would meet their fate backed up against the unforgiving sea. Rom found it hard to imagine how the thousands still fighting across the European mainland could possibly be lifted to safety by the Navy's depleted resources. But the mood on the bridge was clear and resolved. HMS *Grenade* would do all she could to answer their desperate call.

'All we can reasonably do right now, is to be as close as we safely can be, until the point we're needed,' Courtenay-Boyle explained. 'But that's going to be easier said than done. We don't yet know exactly where the ground forces will be forced to make their retreat from the Continent. Calais? Cherbourg? Dieppe? Dunkirk? Le Havre?' He looked down at the charts that were laid out before him. 'The way things currently stand, it could still be almost anywhere within a few hundred miles of coast.

'Meanwhile, we're going to have to be extra vigilant. The U-boat captains don't much like getting themselves into the relatively enclosed space of the Channel. But that doesn't mean they won't risk it. The bigger worry is the threat from the air. The Germans are increasingly enjoying air supremacy for great swathes of the French coast. We're going to have to keep our eyes peeled and our anti-aircraft crews primed for action.'

'Yes, sir,' the group of officers on the bridge responded as one. At that very moment, there was an almighty groan from the bow — the unmistakable sound of metal striking metal.

'We've been hit!' Carter cried out.

'No, I don't think so,' Rom said, leaning out of the starboard wing. 'Actually, sir, we're the one that's done the hitting.'

Courtenay-Boyle and Carter crowded beside Rom as he stood on the bridge wing and took in the grisly sight of a tiny anti-submarine naval trawler, HMS *Clayton Wyke* ahead. Its entire portside had crumpled where the bow of *Grenade* had hit it.

'Dear God, Wheels, where were you looking?' Courtenay-Boyle shouted across to the wheelhouse.

'I'm sorry, sir.' The quartermaster sounded horrified. 'I was listening to your speech, and … well, I just didn't see the wee vessel.'

'Well, pull yourself together, man. These things happen,' Courtenay-Boyle snapped back. 'Turn hard to port and draw up alongside her so we can take a look at the damage. Carter, you head down to the bow and give me a damage report on *Grenade*, though I imagine the little trawler took the brunt.'

'Yes, sir,' Carter said, already heading out of the door.

The entire crew of *Clayton Wyke* seemed to be on the deck, looking over the rail and contemplating the extent of the damage.

'Are you chaps all right?' Courtenay-Boyle shouted down to them as the destroyer turned gently, to draw up alongside the stricken trawler.

'What the hell were you doing?' the angry captain of the trawler boat called back from its bridge. 'You just ploughed straight into us!'

'Terribly sorry, old boy,' Courtenay-Boyle called back. 'These things happen in war.'

Rom fought to keep his composure as he felt a wave of laughter bubbling up within him — you had to hand it to Courtenay-Boyle, he certainly had a way with words.

'Now, look here, are you taking on water?'

'Yes, we're taking on bloody gallons!' the trawler captain bellowed back.

'We'll get a towing rope onto you, then transfer the majority of your crew across to *Grenade*, for safety's sake, while we get you back into Harwich,' Courtenay-Boyle called back, his voice now positively jovial.

Carter returned swiftly to the bridge. 'There's a bit of damage to the rail, but it doesn't look like anything structural, sir,' he reported.

'Good, good,' Courtenay-Boyle said. 'You see, it's not a complete disaster.'

Half an hour later, with a towing line in place, all but three of the crew of the trawler transferred across to the destroyer. Carter was sent over in a lifeboat to collect them. They were all suitably sour-faced. The irate captain of the little vessel remained on board *Clayton Wyke*.

'Go and form a welcoming party, would you, Hutchinson?' Courtenay-Boyle said. 'I suggest you take our guests to the wardroom and offer them all a drink. Cheer everybody up a bit.'

Rom put on his most diplomatic smile, preparing to help the men out of the lifeboat as they stepped aboard *Grenade*. They didn't seem a bad bunch close up, and Rom was becoming somewhat more relaxed when he turned to help the final member of the crew out of the boat. Just as he went to welcome the young rating aboard with an outstretched hand, he stopped in mid-sentence, taken aback to see a familiar face — a distinctively broken nose and a grin that revealed a series of putrid, razor-sharp teeth.

'Tom Charlton?' Rom said at last. 'Bloody hell!'

The youngster he had last seen after breaking his nose while scrapping on the dockside back in Liverpool looked barely altered by his experiences in the navy.

'Bloody hell,' Charlton muttered. 'It's you.'

Rom drew himself up to his full height, as if to better reveal his officer's uniform. 'I think you mean, "Bloody hell, it's you, *sir!*"' he said through tightened lips.

Charlton climbed onto the deck of *Grenade* and looked Rom up and down silently for a moment. 'I suppose I must mean that,' he said at last, casting his eyes down to the deck in defeat.

Rom laughed and gave his old adversary a friendly slap on the shoulder. 'Let's let bygones be bygones, eh, Tom? We've all got bigger battles to fight now.'

'I suppose so, sir.' Charlton allowed the flicker of a smile to cross his face.

Rom turned to the rest of the visiting crew, who were standing around, watching this reunion unfold. 'Now, gentlemen, welcome aboard *Grenade*,' he said, clapping his hands jovially. 'If you would care to follow me up to the wardroom, I'm sure we will be able to offer you some hospitality during your brief stay.'

As he led the way up the nearest flight of metal steps, he could feel *Grenade* turning back for Harwich, with the towing lines tightening in their wake.

By the time *Grenade* had arrived back at Harwich, Rom and Tom Charlton were chatting and bantering like the best of friends. Rom waved Tom off and stood leaning on the rail, watching the two captains who were deep in conversation on the quayside. The repairs to *Grenade* would take just a few days. The *Clayton Wyke*, however, looked as if she would be out of service for quite some time. Indeed, when *Grenade* edged out of Harwich once again two days later, heading for repair work at Sheerness, it appeared that nobody had even begun to work on the bedraggled little naval trawler.

Recovered from this embarrassing incident, for almost two weeks, *Grenade* worked her way up and down the Channel, waiting for the call to action. Wheels, in particular, seemed to be paying more attention to the vessels around him. Luckily, for what was supposed to be one of the busiest stretches of water in the world, it all seemed to Rom to be remarkably devoid of shipping.

Rom had just started his watch on the bridge at four o'clock in the morning when a call came crackling through from the admiralty. A coastal steamship, the SS *Abukir*, had been sunk in the night, and *Grenade*, together with HMS *Codrington*, HMS *Anthony* and HMS *Javelin*, was tasked to support the rescue mission.

The steamship had left Ostend the previous evening, with hundreds of people onboard — more than two hundred British Expeditionary Forces soldiers, RAF and Belgian Air Component personnel crowded on to its decks, along with fifteen German prisoners of war, six priests, and fifty women including a party of nuns from a convent in Bruges and a group of British schoolgirls.

Having been sighted by the Luftwaffe midway across the Channel, her captain had adopted a zigzagging course that had been successful in repelling repeated attacks from dive bombers for more than an hour and a half. But shortly after one in the morning, a 44-knot Kriegsmarine E-boat attacked her off Nieuwpoort. Despite a valiant attempt from the captain to turn the steamship and ram the nippy torpedo boat, she simply wasn't nimble enough to outmanoeuvre the E-boat, which twisted around and hit the coaster with a torpedo that struck *Abukir* amidships, splitting her in two. She sank in less than a minute, scattering survivors into the waves. By the time *Grenade* and the three other destroyers arrived on the scene at first light, most of the passengers were dead.

Rom and Carter spent the next few hours managing a group of ratings, who worked on *Grenade*'s lower decks, pulling from the sea anyone who still looked to be vaguely alive. Only a few dozen survivors were found and rescued, including Morris-Woolfenden, the fearless captain of the coaster, as well as a young sub-lieutenant and two nuns who had survived by treading water, clinging together and taking it in turns to recite prayers. By the time the search for survivors was called off, and *Grenade* had returned to Dover with the lucky ones who had made it through the trauma, it was clear that more than four hundred and eighty souls had been lost on the *Abukir* that night.

The atmosphere on the bridge of *Grenade* was downcast and gloomy.

'We did what we could,' Courtenay-Boyle said at last, breaking a long silence as the ship was refuelled. 'But by God, I wish we could have got there sooner. All those poor people. May they all rest in peace.'

'Amen,' Carter muttered, beside him.

Grenade was still refuelling when word finally came that the army was heading for the beaches at Dunkirk. They were ready for Operation Dynamo.

Courtenay-Boyle wasted no time in setting out to sea. When they approached Dunkirk a few hours later, the rising plumes of smoke coming from every corner of the town were the first indication of the heavy fighting taking place as the expeditionary force made its retreat. By the time *Grenade* had reached the mole — the enormous wooden jetty stretching off the seafront — the smoke was mingling with the mist to create a kind of dense fog.

'It could be a blessing in disguise,' Rom said. 'If it stops the dive bombers from being able to approach, we might get in and out in one piece.'

'My thoughts exactly, Sub,' Courtenay-Boyle said, giving Rom an impressed look, before calling to the quartermaster, 'Bring her aside, Wheels.'

Rom looked down from the bridge to see the mole crowded with men. They looked bedraggled and weary.

'Let's get as many of these poor men onboard as we can,' Courtenay-Boyle muttered.

The men filed onto the ship in an orderly fashion. Within half an hour, every spare inch of *Grenade* was taken up by soldiers, standing shoulder to shoulder and looking back out across to the beach at Dunkirk towards the distant sound of tank fire and the louder cracking of small arms rounds that suggested street-to-street fighting. Still under the protective cloak of fog, *Grenade* slipped silently back out into the Channel, leaving the battle behind.

As they moved back across towards Dover, they passed numerous other Royal Navy ships — destroyers, corvettes, cruisers — but even with such a flotilla taking shape, it was clear the confined nature of the port, with its cramped old wooden jetty, would hamper the rescue operation.

'It's going to take hours,' Courtenay-Boyle said. 'Even with the hundreds of men we've taken aboard, it didn't seem to make so much as a mark on the crowd of men we left behind.'

But after a quick turnaround at Dover to drop off the grateful crowds of battle-weary and bemused-looking soldiers on the quayside, it became clear that something more was taking place. As they returned to sea, dozens of smaller boats were emerging from the mist and all heading towards Dunkirk.

'They've mobilised the civilian crews to support the evacuation,' Courtenay-Boyle said, his voice heavy with emotion. 'Look at all the little boats. God help them. They've mobilised all the little boats. This is bloody extraordinary.'

'It's either bloody inspired, or it's a recipe for a disaster of immense proportions,' Wheels muttered in his dour Scots twang.

Rom looked out to the gathering flotilla of boats and small ships — everything from little pleasure cruisers to sizeable ferry boats. They had come from Portsmouth, Newhaven, Sheerness, Tilbury, Gravesend, Ramsgate, from all along England's south coast, from ports big and small, from fishing villages to yachting harbours. He felt a lump gathering in his throat. Perhaps Wheels was right. Perhaps these brave little boats were motoring to their doom, but you couldn't help but be moved by this show of good old-fashioned grit.

'I think it's marvellous,' Rom said quietly. 'Bloody marvellous. These little boats will be able to bypass the mole and take the men directly off the beach.'

Courtenay-Boyle turned and smiled at him and gave the order to increase their speed to twenty-six knots.

'Aye aye, sir,' Wheels barked back mechanically, as the tone from the engine room deep below them increased to a growl. The route across to Dunkirk was by no means direct, as the ships and boats had to keep to channels that were carefully swept of mines, forcing the vessels together at points to form a ragtag sort of flotilla. But there were so many ships and boats of all shapes and sizes, most were simply playing a game of follow-the-leader.

'We're going to need to be damned careful,' Courtenay-Boyle said. 'Some of these vessels are little more than pleasure boats. I can't imagine the skippers are in any way prepared for this sort of operation.'

'My thoughts exactly, sir,' Wheels grumbled.

The sea had calmed for this makeshift armada and the fog of the previous day had lifted — a mixed blessing, Rom quickly realised, when the first sign of the Luftwaffe arrived in the form of a Junkers JU88 that growled overhead with its distinctive twin-engine throbbing drone. *Grenade*'s own anti-aircraft guns crackled to life, but a moment later a Hurricane appeared in the skies above them, with the eye-catching roundels of the RAF on its wingtips.

The ship's guns halted in an instant and all eyes followed the little fighter that turned tightly to form up behind the JU88. In the work of a moment, its guns had sparked to life high above them, sending the Junkers into a swift tailspin. The German aircraft nosedived straight into the sea a few hundred yards to the starboard of *Grenade*, whose gunners let out a hearty cheer as the aircraft crumpled on impact and immediately began to sink beneath the waves. But Rom's heart seemed to sink with it. He had seen no parachuting pilot emerge from the tumbling aircraft and even after so much firsthand experience of battle, he still found it hard to watch a fellow human plummet from the skies to his death.

The Hurricane gave a little waggle of its wings, partly it seemed in celebration and partly to salute the racing armada below, as it turned and banked back towards Dunkirk, which was now appearing on the distant horizon as a series of vertical lines of black smoke.

'I rather fear we might be in for a rougher ride this time around,' Courtenay-Boyle said.

As they approached the port it was clear that the battle had reached the very edge of the town, with heavy guns bombarding the outskirts relentlessly, and the British and French rearguard battling to hold back the German advance.

Grenade edged its way through water that was now dark with bodies, floating together to form rafts of human flesh. It was only by standing outside on the portside wing of the bridge that Rom and the other officers could confirm that what they were sailing through was a mass of soldiers' bodies, bobbing face-down, their khaki uniforms making them look like a natural rock formation.

'Jesus Christ,' Carter muttered.

'The German fighters must have been over and machine-gunned hundreds of our lads,' Courtenay-Boyle added, before returning to the pilothouse and muttering, 'Take it nice and slow towards the jetty please, Wheels. We'll show these poor devils what little dignity we can.'

The mass of little boats and larger ships were queuing and jostling to find a space on the mole ahead, with civilian sailors calling out for men to move up and let more climb aboard. Many more of the smaller vessels had made it all the way to the beaches of East Dunkirk, where they were getting close enough to the shore to allow men to wade out to them. Rom cast his eyes across the scene that was unfolding and he was momentarily overcome by the feeling that something truly extraordinary was being achieved. Could they really be snatching some sort of victory from the very jaws of defeat?

The bedraggled soldiers standing shoulder to shoulder on the jetty had swelled in numbers since *Grenade*'s last approach, and Rom was struck by how different in scale this evacuation felt to their previous experience of plucking soldiers from the hands of the enemy in a distant Norwegian fjord. But still they moved in a disciplined shuffle, observing orders and valiantly refusing to be panicked into a frenzy by the ever-present threat from the skies above.

Further down the mole there was even more frenetic activity, where it seemed a cruiser had earlier left half a dozen of its lifeboats in the water and a ragtag collection of civilian sailors and naval ratings were being directed to one lifeboat apiece, each taking aboard twenty-five or thirty men with barely room to take breath. They were driven out with tiny Britannia outboard motors taking on the mighty expanse of the sea. But a few hundred yards out, they clustered and were roped together into a bobbing mass, ready to be towed behind a tug, which also had its decks completely filled with a mass of humanity.

Rom watched the collection of lifeboats being towed out to sea as *Grenade* waited patiently for its turn at the mole. As he watched, the ominous rumble of a squadron of low-flying aircraft passed overhead. He dashed across the bridge to join a group of the other junior officers who had moved to the starboard side to try to identify the threat. He sensed the crowd of soldiers on the mole tense as one at the sight of the distinctive, gangly shape of a Stuka dive bomber.

But Rom, his brother officers and all the men outside on the quay seemed to breathe an audible sigh of relief at the sight of three Spitfires chasing almost line abreast, with the middle of the three slightly ahead, leading the pack. A fourth Spitfire followed shortly behind, racing to regain its place in the formation. The Stuka pilot twisted and turned as he tried to shake off his attackers, banking hard inland towards the centre of the town with the RAF aces in pursuit.

Moments later two Heinkel He111 bombers rumbled high across the scene, releasing a peppering of bombs over the beaches of East Dunkirk, which were crowded with soldiers waiting to evacuate.

'Where have those Spits gone?' Rom wondered aloud. He could see a flowing movement to the distant crowd, as the men on the beach attempted to scatter to get away from the bombs, but as they fell over such a broad section of the beach, it must have been impossible for everyone to avoid the blasts.

The explosions, when they came, seemed strangely muted, as if the sand was absorbing some of the impact. But Rom couldn't avoid contemplating the impact that the blasts must be having on the men crowded there. Some of it — the tumbling of limbs and body parts — he could see, even from this distance. Much more of it he could see when he closed his eyes to try to protect himself from the horror, but it had imprinted itself on the inside of his eyelids. He shook his head from side to side, as if the gesture might somehow shake away all that he had just witnessed.

'Come on, Wheels,' Courtenay-Boyle said. 'This is taking far too long. We need to get in and out as swiftly as possible, otherwise we're a sitting duck here.'

Another engine noise rumbled overhead. It was the Stuka dive bomber turning back, with two of the little Spitfires still in close pursuit. The German and British aces seemed to be working to outmanoeuvre each other, giving the impression of a display being put on to impress a crowd. But Rom knew that the leather-clad Luftwaffe pilot would not be giving a thought to the thousands watching on — he was in a battle to survive.

Rom looked away, turning back to the charts in front of him. He couldn't bring himself to watch while anyone else was killed. Biting his lip, he examined the charts needlessly, muttering to himself about tide times.

A cheer rose up from the men outside on the mole. The Stuka must be down. Rom walked back across to the portside and stepped out onto the wing. Sure enough, a new acrid column of smoke was rising from the middle of the town, and a pilot was floating down towards it beneath fluttering silk. The

Spitfires were already just specks of light, banking back around in formation far in the distance.

The ship ahead of *Grenade* had finished taking soldiers aboard; it now raised its gangplank and was casting off.

'We're up next, I think, sir,' Rom said, stepping back inside the pilothouse.

'Take her alongside then, Wheels,' Courtenay-Boyle muttered wearily.

Grenade tied up portside towards the quay. They were about to lower the gangplank, when Courtenay-Boyle took a message from the flotilla leader on the voice set. He replaced the receiver, looking irritated. 'We can't get the men on board just yet,' he said. 'We've got to wait.'

'What are we waiting for, sir?' Rom asked.

'General Viscount Gort and his staff, apparently.' Courtenay-Boyle took in Rom's blank expression. 'He's the commander of the BEF. They're thinking about getting him out of Dunkirk.'

'Thinking about it, sir?' Rom asked incredulously.

Courtenay-Boyle raised his eyebrows. 'Yes, Hutchinson, and until they make their mind up, we just have to wait here.'

'What's more,' Carter chipped in, 'we're taking up valuable space on the mole. If we wait here, the other ships can't get in and continue the evacuation.'

'I know, it's a bloody good point, First Lieutenant,' Courtenay-Boyle muttered. He returned to the voice set and had another conversation with the senior officer. A few moments later, he replaced the receiver and stepped back across the bridge. 'We are going to cast off and wait a few hundred yards off. Prepare to tread water for a good few hours, Wheels.'

'Aye aye, sir,' the quartermaster called from the wheelhouse.

*

It was eight long hours with *Grenade* sitting-to off the mole before the call finally came through for them to take action. Courtenay-Boyle returned from the voice set at the aft of the pilothouse, seemingly more frustrated than ever. 'He's not leaving,' the captain said.

'Sorry, sir?' Carter sounded confused.

'Bloody General Viscount Gort has said he is not leaving Dunkirk. Not yet, at least. So we are to head back to the mole and return to taking part in the evacuation.'

'Thank heavens for that,' Carter muttered.

'Take her alongside as swiftly as you can, please, Wheels.'

'Aye aye, sir.'

Rom gazed out of the pilothouse window. They must be different men now standing shoulder to shoulder like sardines filling every square foot of the jetty. But they looked just the same to him as the men that had been there eight hours before — with their strikingly world-weary expressions and haunted eyes staring up towards the bridge of the destroyer.

Finally, he heard the clatter of the gangplank being lowered and the steady thunder caused by the soldiers' feet making their way up and onto the ship's lower decks. At that very moment a cry rose up from the lookout, perched high above them, and there was a gasp from the men left standing on the mole. Two Stukas were approaching at steep angles, one coming in from the east, the other from the west, moving with a fluid choreography through the air like synchronised swimmers.

The scream from their engines filled the scene, while Courtenay-Boyle bellowed, 'Fire at will, Mr Lake!' to the armourer, who swiftly relayed the message via the voicepipe — though it was something of a formality. The anti-aircraft gunners had already started to send a hail of bullets towards the attacking aircraft.

Rom ran to the window and his eyes followed the spray of bullets, flickering and sparking from the forward deck, but he somehow knew, deep in his gut, that this time the Stukas would not be caught out. Rom saw the bomb dropping from one of the planes. He saw how it seemed to hang in the air, poised and vivid with all the potential destruction still curled up inside it for a moment more. Then it struck the forward deck. Almost simultaneously, the bomb from the other Stuka struck *Grenade* towards her aft. Two deafening booms, and the combined burst of energy from the two bombs shook the ship violently. A frantic glance out of the window revealed the whole front half of the ship appeared to be alight.

'Damage report, quickly!' Courtenay-Boyle barked.

'We're well alight across the fo'c'sle, sir,' Carter called out.

'Severe damage to the aft, sir!' Rom shouted. 'It looks like a gaping hole where the starboard side was.'

'Carter, get down there and lead the firefighting!' Courtenay-Boyle shouted back. 'Hutchinson, take charge of getting those bloody soldiers back off the ship. Lake — make sure the gunners are prepared to respond if those bastards return.'

By the time Rom had reached the lower decks, the mass of soldiers was already moving back towards the gangplank in panic. He called for calm, but nobody was listening to him, and he watched on in horror as men trampled each other and others slipped and fell from the gangplank onto the edge of the mole below. A moment later, the abandon ship alarm was sounded. He dashed back to the bridge.

'It's no good, Hutchinson. She's too well alight — we're going to lose her,' Courtenay-Boyle said in a resigned sort of tone. 'Try to manage as calm an evacuation as you can, and then get yourself off on to the mole as quickly as possible.'

Rom ran back down the steps and took to guiding ratings towards safety — down the gangplank on the portside, and into the swiftly launching lifeboats that were already being lowered on the starboard side. Within minutes, the ship's decks were deserted. He ran towards the bow and met Carter, who was running towards him against an unreal-seeming backdrop of flames.

'We're buggered,' Carter gasped. 'She's going to go down.'

A tug pulled up alongside and Courtenay-Boyle called down to them from the wing of the bridge. 'We need to cast off, or we're going to block the evacuation completely!'

'We'll make sure she's cast off, sir!' Rom called back.

He and Carter drew together a group of young ratings who were still heading for the gangplank and coordinated a series of deft actions that sent the remaining crew scurrying left and right in a frenzy of activity that somehow released the destroyer from the mole. Then they leapt towards the gangplank, seeking the relative safety of the jetty. Carter and the ratings were caught by the tangle of soldiers, who grabbed at them to prevent them from slipping back towards the water's edge as the burning ship edged away from the mole. Rom was not so lucky. He tripped and tumbled halfway along the gangplank, and in the jumble of limbs, flipped unceremoniously over the edge, crashing into the water midway between the ship and the jetty. The splash as he entered the water was met with a cry from the men as they looked on.

The ship was turning to starboard already, and by the time Rom's head had emerged from the water, he was met by the great hulk of *Grenade*'s stern careering towards him at pace.

From the back of the ship, he could see the white water created by the force of the ship's engine spluttering momentarily back to life. Deep below the waterline, Rom knew the two enormous propellers would now be turning at a dizzying rate, capable of cutting him to shreds in moments.

In his panic, he momentarily forgot to swim, and his head was submerged by the wake generated by the 1,300-ton ship as it twisted and writhed in its final moments, oblivious to Rom's miniscule strip of flesh and blood that battled to survive at its side.

Below the waves, Rom briefly opened his eyes and looked around at the boiling tumult. He fully expected it to be his last sight of this world, but in another moment, the undercurrents that had threatened to drag him towards the propellers now thrust him upwards. Rom's face resurfaced for a moment and he coughed and spluttered as a mouthful of ocean spewed across his chin. He desperately fought to take another lungful of air before the propellers sucked him back down beneath the surface. But in another dizzying moment, he heard the distant cry of the men on the mole and saw a rope being thrown towards him. It landed a few yards off, but the mere sight of the rope was enough to fill his legs with another burst of adrenalin.

He dived once more beneath the waves, but this time he used the calm waters below the surface to his advantage, kicking his legs frantically to drive himself forward. He resurfaced within grasping distance of the rope. Rom reached out and felt the rope brush his hand for a moment, before he tightened his grasp and with an outpouring of utter relief, knew he would survive. This would not, after all, be the day of his death.

The men on the jetty began to rapidly pull him in. Once at the mole, he somehow found the strength to clamber up, dragging his body agonisingly up against the rough wooden edge of the jetty, covering his chest and stomach with countless gashes and great fleshy swathes of wood splinters. But he didn't care about the pain. He felt the beautifully solid wooden boards of the mole beneath his body. He felt the arms of countless soldiers clinging to him. He looked up and saw Carter's face looking directly at his. The first lieutenant was clinging to Rom's shoulders with an unexpected passion.

'For God's sake, Hutchinson,' Carter gasped. 'You nearly killed yourself!'

Rom took another moment to regain control of his breathing before he finally spoke. 'I'm so sorry, sir,' he said at last. 'I think I lost my footing.'

Carter leaned forward and gave the youngster a relieved embrace, laughing heartily. 'Well, that's the understatement of the century, my boy!' he shouted.

Rom looked up. The ship was now some yards distant and still drifting away from the mole. He could see the captain and the quartermaster at work on the bridge, driving the ship out from the jetty, with a supporting nudge from the tugboat. *Grenade* then, caught by the wind, glided a little further away from the land, its forward decks well alight, looking for all the world like a Viking burial on a giant scale. Once the dying ship was floated to a safe distance, Courtenay-Boyle and Wheels made their escape down onto the waiting tug.

The crowd of men stood silently and watched *Grenade* as she was consumed by the flames, and within moments she began to creak and groan. Then, in a series of shuddering death throes, she slipped swiftly beneath the waters of the harbour as a merchant vessel moved in to moor at the mole.

Rom felt himself becoming overwhelmed by emotion at the loss of the ship. She had become more than a ship. She was home and workplace, and somehow the fabric that bound together the ship's company into a single soul, a resolute fighting unit. Her sudden absence, leaving behind just a scattering of flotsam and wreckage, felt like a gaping wound.

CHAPTER FOURTEEN

The *John Holt*'s rendezvous with the Atlantic convoy had been smoothly met and the little ship had slipped into her place at the aft end of the portside column, under the watchful gaze of both the commodore and comescort.

Taylor had returned to full consciousness only briefly in days, and then he had merely taken some water and asked hoarsely about Remmie's shoulder.

'The chief sorted you out?'

Remmie smiled. 'The chief certainly did sort me out, thanks, Taylor. How are you feeling, pal? You've been unconscious a long time.'

Taylor grinned weakly. 'I've felt better,' he admitted before closing his eyes once again.

Sleep consumed him for another few more days, but he slept on more calmly now, unconscious for hours at a time, waking briefly to take a sip of water, before rolling back on his pillow and falling straight back into sleep.

Mercifully, the convoy was relatively peaceful. Just one merchant vessel — a tanker at the head of the column met a torpedo on the fifth day, leaving a great plume of inky black smoke that could be seen for miles as the convoy left her behind slowly sinking towards her fate. The U-boat that had fired the torpedo seemed to lose interest in the convoy, contented with its one kill, or distracted by orders to manoeuvre swiftly to another place.

Who knew why it had taken flight? But Remmie was certainly grateful that it had done so. The convoy steamed on in peace. It was within sight of the Irish coast when Captain

Hime came across on the Tannoy to announce the ship would be leaving the convoy to make a slight detour.

Detour? What the hell are they playing at? Remmie wondered, as he looked down at Taylor, still a sweaty, barely conscious mess, twisted up in his bedsheets.

He left the sick bay, momentarily blinded by the bright light as he stepped out onto the deck. He lifted his hands to shield his eyes and leaned into the wind as he made his way determinedly towards the bridge. The pilothouse was alive with activity when he got there, with the chief engineer, the captain and all the senior officers apparently in the middle of some kind of debate. They turned as one to look at the young deckhand who was standing in the doorway.

'Excuse me, sir,' Remmie muttered.

'That's quite all right, Hutchinson,' Captain Hime said. 'How's the patient?'

'He's much the same, sir. Still very feverish. He's asleep most of the time. I'm concerned, sir — he needs to get to a hospital. I heard you on the Tannoy. You mentioned a diversion?'

'Yes.' Captain Hime rubbed his eyes wearily. 'Can't be helped, I'm afraid, Hutchinson. They need us to head on up the Channel to support the evacuation of our boys from France. Jerry has them with their backs to the wall. They've requested every ship that can help and that can get there.'

Remmie cast his eyes down. Captain Hime stepped away from the group of officers gathered around the chart table, formally handing over command of the bridge to Chief Officer Daniels. Hime put a tobacco-scented hand on Remmie's shoulder and gently led him out to the deck. 'We all know you're doing a tremendous job down there, Hutchinson,' he said, bending forward to look into Remmie's eyes earnestly. 'You've turned a disused cabin into a sick bay and nursed

Taylor all the way from Lagos, as if you've been a medical man for years. But I'm afraid we're going to have to ask you for even more. Remember what I said to you the other day, about needing to prioritise the many over the few?'

Remmie nodded.

'We need to do it again now. You're going to have to just keep on doing all you can for Taylor. In a few days' time we're going to be at the very heart of this war and I imagine your impromptu sick bay is going to get very busy indeed. Do you understand, Hutchinson?'

'Yes, sir.' Remmie nodded again, his lips tightening with determination. 'Of course, sir, I'll do what I can.'

Captain Hime slapped him cheerfully on the shoulder. 'Good man, Hutchinson, good man.'

Taylor's chest rose and fell beneath the sheets so gently, Remmie found himself spending much of his time watching the stoker's body, willing him to take another breath. His flushed complexion had now gone and his skin seemed waxy and pale. He appeared to have stopped sweating too, but the gauge of the thermometer revealed that these outward signs of improvement were masking the real truth. He was getting worse. He had a fever of 104°F, but it was as if his body had stopped reacting to it.

The earlier flashes of consciousness now had also passed. As the *John Holt* worked her way carefully along the mine-swept corridor of the Channel, it felt as if Taylor was slipping away, forgotten by all but Remmie.

'I don't know what else I can do for you, pal,' Remmie whispered. 'I tried to tell the captain that you need to get to a hospital sharpish, but we've been redirected to help get the bloody BEF out of France.'

He reached out and held the stoker's muscular hand, sensing that it was desperately important that Taylor should know he was not alone in this moment.

'I don't know, Taylor,' he went on, talking directly to the motionless body. 'It's like the whole world is falling apart — the whole God-damned deck of cards is collapsing around us somehow. I've never said this to anyone before, but you know what, I reckon the Jerries are going to win this time around. Don't you think? I know it's unpatriotic and all that. But the more you look at it, the more you realise we don't stand a chance against this lot, with their tanks and their planes, blitzkrieging their way across Europe — an unstoppable force, like a cloud of locusts destroying everything in their path.'

Remmie glanced towards the light emerging from behind the flimsy sheet that acted as a curtain, hastily arranged across the porthole of the makeshift sick bay.

'The dawn,' he muttered. 'We'll soon be there, pal — right in the very heart of this war. If you'd only wake up, you might be able to see a bit of the action like the rest of us. Come on, stop being lazy,' Remmie joked. He turned his eyes back towards the stoker's chest, with its tangled twists of body hair peeping over the edge of the bedsheet. He watched it for ten seconds, fifteen, twenty. It didn't rise. Not even a fraction. 'Come on, pal,' Remmie whispered. 'Breathe, damn you.'

He released his grip on Taylor's lifeless hand and reached out to rest his hand on Taylor's forehead. It felt cooler and somehow waxier than it had previously. He reached for Taylor's wrist and tried unsuccessfully to feel for a pulse. The panic rose in his chest as he thrust his fingers towards the stoker's neck. No pulse there either. Not even a flicker.

'You've gone, haven't you?' he whispered. 'Why couldn't you hold on just a little longer? We could have got you help the minute we docked. Christ, Taylor. Why couldn't you just hold on?'

Remmie wearily pulled himself to his feet, pushing back the little metal chair with a scraping noise, and walked out of the sick bay to face the sunrise that was casting its amber glow across the deck. He walked slowly along the deck and made his way up the metal stairs and stepped into the pilothouse. Captain Hime was on the bridge. He turned immediately to look at Remmie and nodded silently.

'You did all you could, Hutchinson,' Hime said.

'He just slipped away, sir,' Remmie said softly. 'I never knew you could die so gently.'

Hime walked across the bridge and put a paternal arm around Remmie's shoulders. 'That sounds like a bloody blessed way to go amid this damned war. You gave him that peace at the last. That was down to you, Hutchinson, and all you'd done for him these past two weeks.'

'I think you should check, though, sir,' Remmie added. 'You can't take my word for it that he's gone. What if I'm wrong?'

Hime nodded with a sad smile. 'As you like, young man. Come on then,' he said, pausing to call back, 'Daniels, you have the bridge.'

'Aye aye, sir,' Daniels responded, as Remmie and the captain stepped back out towards the new dawn.

When they reemerged from the sick bay a few moments later, Hime's face was ashen. He and Remmie were met by the chief engineer, who was pacing on the deck with the stub of a cigarette between his fingers. He looked without hope at the pair as they emerged.

'He's gone, Stan. Taylor's dead,' Hime said.

'Damn,' Clensy whispered hoarsely, shaking his head. He lifted the cigarette back to his lips. 'I had no idea he was so bad.'

'Bad luck, these tropical diseases,' Hime said. 'You can seem fine one moment and then…' He clicked his fingers.

'He'd been going downhill, but I'd hoped we would get him home in time,' Remmie said quietly.

'You did all you could, lad,' Hime repeated. 'You have nothing to reproach yourself for.' He turned his gaze out to the sea as he spoke. 'We'll need to bag up the body and get him down below. There simply isn't time for a proper burial at sea right now. I'm sorry, but we have more important things to do for the living. We're only an hour off Dunkirk. Let the dead bury the dead.'

Remmie looked at him.

'I'm sorry, just a turn of phrase, Hutchinson,' Hime muttered, placing a hand on his shoulder. 'Don't worry, we'll deal with him with all due reverence just as soon as we can.'

Hime returned to the bridge and the chief to the engine room, leaving Remmie to stand at the deck rail and contemplate the sea as the *John Holt* raced across it. He stood there for some time, trying to take in the events of the morning. Nobody approached him or gave him a job to do. He wondered if the captain had told the crew to lay off him for a while.

The first indication that the ship was approaching Dunkirk was the massing of other ships around them — destroyers, cruisers, corvettes, troopships, ferry boats and increasingly lots of little boats — trawlers, pleasure boats and even yachts.

Remmie turned his eyes to the coastline and saw for the first time the dirty black smudge of rising smoke, and he knew instinctively that he was looking at the very fulcrum of the war.

If all these boats and ships could successfully get the BEF home, perhaps their little island nation stood a chance of defending itself against the oppressors? If not, then who knew how quickly Britain would fall to the Germans?

One of the junior officers passed him on the deck and caught his attention. 'Hutchinson, prepare the sick bay for action — you seem as well qualified as anyone aboard, given what you've been through these last couple of weeks.'

Remmie turned to look at the young, ginger-haired officer. His face, with its pallid and freckled complexion, looked wholly unprepared to be approaching the heat of battle.

'Yes, sir,' Remmie muttered.

'Taylor's been taken down below, so get it all cleaned up. We're going to be taking on a lot of injured men. You'll just have to do what you can until we get them back across the Channel, understood?'

Remmie nodded, and the young officer strode off along the deck.

Inside, the sick bay still smelt of Taylor's sweat. Remmie wearily stripped down the bed and replaced the sheets. He pulled the makeshift curtain from the porthole and let the light shine in on this place of darkness.

By the time he reappeared on deck, a mop and bucket in his hands, he was surprised to see that the *John Holt* had arrived at the edge of Dunkirk's crowded mole. The sea was alive with boats and ships of every conceivable shape and size. Bodies floated face down in the water everywhere he looked, gathered into clusters like jellyfish. He turned his horrified eyes up towards the town where a battle seemed to be raging. He could hear small arms fire ricocheting from walls, and to the east a beach filled with a great mass of men — soldiers, thousands of them crowded towards the waterline, as small boats came in close to the shore to take on board what seemed like a pitiful number of men each time.

He put down his bucket on the deck and turned back to face the town, as the ship edged ever closer. Ahead the wooden jetty was crammed to breaking point with hundreds of battle-worn soldiers, while just a few hundred yards away, a drifting British destroyer was well alight. Two men were being taken off into a tugboat that was up alongside, and then a moment later, the great ship creaked and groaned and began a swift progress beneath the waves. He had no idea that it was his twin brother's ship sinking before him. But his mind did wander to Rom, knowing he served on a destroyer. He wondered, with a twinge of terror, what kind of horrors his brother was enduring out there, facing the nautical front lines of this Godforsaken war.

Within moments, the *John Holt* nosed her way into the mole and he heard the gangplanks fall on the portside decks. Before Remmie knew what was happening, every square inch of the tramp steamer became alive with a great crush of humanity. Soldiers shuffled into every available space, many looking dazed and confused, many more carrying bandaged arms and dragging injured legs. He felt a rise of panic in his core — there was nothing he could do for these people with his makeshift sick bay and his small first aid kit. So he turned to busying himself with handing out mugs of tea.

Eric Curtis, a pencil-thin fellow deckhand with a few more years' service than Remmie, came over to assist him, carrying a tea urn out of the galley and onto the deck.

'Remmie!' Curtis said over the soldiers' din. 'The queerest thing. There's a fella over there who looks like your absolute double.'

Remmie looked up immediately and followed Curtis's pointing finger. There on the deck ahead of him was indeed his own mirror image, only his doppelganger was dressed in the bedraggled, sea-soaked uniform of a RNVR sub-lieutenant, and had a dripping crimson gash across one side of his face. Remmie dropped the two mugs of tea he was holding and ran across the deck, pushing men aside as he fought his way through.

'Rom!' he cried and embraced his twin brother. 'Jesus, Rom, what happened to you?'

Rom looked up, blinking through the dripping blood. 'Remmie? Christ, Remmie, what the hell are you doing here?'

Remmie laughed. 'What the bleeding hell do you think? Welcome aboard the SS *John Holt*.'

'This is the *John Holt*?' Rom laughed. 'Christ, I'd not even noticed. I was just shoved onto the first ship that appeared.'

'What happened? Where's your ship?' Remmie asked impatiently. But the moment he asked the question he realised he knew the answer. 'That was your destroyer — the one that was well alight when we arrived at the jetty.'

Rom nodded. 'That was *Grenade*, God rest her. We took an absolute battering.'

Remmie noticed for the first time that his twin brother's hands were shaking. 'Come over this way,' he said, taking Rom by the arm. 'Let's sort you out a bit.' Remmie pushed and shoved his way back across the deck and directed his brother into the makeshift sick bay. 'Sit on the bed, Rom, and let me take a look at that wound.'

Remmie busied himself with the first aid kit, finding a bandage and some antiseptic powder, labelled Sulphanilamide. He found a box of Ethicon sutures and made his first attempt at stitching a wound, closing the gash across Rom's forehead.

Rom winced each time the needle pinched in through the tight skin of his forehead. But otherwise, he sat silently, his shaking hands gradually easing the longer he spent in his brother's company.

'Fancy finding you of all people,' Rom said at last, breaking the silence that had gathered as Remmie concentrated on his work.

'It's a funny old world, especially when you're a twin,' Remmie said, still focusing on tying off the end of the stitches. He took a step back and holding his brother by the shoulders, examined his handiwork. 'Not bad, even if I do say so myself,' he mused.

'I suppose I'm going to have a hell of a scar?'

'Maybe, but at least people will be able to tell us apart now,' Remmie laughed. 'Anyway, any sailor worth his salt needs a decent scar or two. How else are you going to impress the ladies?' Remmie began to tidy away the first aid kit. 'So what actually happened?' he asked, as he reached for a grey woollen blanket and wrapped it around his brother's wet shoulders.

'We were attacked by two Stukas simultaneously,' Rom said. 'She was well alight before we even knew what was happening. The captain managed to get her away from the mole, otherwise the evacuation would have ground to a halt. But there was nothing he could do for *Grenade*. She went down in minutes.' Rom looked out towards the light of the porthole with a glint of profound sadness. 'It was such a shock to lose her so swiftly. She was there one minute and gone the next. I loved that ship.'

Remmie shrugged. 'Don't fret — there'll be other ships. You got out alive and just about in one piece. That's the main thing.'

'I took a tumble getting down the gangplank and ended up in the sink — it was the stupidest thing,' Rom said. 'Then I knocked the hell out of myself trying to get back up onto the jetty.'

'Let me find you some tea,' Remmie said, fussing around his brother and straightening his blanket, before dashing back out onto the deck. He returned a few moments later with two steaming mugs. 'They've cast off already,' Remmie beamed. 'You'll be back in Blighty before you know it.'

'God willing,' Rom added, with a superstitious shudder.

'I expect you'll go into Dover. They'll check you over properly there. Then they'll have you on a train and back up to Liverpool for some R and R, no doubt.'

'Who knows?' Rom said. 'What do they do with the crew of a ship that's gone down? I've never even thought about it.'

'Maybe they'll keep you all together and put you on a new ship?'

'Or maybe we'll get distributed around other ships as required. Men are being lost everywhere, all the time.'

'That's true,' Remmie said, and unexpectedly began to sob.

'What's the matter?' Rom looked up, baffled, before getting to his feet and putting a supporting arm around his brother.

'Sorry,' Remmie said, flustered. 'I'm being stupid. It's been a bastard of a voyage up from Lagos this time. I've been nursing a dying stoker who had some God-damned tropical bug. It was grim, Rom — really grim.'

'They've got you nursing?' Rom was clearly appalled at the notion.

'Basically, yes,' Remmie said, wiping away his tears. 'Somebody had to look after him. We didn't even have a working sick bay. This was a cabin that they fitted out as best they could. He only died a few hours back.'

'Poor lad,' Rom said, shaking his head. 'We lost a fair few of our chaps. More than I care to think about, if I'm honest.'

'Best not to think about it. None of us knows when it might happen, do we?'

As if to emphasise his point, the noise of an aircraft engine raced overhead, and both brothers looked up from their mugs of tea and allowed their eyes to follow the aircraft as it passed.

'You can say that again,' Rom muttered. 'Well, I suppose we can properly say we've done our bit now, whatever happens.'

'I suppose so,' Remmie nodded. 'For what it's worth.'

The two men sat and considered their own thoughts, submitting to the silence for a beat, before Remmie spoke again. 'I suppose I'd better go and carry on helping the others.'

Rom nodded. 'Duty calls. Go on, Remmie, get to it. I'll make sure I see you before I disembark.'

Remmie laid a hand on his brother's shoulder. 'I'm glad you're all right, Rom. Wait until Mother sees your forehead, mind. She'll blame me, no doubt, when she knows it was me that stitched you up.'

Remmie returned to the deck, leaving the door ajar so that the sunlight slanted into the cabin. Rom put down his empty mug and walked to the doorway, wishing he had a cigarette on him. He scanned the weary faces of the soldiers that stood and sat about in various states of decrepitude and dirt. The whites of their eyes seemed to stand out against their unwashed skin. Few were talking. Mostly, they seemed to be processing the experiences they had just gone through — the near misses each of them must have had to make it safely onto the deck of a ship heading for home.

Then Rom recognised one of the faces in the crowd as Bill Ridgewell — the anti-aircraft gunner from *Grenade*. He walked across to him and slapped him on the arm. 'Good to see you, old pal,' he beamed.

Ridgewell winced, then tried to cover up the pain. 'Hello, sir — you made it through too then. I'm jolly glad to see you.' Ridgewell tilted his face up and Rom saw the burns across his cheeks, nose and forehead.

'Are you injured, Bill?'

'The burns hurt like hell. But it's also my back, sir,' Ridgewell explained, lifting the tail of his shirt to reveal a sickeningly black mottled bruise that stretched across the entire small of his back. 'I was on the Lewis gun when the first bomb hit. The blast lifted me up and cracked the small of my back against the metalwork of the signalling sponson. I'll be all right, I'm sure. I couldn't move for a bit. But I think it just winded me. I certainly moved sharpish when they signalled the abandon ship!'

'I bet you did,' Rom said. 'I'm going to ask the medics to see if they can give you anything for the pain. But you will need to get that back checked out properly once you're back in Blighty. It looks nasty. Let's hope there's no real damage.'

'I may have chipped a bone or something, but I'm still walking, just about, so it can't be too bad.'

'But how did you get the burns on your face?'

'My face, my hands, my arms. Every exposed bit of skin seemed to get burnt by the blast.'

'On *Grenade*?'

'No, I got onto a paddle steamer that pulled up alongside, but then she was hit by a bomb moments later. She'd barely got out of the harbour. I got a face full of that blast and ended up in the sea.'

'Jesus, Ridgewell, you're lucky to be alive. Did you swim back to shore then?'

'Christ, no, I'd seen what was happening on the beaches. I just kept swimming out to sea. I knew somebody would pick me up if they saw me swimming. God knows, there were enough boats about.'

'And somebody did?'

Ridgewell nodded. 'A little motorboat, it was. Amazing to think it had crossed the Channel. But the skipper was taking her across to try to help with the evacuation. So he took us back to the jetty. I made way for the soldiers climbing aboard, then fancied my chances better when I saw the *John Holt* coming in, and Lieutenant Carter climbing aboard.'

'You saw Carter boarding this ship?'

'I did, sir,' Ridgewell said with a nod. 'So I thought, best if we stick together, as much as possible. He must be about somewhere, but I've not found him yet. But what about you, sir? What happened to your head?'

'Oh, don't worry about me — just a flesh wound. I tumbled into the bloody sink, worse luck. My pride was hurt more than my head.'

'Well, as long as you're in one piece, sir,' Ridgewell went on. 'I reckon we must have lost a good dozen or more when those bombs hit.'

'I know, Bill — it doesn't bear thinking about.'

Ridgewell reached into his pocket and produced a packet of cigarettes. 'Would you like one, sir?'

'Would I like one? Good God, Ridgewell, you'll be my best friend for life,' Rom laughed and gratefully took a cigarette. 'My hands have been shaking.'

The resilient gunner lit it for him with a silver lighter, before moving the flame to his own. 'Well, let's just get back to Dover in one piece now,' Ridgewell said, expelling a cloud of smoke into the air above him. 'And we might get a moment to regroup and work out what the blazes our country is going to do next.'

Rom nodded and turned his attention to his own cigarette and the distant sight of white cliffs that were just emerging over the barrelling edge of the horizon.

A couple of Army medics, who were walking around the deck and helping those most in need, eventually reached Ridgewell shortly before the ship arrived into port. They gave him a shot of morphine and placed strips of gauze, soaked in cold tea, across his burnt skin.

'Do you know, sir,' Ridgewell said to Rom as the medics wrapped his forearm in gauze, 'it's the funniest thing, but there's a seaman over there that's your absolute dead-spit.'

Rom laughed. 'How extraordinary.'

It was not Dover, but Ramsgate that Rom found himself in when he was ushered off the *John Holt*, feeling somewhat bewildered. Remmie had accompanied him to the top of the gangplank and embraced him before allowing him to disembark.

'Look after yourself, Rom,' Remmie said, clearly battling his emotions.

'You too, Remmie,' Rom said, affectionately tousling his brother's hair. 'It's anyone's guess if you'll get home before I do, but if you see Mother and Father when you're back in Liverpool, just tell them I'll be absolutely fine. Don't let them worry.'

Remmie nodded. 'You *are* fine, Rom. Now, get lost,' he said.

Rom laughed and gave his brother one final handshake before turning to face the crowds on the quay. Moments later he was ushered into the hands of a Red Cross nurse who checked him over, took his details, and assigned him to a hotel on the seafront.

It was a big, white, three-storey Victorian townhouse, perched on the cliff edge overlooking the harbour. Inside he was welcomed by a buxom elderly woman called Mrs Barker, who fussed over him as though he was her own son. She sat him down in the guests' lounge and served him cups of sweet tea, while the hotel gradually filled up over the course of the next hour with a ragtag collection of Royal Navy officers and men — many of whom were survivors from *Grenade*. With each familiar face that appeared looking bemused in the hallway, he felt another wave of relief. It seemed the great majority of the ship's company had made it through, mostly in one piece.

One of the last to arrive was Courtenay-Boyle, who was in the company of Wheels and Carter. Rom got to his feet and, foregoing all sense of naval decorum, embraced each of them in turn, shaking their hands vigorously while telling the newcomers repeatedly how thrilled he was to see them back safe and sound.

'Thank you, Hutchinson,' Courtenay-Boyle said. 'It was a bad business, but these things happen in war. Onwards and upwards.'

Carter smiled at Rom while Mrs Barker took to fussing around the captain and the quartermaster.

'Well, sit tight, Hutchinson,' Carter said. 'Sounds like we'll get a few days here before the admiralty decide what they're going to do with us.'

'Do you think we'll get some leave?' Rom asked hopefully.

Carter shrugged. 'I'm not sure. We might be needed elsewhere. I have a terrible feeling that the whole damned thing is collapsing like a deck of cards around us.'

'What thing?'

Carter waved towards the sweeping view of Ramsgate out of the window. 'The whole thing — dear old Blighty. Now our boys are out, the whole of western Europe is in the hands of Hitler and his lot. You don't have to be a tactical genius to imagine what his next move might be.'

'You think they'll invade?'

Carter frowned. 'Let's just put it this way: the sooner we're back on the bridge of a destroyer, the better I'll feel. Drinking tea in Ramsgate, we're not much use to anybody.'

Rom returned to the lounge and seated himself by the window with his cup of cold tea. A moment later, he was joined by a middle-aged Royal Navy chaplain, with a kind, if slightly world-weary face. 'How are you, son?'

Rom shrugged. 'Bearing up, thanks, Padre.'

'Jolly good. Glad to hear it. Bulldog spirit and all that,' the clergyman said. 'Now listen, I'm here to help. Is there anyone you would like to send a telegram to?'

Rom didn't have to think for long. 'My mother, I suppose. Best to let her know I'm all right.'

'Excellent,' the chaplain replied, handing Rom a slip of paper and a little pencil. 'Scribble down your message, and I'll be around to collect up the cards in half an hour or so. Keep it brief.'

'Right you are, Padre,' Rom said and put down his teacup. He filled in the details of his home address and following the chaplain's advice, kept the message brief:

Am currently between ships, but am fit and well, bar a few scrapes and bruises. Met Remmie. He sends his love too.
  Rom.

That should do it, he decided and looked around for the chaplain. He was busy talking to Courtenay-Boyle, so Rom sat back down and gazed out of the window towards Ramsgate. The shipping coming in and out of the harbour seemed frantic. He wondered how many of the vessels were coming from Dunkirk, filled to bursting point with men plucked from the beaches. It really had been miraculous, what all those ships and little boats had achieved. Rom felt a kind of pride swelling within him. He had been part of something significant. Carter was right, of course. Britain was now more vulnerable than ever. But it was strange how little the whole evacuation had felt like a defeat.

He caught the chaplain's attention and handed him the little telegram card. 'Thank you, Padre.'

'You're very welcome, my boy. Now, help yourself to one of the Red Cross packs in the lobby. It just has some essentials in it — a dry shirt, a pair of pyjamas, some soap and so on. It's not much, but it's a start.'

The following morning, the breakfast room was bustling with men from a variety of ships. Rom took his tea and toast at a table with Courtenay-Boyle.

'The ship's company will be split up,' the captain explained. 'We'll all get assessed medically back in Chatham in the coming days, then we'll be assigned a new ship. Could be anything. You'll have to take what you're given, I'm afraid.'

Rom nodded. 'I hear Bill Ridgewell, the gunner, was taken up to Southern General Hospital at Dartford.'

'Was he?'

'I was with him on the *John Holt* on the way back over. He had some fairly bad burns. I'd like to call up there and see him, if that would be all right?'

Courtenay-Boyle nodded. 'I suppose so. Send him my best, won't you? Once you're finished there, you can head straight into Chatham for your medical. Take the train. You'll have to change at Gillingham.'

Rom finished his piece of toast and brushing the crumbs from his hands, he rushed to finish his tea and got to his feet. 'I wanted to thank you, sir, for everything,' he said.

Courtenay-Boyle smiled up at him and put down his half-eaten piece of toast. He stood and shook Rom's hand. 'Best of British, dear boy,' he muttered. 'I'm sure I'll see you around. It's a small world, you know, in the Royal Navy.'

'Thank you, sir, and all the very best.'

Rom waved and shook a few more hands as he left the bustle of the room and went upstairs to pack the small bag of essentials that had been given to him by the padre the day before.

It felt strange to walk through Ramsgate, to make his way to the railway station and into the barrel-vaulted ticket office, passing people all the while — ordinary people going about their business with no knowledge of the horrors Rom had witnessed.

They don't have a clue, Rom thought to himself, watching a striking, middle-aged woman walking with two children out towards the platform, then turning his attention to a young girl in a Land Army uniform, who was walking in the opposite direction. *None of them really know what it's like over there.*

He felt extraordinarily weary this morning, and he found himself being rather short with the little old man in the ticket office, who seemed to be keen to chat.

'Come on, please, I've not got all day,' he snapped, reaching through the gap in the counter to show he was keen to receive

198

his ticket swiftly. 'Thank you,' he added, as he took it and turned towards the platform.

He stood waiting for the train, his legs shaking after so long at sea. He wished more than anything that he could be back on the bridge of *Grenade*.

It was difficult not to continually replay the events of the previous few days during the train journey. The rocking motion of the carriage brought back the sensation of the lurching ship as he had left her, perilously aflame and already taking on water. The broad open fields of the Kent countryside flickered past the window, but in his mind's eye he was still seeing *Grenade* sinking beneath the waves, and reliving that curious feeling of hollowness that had come over him as he had stood panting and shivering on the jetty.

He changed trains at Gillingham and found himself sharing a carriage with an elderly nun, who chuntered about the weather and the state of the railways and how things hadn't been like this when she was younger. Rom nodded and forced a smile, but he wished she would just be quiet. He could feel a sharp headache coming on.

'You look a little peaky, my dear,' the nun said, frowning at him with gentle consideration.

'I'm fine, thank you,' Rom said with a shrug. 'It's just been a busy few days, Sister.'

The elderly nun nodded and turned to open a bundle in her lap. Tearing away the paper, she revealed a large, glistening rock bun. Offering it up for Rom to see with a glint in her eye, her face lit up with a playful smile.

'Sister Cecilia makes the most wonderful cakes,' she said. 'I really don't know where she manages to get hold of enough sugar for them. But ask no questions, and all that.' She gave a curiously childlike giggle, before breaking the cake in two. 'Please, take some.'

'No thank you, Sister. I couldn't possibly.' Rom raised a hand and gently pushed the bundle back towards the nun.

'Oh, but you absolutely must, or else I shan't be able to eat my half.'

Rom shrugged and laughed a little. 'Well, in that case,' he said, reaching forward and taking his half of the cake, 'I can't stand by and watch you suffer.'

'Good,' the nun smiled. 'That's the spirit. Our lives are all about the little details. How did Sister Cecilia get enough sugar to make rock cakes? What makes a young naval officer so world-weary that he doesn't want to eat cake? But the most important thing is compassion for others. You do yourself justice in eating the cake for my benefit.'

Rom stopped chewing for a moment and stared up at the nun with undisguised curiosity. 'What did you say, Sister?'

'Where did Sister Cecilia get enough sugar to make rock cakes?'

'No, no, the bit about detail and compassion?'

'I'm not sure, my dear.' She seemed puzzled by his response. 'All I meant is that I'm grateful for your kindness.' Lifting her half of the rock cake in a little salute to the young naval officer, she took a bite and turned her eyes back towards the window and the racing Kentish countryside.

It turned out that the nun was also heading to the hospital in Dartford. Rom walked with her as far as the main gate, where she pointed him in the direction of a reception desk where somebody would help him find his shipmate's ward. 'God bless you, my dear,' she said, giving a cheerful wave as she bustled off down a long corridor.

The woman behind the desk tracked down Ridgewell's details and directed Rom towards the unsuitably jolly-sounding 'Tulip ward'.

When he first walked in, he didn't recognise Ridgewell. All the men in the beds seemed to be covered in a black, tar-like substance — it was lathered across their faces, arms, legs and chests. It was Ridgewell who recognised Rom.

'Sir! It is you — I thought it was. Whatever are you doing here?' Ridgewell called from the far side of the ward.

Rom turned and walked over to him. 'I thought I'd look in on you, Bill — see how you're settling in. What on earth have they done to your face?'

'Oh, it's a black paste — tannic acid and silver nitrate — it's for the burns,' he explained with a shrug. 'Apparently, when the skin is properly healed, the paste will flake off. It's a bloody devil, though, sir — it doesn't half itch.'

'You're doing a grand job, Ridgewell,' Rom said, taking a seat beside the bed. 'You just need to concentrate on getting better now and enjoy the attention of all these lovely nurses.'

'You'll never believe it, though, sir,' Ridgewell added with a chuckle. 'The two doctors treating me are both bloody Germans. Schurtenberger and Muller. Would you credit that? They've been resident here for years, apparently. But they still have the accent. It's a funny old world, sir, ain't it?'

'It certainly bloody is, Bill,' Rom said. 'I can't fathom any of it, if I'm honest.'

CHAPTER FIFTEEN

The *John Holt* seemed to make record time getting back around the coast to the Mersey. Remmie got on with his work quietly, trying to process his experiences and the horrors he had seen on the French coast. He slept poorly and would occasionally drift off into something like sleep while on the deck with a paintbrush in his hand, or leaning on a mop, or clinging to a spool of rope. Then with a shift in the breeze or the cry of a gull or the sound of a fellow deckhand at work, he would snap back awake.

But it was a peaceful journey back up the Irish Sea — the waters were calm and there were no signs of enemy ships or U-boats, for which the entire crew seemed grateful. By the time the mouth of the Mersey stretched out before them, with its waves kicking up around the ship in khaki tones of mud and sand, Remmie had never been so pleased to be arriving back home.

He felt changed beyond all comprehension by his recent experiences. He was coming back to Liverpool as a different person — more grown-up than his years would attest, wearier than his young bones should feel. But it was reassuring to see the Pier Head emerging before them, with The Three Graces — the Royal Liver Building, the Cunard Building and the Port of Liverpool Building standing proud and sturdy, an unchanging constant in what felt like an extremely uncertain world.

As his watch came to an end, he stretched and yawned, lingering on deck, leaning on the rail to watch the *John Holt* come up alongside at last, while an army of dockers set to work on unloading her cargo. Then he looked on as a coffin was carried onto the ship and moments later, was taken back off and carried with little solemnity towards a waiting hearse.

'Goodbye, Taylor,' he muttered under his breath. 'I did my best for you. I'm sorry it wasn't enough.'

At that moment Captain Hime walked up and stood beside him. He watched the coffin being manoeuvred in silence.

'I wondered if I could attend Taylor's funeral, sir?' Remmie asked. 'We had become close, what with me looking after him in those final weeks.'

'I'm afraid that won't be possible, Hutchinson,' Hime said. 'I would have gone myself, if we were still in port. But we won't be. It'll be a quick refuelling and straight back out, I'm afraid. We've been ordered back down south. We're going back to continue with the push to get the men out of France.'

'I thought that was all finished, sir?'

Hime shook his head. 'We're not going back to Dunkirk. We will be part of a convoy of ships getting British nationals out of the French Atlantic coast.'

'Good Lord,' Remmie muttered, feeling more exhausted than ever.

'But not a word to anyone, Hutchinson — it's all hush-hush at the moment.'

'Aye aye, sir, loose lips and all that.'

'Quite.' The captain strode off towards the bridge. Remmie walked back towards his own cabin, where sleep beckoned. To get back to Liverpool and not get any shore leave at all was a tough prospect, but in that moment, all he wanted to do was sleep.

The medical assessment at Chatham was remarkably swift, and was unencumbered by much in the way of detail or compassion.

'You look well enough,' the surly-faced lieutenant said, looking Rom up and down. 'Any serious injuries?'

'I banged my head on the jetty, sir. I had a few stitches. Other than that, it's all scrapes and bruises.'

'You feeling all right in yourself, Hutchinson? Managing to keep chipper?'

'I'm feeling exhausted, sir, truth be told.'

'Aren't we all?' the medical officer snapped back impatiently, stamping and signing a document that passed him with a clean bill of health. 'You're set to join HMS *Havelock* at Plymouth in two days' time,' he added, without looking up.

'She was at Narvik too, when we were there on *Grenade*,' Rom said, taking the sheet of paper.

'Good, good — old pals then,' the officer muttered. 'Go and get yourself a meal, Hutchinson — the mess is on the ground floor. Your rail tickets for Plymouth can be collected from the front desk.'

'Yes, sir.' Rom replaced his cap, saluted and left the room.

Rom slept for much of the train journey down to Plymouth, and stepped off the platform late in the evening feeling groggy, as he went in search of the digs that had been assigned to him until joining the ship on Tuesday morning.

He awoke early the next morning in the former hotel, which had been requisitioned by the Navy for the duration and took a walk around the city's docks. He was propositioned by one of the oldest prostitutes he had yet seen — ladies of the night had become a familiar sight in all the ports he had visited. As usual, the brief interaction involved in declining such advances was enough to send a blush across his cheeks. His flushed response amused the woman enormously — and he could still hear her cackle as he turned the corner with his head down and his coat collar lifted against the wind.

He walked around for some time, exploring the docks, before heading on into the city centre. When the shops opened, he visited a stationer and bought some paper and envelopes with the intention of writing to his mother and also to Charlotte, to let them know he was joining a new ship. He found a Lyons teashop and sat for a long time with a pot of tea and a bun, watching the steam rising from the cup and listening to the chatter of strangers, before he finally found the capacity to get out the paper, find a pen in his inside pocket, and begin to write.

He didn't want to go into the grisly details of everything he had been through at Dunkirk — partly because he was keen to keep both letters light to prevent the two women in his life worrying about him. But he also suspected that too much detail wouldn't get past the censor. He told them that he was joining HMS *Havelock* at Plymouth and wondered how much of that line would get past the censor too. In the letter to his mother, he told of how he had met up with Remmie after hitching a ride on the *John Holt*. In his letter to Charlotte, he asked if she had chosen between the Land Army and the WRNS. He felt strangely lonely after sealing both envelopes and heading out of the teashop to post them.

He went to a matinee showing at a cinema in the city centre — partly to pass some time and partly to feel less conspicuous. He somehow felt like a deserter being back in an ordinary English port like this and felt a strange compulsion to tell the strangers around him that he was only waiting for his ship to come in the following day. In the darkness of the cinema, he could relax a little, and quickly became engrossed in the film, in which Laurence Olivier's character, a wealthy widower, was trying to build a new life with an innocent young girl played by Joan Fontaine.

It was the first time he had been to a cinema since he was last with Charlotte, and the flicker of the screen, as well as Joan Fontaine's big blinking eyes, made him think about Charlotte constantly. He wondered if she really might by now be serving in uniform. She may even have joined the Wrens. Gradually the truth of what had really happened to Laurence Olivier's first wife came to the fore, and Joan Fontaine was met by a dim-witted old Cornishman at a boathouse. '*She's gone in the sea, ain't she? She'll never come back no more.*' With a sudden jolt, that single line, spoken by the wild-eyed old man on the screen transported him back to Dunkirk, gasping and blood-soaked, watching in horror as *Grenade* slipped beneath the waves.

In the darkness of the cinema, Rom felt tears running down his cheeks, not for a lost love or a fallen comrade, but for a ship, a big hulking lump of metal that had been his home and was gone.

The next morning Rom was out of his hotel room and waiting at the quayside as HMS *Havelock* came alongside. He strode aboard the moment the gangplank was in place and was ushered towards the captain.

'Sub-lieutenant Romulus Hutchinson, reporting for duty, sir.'

'Captain Eric Stevens. Jolly good to meet you.' The captain glanced at his watch. 'Dear God, man, you're keen — we've only just moored.'

'I like to be punctual, sir.'

'Excellent. Now, what do people call you, Sub? I can't imagine you get Romulus — unless you're being told off by your mother.'

'They call me Rom, sir.'

'Rom it is. Jolly good. Now, get yourself settled. You'll be bunking up with Sub-lieutenant Archibald Coles. Nearly as bad as Romulus Hutchinson, what? Don't worry, though — he gets Archie.'

The captain was in his mid-forties, greying around the temples and walked with a slight limp, as if he had suffered an injury in the not too distant past. He led Rom across the bridge and introduced him to Coles — a fresh-faced, handsome young chap — and First Lieutenant Chapman, who was older, frowning and tight-lipped, as if he was always on the verge of asking a question.

'Show Hutchinson his bunk, would you, Coles?' Captain Stevens asked. 'He'll be wanting to unpack. Though you seem to have packed rather light.'

'I lost all my gear when *Grenade* went down.'

Stevens rubbed at his cheek in a sympathetic sort of gesture. 'Gosh, what a blow,' he muttered. 'Well, we'll get you fully kitted out again in no time. You can't live in just one uniform.'

'Thank you, sir.' Rom nodded. 'That would be wonderful.'

'Get yourself settled in while we're refuelling and head back up to the bridge in an hour or so, and I'll introduce you to everyone. We're heading straight back out tomorrow morning — we're to escort a convoy of troopships heading down to the Atlantic coast to get more men out of western France. They're rather being squeezed down there as well as at Dunkirk, so I'm told.'

'Right you are, sir.'

'Come on, chap,' Coles said, giving Rom a friendly pat on the shoulder. 'Let me show you the digs.'

He led Rom through the ship, nodding towards any points of interest — although a H-class destroyer wasn't so very different to a G-class destroyer, and it all felt rather familiar.

'This is our cabin, home sweet home,' Coles said. 'I've got the top bunk, but I can move down, if you feel particularly passionately about it.'

'No, that's fine, thank you,' Rom said. 'I'm happy with the bottom bunk.'

'Well, throw your bag down. Make yourself at home. It's good to have some company. My last cabinmate bought it at Bjerkvik. Poor chap took a face full of shrapnel. Survived for a few days, but well, it was probably for the best for him to check out. He wouldn't have had much of a life.'

'How awful. I lost my cabinmate too, during the Norwegian campaign. A bloody U-boat surfaced and took him out with machine-gun fire. He was a decent fellow.'

'Well, let's hope that means we're the lucky ones, eh, chap?'

'Quite,' Rom said.

Coles excused himself to return to the bridge, leaving Rom alone in the cabin. The memory of Chubby Smith had left him feeling a little down, and he noticed that his breathing was unusually rapid. The longer he sat there alone on the edge of the bunk, the more he felt the walls closing in on him, leaving him in a tighter and tighter space, reminiscent of a coffin.

Rom received a letter from Charlotte among the small sack of mail that was brought onto the ship just half an hour before she was due to set sail. The letters were quickly handed out and Rom's heart had seemed to skip a beat when he saw Charlotte's handwriting on the envelope.

He read it quietly in his cabin before the start of his watch — reading and rereading every line, as if to somehow bring himself closer to her.

*

Dearest Rom,

Well, you will be happy — I decided to go for the Wrens. I started work at the Royal Navy's Plymouth Command headquarters. I almost didn't get in — I came up too scrawny at the medical, but Mother fattened me up and we cheated a little by sewing coins into the lining of my jacket — but it was all worth it when I finally got accepted.

The work was hard and I missed Mother terribly — I understand now how hard it must be for you being away for so long — but they must have been impressed with me because they offered me additional training, and I am to be a plotting officer. I'll be keeping track of convoy ship positions, U-boat positions, and wind speed and direction. It's a lot of numbers to hold in your head, but I'm looking forward to the challenge.

I can't wait to be part of the action — to know exactly what is happening out there. It feels as if I'll be almost like a guardian angel for you and Remmie — like the words of that Gershwin song, someone to watch over you.

The plotters work in watches, just like you do on the ship. There are four watches and I'm told they're very long, because of the need for continuity. I'll be working shifts of 8am to 6pm or 6pm to 8am. You have to concentrate for all that time. I do hope I'll be able to manage it without making a fool of myself. I'll be thinking of you for every minute of every watch (though of course, I'll be keeping a careful watch over all the ships too — not just yours!)

I hope you are well and maybe you think of me sometimes.

All my love,

Charlotte

So, his own Charlotte was a Wren. What an extraordinary thought — Charlotte, the carefree, artistic soul, with her flowing red hair and her passion for poetry. It was almost impossible for him to imagine her neatly clipped into the uniform of a junior officer. But he had loved the line about her being a kind of guardian angel — someone to watch over him from back home. He imagined the *Havelock* as a little ship-shaped symbol on an enormous, floor-to-ceiling map of the Atlantic, with his own dear Charlotte one of those who would climb the stepladder to move its position as the destroyer cut her way through the waves far away, out in the real world. They were once again connected. Only now it was by the plotting strings that she would pin to the board. Someone to watch over him indeed.

He slipped the letter beneath his pillow for safekeeping, and took a deep, unexpectedly nervous breath as he picked up his cap and headed to the bridge for his first watch on his new ship.

'Good morning, Hutchinson,' Captain Stevens said cheerfully as he arrived at the pilothouse.

'Morning, sir.'

'You've already met the first lieutenant.'

'Yes, morning, sir.' Rom turned to Chapman, who acknowledged him with a nod.

'The quartermaster is on the wheel. We call him Wheels.'

'Of course,' Rom said with a wry smile. 'Good morning.'

'Good to meet you, sir,' the quartermaster said. He was quite different from the previous Wheels. He was a smooth-faced young man, with the distinctive hardened vowels of a Yorkshireman.

'Is that a Leeds accent?' Rom asked.

'Sheffield, sir.'

Rom nodded. 'Long way from the sea.'

The quartermaster laughed. 'That's true enough, sir. But I suppose I fancied a change of scenery.'

*

As *Havelock* slipped out of the bustling Plymouth Sound, she was surrounded by Royal Navy vessels — including countless other destroyers and corvettes. But within half an hour *Havelock* was alone, cutting through the waves as she followed the coast of Cornwall — Rame Head, St George's Island, Gribbin Head. She had not travelled for long before the Lizard hove into view — a great flat-topped, rocky-edged peninsula of land reaching into the sea. A mile or so off the tip of this outcrop, the convoy was forming up — nineteen vessels that made for a ragtag collection of every shape and size ship that Rom could imagine, with the magnificent RMS *Lancastria* at its heart. The beautiful Cunard liner was a familiar sight to Rom from her regular visits to Liverpool before the war — she had offered one of the most regular crossings between his home city and New York throughout the 1930s. But the previous year, she had been requisitioned for the duration as a troopship — albeit a rather grand one. In peacetime she could take two thousand passengers, but as a troopship, with a bit of pushing and shoving, she could take up to nine thousand men — a guardian angel that could lift a whole brigade out of the clutches of the enemy and sail them to safety. To see her now, looking magnificent against the icy blue Cornish waves, made Rom's chest flutter. It was like bumping into an old sweetheart far from home and suddenly remembering how beautiful she was.

As the convoy formed up in columns, with the escort gathering into a protective ring around it, the great maritime machine, of which *Havelock* was just a single part, began to move as one out towards the open ocean. As it did so, Rom took pleasure in examining each of the ships through his binoculars — it made for an eclectic mix of merchant and passenger ships, all with one goal — to come to the rescue of those men who had not reached the relative safety of evacuation at Dunkirk, and who had been pursued at pace across France and were even now backing up to the great wall of the Atlantic ocean at St Nazaire. The sooner they could get there and get them out, the better.

Rom moved the glasses from one ship to the next, roughly assessing their capacity to hold men — some could take a few hundred, some, like the *Lancastria*, many thousands. Then two black-edged circles of his magnified vision swept onto the peculiarly familiar outline of the SS *John Holt*. It had to be, Rom thought — he would know that ship anywhere.

'Is that the *John Holt?*' he asked the captain, although he already knew the answer.

Stevens turned his own glasses towards the familiar silhouette. 'Yes, she's been pulled into this business, along with lots of other vessels from your native port,' he said.

'My brother is on that ship,' Rom said. 'He only joined the merchant navy last year. We both signed up when we turned sixteen. We're twins.'

'Of course — Romulus. Makes sense.' Stevens smiled. 'I bet I could guess your brother's name in one.'

'I bet you could, sir.' Rom laughed.

'Well, it's a good job that he has you so close at hand, to keep an eye on him. A bit of fraternal protection never did any harm. We could see a fair bit of action over the next few days.' He patted Rom on the shoulder. 'Don't worry, we'll keep a very careful eye on the *John Holt* and make sure we get your brother back in one piece.'

Rom nodded and flashed a nervous smile before returning to his duties.

*

The evacuation of St Nazaire began the following morning, with a five-mile queue of battle-worn soldiers shuffling patiently towards the steady flow of vessels at the port's docks. Some were lucky enough to step straight aboard the ship that would be taking them home. Others had to settle for being ferried out to the larger ships that were waiting off the headland.

Loading went on throughout the day, all through the night and into the Sunday morning. *Havelock* maintained a protective position off the harbour entrance, and Rom kept a particularly careful watch as the *John Holt* moved towards the quayside, emerging some time later with its decks tightly packed with men.

On the forward deck of the *John Holt*, Remmie was back into the swing of his newly found role of making a massive urn of tea and handing mugs out to thousands of grateful men.

'Thanks, pal.' A soldier with his leg in a metal brace beamed up at Remmie as he handed him a steaming mug.

'Are you all right there?' Remmie asked, looking down at the injured leg.

'Yes, thanks. I'll be just fine now I'm homeward bound. I was in a bloody hospital with this thing.' The man nodded down towards his leg. 'We had no idea what was coming. A captain marched onto the ward. "Now, let's be having you chaps," he said, and before we knew what was happening, we were all being put into wheelchairs and wheeled out towards a waiting lorry. We had no idea Jerry was getting so close. It certainly put the frighteners up the nurses, the poor loves.'

'We were getting men out of Dunkirk just a few days ago,' Remmie said, shaking his head. 'It's like the whole bleedin' continent is being emptied out.'

The injured soldier nodded and frowned down towards his tea. 'It's not looking good, is it? Not good at all.'

Remmie patted his back. 'Chin up, mate,' he said. 'You're safe now.'

CHAPTER SIXTEEN

The arrival of the *Robert Holt* on the scene was almost as much of a shock for Rom as the sight of the *John Holt* had been a few hours before.

'Christ, it's a family affair,' he muttered, lifting the binoculars away from his eyes.

'What's wrong, Hutchinson?' First Lieutenant Chapman asked.

'Nothing, sir. My father is captain of that ship.' Rom pointed at the vessel that was passing by, the bow waves dancing against its low-slung, straight-lined hull. The bridge was raised before the modest steamer's single funnel, and standing at the helm, Rom could distinctly see the familiar, burly silhouette of his father. The old man turned his head towards the portside bridge wing and raised a hand in salute at the *Havelock*, not knowing that it was his son waving back.

'I thought they tried to stop families from serving in the same field, as it were, after the mess of the pals' battalions in the last war,' Chapman muttered with a frown.

'Evidently they didn't spot it,' Rom replied with a shrug. 'Desperate times, I suppose, call for desperate measures.'

The *Robert Holt* swept in towards the port, disappearing behind the harbour wall, beyond which she would be up alongside the quay within minutes. Over to the *Havelock*'s starboard side, the convoy was forming back up into columns, with the fully laden ships, including the *John Holt*, now visibly bustling with life. At the heart of the scene rose up the sheer sides of the mighty RMS *Lancastria*, with tenders motoring back and forth, delivering men to the liner turned troopship, which was too big to make the quayside. Beyond them, the great green arcing strip of land that defined Quiberon Bay stretched out, offering a protective embrace.

'The bay is probably too shallow for U-boats to be a real threat,' Captain Stevens said contemplatively to Rom. 'But when the Luftwaffe gets wind of us, we'll be bobbing around here like sitting ducks. They have complete control of the skies this far south.'

As if on cue, a rumble of engines came out of the blue skies, and a lone JU88 twin-engine bomber soared high overhead, passing across the convoy, before heading out to sea and turning in a great long arc that left a contrail in its wake that almost perfectly mirrored the shape of the bay. The officers on the bridge of the *Havelock* watched fretfully as the bomber turned back towards the gathered ships. Stevens grabbed for the voicepipe and readied the anti-aircraft gunners. Then he stood alongside Rom and Chapman, and for a long moment all three men were thinking the same grim thought — which ship would it aim for?

'Turn her hard to port, Wheels. Let's see if we can give the gunners a better shot at the bastard,' Stevens growled and with a groan from the engine room, the destroyer lurched heavily beneath them.

The bomber passed over the *John Holt* and the mighty *Lancastria*, much to Rom's relief, but made for another liner turned troopship — the twin-funnelled SS *Oronsay*. Rom saw the bomb drop from the JU88's clutches; it seemed to hang for a moment in the air, somehow defying gravity, before making a determined descent straight towards the bridge of the troopship. The blast that followed created a searing flash and a mushroom cloud of smoke and debris that rose up from the deck of the ill-fated vessel, before rising to reveal that half of the bridge had become a twisted wreck.

Rom lifted his glasses and surveyed the damage to the *Oronsay* as best he could. 'She's badly hit, Captain,' he reported. 'But it doesn't look like she's taking on water.'

'No,' Stevens agreed. 'It's a flesh wound; I don't think she'll go down. Whether she can be manoeuvred with the wheel room taken out is another matter. Christ knows how many good officers were lost on that bridge.'

A voice radioed through from the commodore's ship five minutes after the strike that confirmed Rom's assessment. But before the captain could respond, the menacing outline of the bomber returned back across the bay. This time, Rom saw it before he heard it. But then its distinctive rumble seemed to catch it up, as it made straight back towards the centre of the convoy.

'God help us. She's coming straight back for more,' Rom muttered.

The anti-aircraft guns on *Havelock* and the other destroyers burst into action, sending bullets wildly, and from this distance, impotently into the sky. The JU88 lived up to its nickname — the "Schnellbomber", or fast bomber — twisting and turning as it dived across the top of the convoy, its bulbous glass cockpit giving it the unsettling appearance of a giant wasp.

Once again, Rom could only watch on in sickening terror and time seemed to slow down as four bombs were simultaneously released and sent careering straight down towards the unmissable mammoth presence of the RMS *Lancastria*. In those final seconds of the Schnellbomber's shallow dive, several Bren gunners on the deck of the *Lancastria* opened fire, but offered too little, too late to drive the plane off.

The first two of the bombs disappeared. Rom could not quite see an impact — could they somehow have missed and gone tumbling towards the sea? He couldn't be certain. But the other two hit their target for sure. One smashed through the dining saloon, and the explosion in the lower decks rocked the ship laterally, like a canoe crossing rapids. Almost at exactly the same moment, the last of the bombs made the ultimate strike — slipping like a cyanide pill straight down the funnel and impacting deep in the engine room with an otherworldly boom and metallic groan. When the smoke had cleared, it was immediately evident that the bombs had blown gaping holes in the side of the ship — fatal wounds that would in moments send her careering down to meet the sea's own morbid embrace.

Vast quantities of oil were pouring out like blood and settling across the sea in a thick soup. At an extraordinary speed the mighty ship lurched, twisted to port, and bobbed up into a vertical position before slipping down beneath the waves even as hundreds of men dived from the decks, taking their last chance to fling their bodies clear of the wreck.

The sight of that waterfall of men, tumbling over each other as they barrel-rolled down the upturned decks, sent a wave of horror across the bridge of the *Havelock* and throughout all the other ships that were fanning out from what had moments before been the rough outline of a convoy formation. The whole process of the great ship's death throes had taken little more than twenty minutes. Rom could hardly believe what he was witnessing — the thousands of men, sailors and soldiers, that must have slipped, tumbled or been sucked down beneath the sea along with *Lancastria* hardly bore thinking about.

As *Havelock* and other ships moved in to assist with the rescue operation, Rom felt as though his mind was somehow switching itself off, unable to deal with the trauma.

Thousands of men were now in the oil-coated water, desperately trying to swim through the greasy liquid, mingling with the dead, being choked by oil, and all the time being dragged down by their heavy uniforms. The JU88 returned over and over again, seemingly immune to the anti-aircraft fire from the convoy's escort. The aircraft was machine-gunning the survivors from the air, and as Rom gazed on impotently, he knew there was a real danger that this would cause the oil to catch fire at any moment.

The *Havelock* sent out all its lifeboats to collect survivors, with Rom given command of one of the little boats. 'Detail and compassion,' he muttered to himself. 'Detail and compassion.'

Within moments the boat was being pulled through the slimy film of oil, and Rom began leaning over the edge of the boat and pulling men aboard. Many had removed their uniforms in the water to try to keep afloat, and he found himself wrestling with the slippery naked forms of soldiers and sailors bewildered by the situation in which they found themselves, shaking violently with shock and barely able to pull themselves aboard. It was a brutally physical process for Rom, with the two ratings who had accompanied him eventually having to put down their oars to help the young officer to gain purchase on the bodies of the survivors. There seemed to be barely any lifejackets, which would have given Rom something to cling on to. Perhaps there had been insufficient numbers of lifejackets aboard the troopship. Perhaps they just hadn't had time to put them on, given the speed with which the great ship had been hungrily consumed by the waves.

As they struggled to rescue men from the water, Rom, his own uniform now lathered with oil, paused to look up at the rumbling skies. He saw the distinctive outline of more JU88s, flying in a swarm, each with their MG17 machine guns peppering the water. Rom and the rescued men dived onto the deck of the boat as the bullets tore around them, igniting a section of oil into an immediate inferno.

A moment later and the planes were gone. Rom straightened up to see the grisly sight of swimmers and bodies alike consumed by flames. One of the junior ratings from *Havelock* who had been rowing lay dead, hanging from the side of the boat like a piece of meat in a butcher's shop window, half of his head blown away by a bullet. Rom stepped carefully forward to pull the body back onto the deck of the boat. As he turned it over, he could see that most of the man's face was missing. Rom felt his chest tighten and he made a quick decision, twisting the body back up and allowing it to slide over the edge of the boat and into the oily sea.

'Better to get as many living men aboard as possible than to take the dead back to *Havelock*,' he said firmly. 'Come on,' he added to the wild-eyed rating who had survived the attack. 'Give me a hand.'

They picked up the oars and moved the boat away from the worst of the flames, then stopped once again to pull more men aboard. Eventually, when there wasn't a single inch of space left on the heavily overloaded lifeboat, Rom and the junior rating returned to their oars and began to wearily pull the boat back towards *Havelock*.

The blackened, oil-encrusted faces of the survivors gazed at the scene of utter devastation where *Lancastria* had gone down. The silence was broken by one man singing a quiet, mournful rendition of 'There'll Always Be an England'. By the time the boat was within touching distance of *Havelock*, all the survivors were joining in with the refrain.

Rom found himself so overcome by emotion that he couldn't risk speaking, so he simply clung in silence to *Havelock*'s rope ladder, and helped each survivor in turn to climb up onto the first rung. With the last man aboard, Rom was relieved of his command of the rescue boat by Coles, who boarded with two more junior ratings. They cut away back towards the oily wreckage. A short time later they returned, and Rom retook his place in the boat. The pair worked together to continue their rescue efforts for two hours, before the captain finally gave the signal for all the lifeboats to be winched back aboard. By this time, finding a man still alive in the water had become a rarity and the commodore had made it clear that he was keen to get the convoy moving back towards Plymouth.

A few hours later, Rom was back on the bridge of *Havelock*, his uniform still caked in oil, as the destroyer slipped into its place in the protective wall of steel that the escort was attempting to build around the convoy. He looked through his glasses towards the *John Holt* and ahead of it, her sister ship, the *Robert Holt*. His family was heading home.

Rom returned to his cabin, but he could not sleep. It was as if the walls were shifting towards him. He knew logically that this could not happen, but it did not help him to cope with the terror when the walls seemed to lurch a little closer, making the cabin a few inches smaller each time.

Coles was on the opposite watch, so Rom had the cabin to himself, but he was feeling increasingly claustrophobic in the space. After an hour of trying to cope with this, he climbed wearily from his bunk, slipped out of the cabin and made his way down the deserted corridor towards the open deck. Carrying his blanket and pillow under his arm, he settled in a quiet corner behind a bulkhead close to the aft of the funnel. The warmth from the engine room below eased the chill, and he curled up beneath the stars and fell into a fitful sleep.

Early the following morning, Rom slipped back to the cabin in the dawn light and washed and dressed. Back up on the bridge the ship was being readied for its approach into Plymouth Sound, and Rom worked hard to focus through his exhaustion on the tasks set for him.

Plymouth emerged out of the haze like a grey, otherworldly landscape in the watery sunlight. Moored up alongside, Rom stood on the port wing of the bridge and watched the beleaguered survivors of the *Lancastria* step ashore, cloaked in heavy woollen blankets. They were met on the quayside by a bustling army of Red Cross volunteers, who led them away into the compassionate embrace of the city.

Captain Stevens stepped out and stood beside Rom. 'The world has gone mad,' he muttered after a while. 'You wonder where it's all going to end.'

Rom looked out across Plymouth. 'I dread to think about that,' he said.

'Your brother made it back in one piece anyway.'

Rom nodded. 'Yes, both the *John Holt* and *Robert Holt* continued on towards Liverpool. It was the strangest thing, to be serving alongside them both like that.'

Stevens nodded. 'It's certainly something to tell the grandchildren about.'

Rom laughed. 'Yes, sir.'

'You look tired, Hutchinson,' Stevens added, surveying Rom's face carefully. 'Have you been sleeping?'

'Yes, I'm fine, sir,' Rom lied. 'It's been a tiring week for everyone. Quite a strain.'

Stevens nodded and reached into his pocket for his pipe. He didn't light it, but put it to his lips and gently chewed on its tip as he gazed out at the city. Rom wondered if it helped the older man to think clearly. He reminded Rom distinctly of his own father.

Once refuelled, the *Havelock* was sent straight back out on anti-submarine manoeuvres in the Channel. Rom wished desperately that they could have some shore leave, but it was straight back to sea without a moment to recuperate. That night he found himself having to sleep out on the deck once again. The weather had worsened and even the idea of getting any real sleep was absurd. But at least out on the deck he didn't have to watch the walls moving towards him threateningly.

The following morning, he returned to his watch on the bridge, his head spinning with exhaustion. Captain Stevens, who had just done two back-to-back watches on the bridge, apologetically muttered something about taking a break.

'I'm going to get a meal, take a shower and get my head down for a few hours,' he said to nobody in particular, as he stretched and yawned. 'It's been exceptionally quiet, but do alert me if the enemy is sighted. Hutchinson, you have the conn.'

'Yes, sir,' Rom agreed, before turning towards the quartermaster and mechanically firing the next steering instructions. 'Steady on course one, zero, four, Wheels.'

'Course steady on one, zero, four, sir,' the quartermaster replied.

The ship was making enormous figures of eight, providing a visible presence at the widest point of the English Channel, while giving the ASDIC rating an opportunity to go fishing for U-boats. It was a dull, tedious operation, with little chance of seeing any action, and the steady rumble of the engine far below was having a soporific effect on Rom. Within minutes, his work plotting a course on the charts saw him leaning against the chart table, his head slumped down, as if in careful examination of a point on the map. When he opened his eyes, he had no idea if he had been asleep for minutes or seconds. He glanced around nervously and determined he must only have closed his eyes for a moment.

Rom was roughly awoken by Captain Stevens, who had returned to the bridge in search of his wristwatch. He found Rom fast asleep, in a sort of puppet-like slouching position, propped up against the gyro-compass repeater. He grabbed him by the shoulder and gave him a vigorous shake.

'Mr Coles, you have the bridge,' Stevens growled.

'Aye aye, sir,' Coles replied. He stepped forward, with an anxious glance towards Rom.

'You,' Stevens hissed at Rom, 'come with me.' The captain didn't say another word until he had marched Rom out onto the quarterdeck. 'What in God's name do you think you're doing?' he snarled.

Rom had never seen the captain so incensed. 'I'm sorry, sir.'

'You're sorry? You had the bridge of a destroyer. What the blazes is wrong with you?'

'I've not been sleeping, sir.'

'Why the hell not? For how long?'

Rom didn't know which question to answer first. His face crumpled. 'Not properly since Dunkirk, sir. Ever since *Grenade* went down, I just…' He paused as he struggled to articulate why exactly he had not been able to sleep. 'I've just not been able to stand being below decks. The cabin walls close in on me, sir. I've been slipping out and sleeping on deck — hidden at the aft of the funnel.'

For the briefest of moments, he thought the captain was going to strike him, but the rage seemed to subside as swiftly as it had arrived. Stevens looked out towards the sea as he spoke to Rom. 'You're not the first, and you certainly won't be the last, Hutchinson,' he muttered. 'You're still a very young man. You will have time to come back from this, I'm sure. But you are going to need to go ashore for a while.'

'Ashore, sir?'

'You're going to need some treatment, I think, Hutchinson.' Stevens seemed embarrassed by the conversation. 'The Royal Navy has specialist physicians for this kind of thing. They'll get you sorted out in no time.' His face broke into an unconvincing smile.

'Will they, sir?' Rom said, casting his eyes towards the deck as he felt himself being consumed by a wave of shame. He had expected to be put on a charge, but not this — this awful, calmly spoken dismissal from the ship. It was followed by another wave of shame and another, crashing against him like the sea battering the Eddystone Lighthouse in a storm. Within moments he was drowning in it.

CHAPTER SEVENTEEN

Remmie stepped ashore at Canada Dock in Liverpool and shouldered his bag without turning to take another look at the *John Holt* at the quayside behind him. He had two days' shore leave and he had never felt more in need of it. Everything around him looked eerily familiar, but he had changed. Something in his nature had been reworked by his experiences over the past few weeks.

He took the Overhead Railway as far as Seaforth, where he would need to change onto the Crosby train. Remmie had always had a soft spot for the Overhead Railway. Locally, they called it the Dockers' Umbrella — for obvious reasons — and in fact the sight of dockers sheltering beneath was a distinct childhood memory that seemed to have been burnt onto his brain. But he couldn't be entirely sure whether he had ever seen those dockers sheltering there, or whether it was one of those imagined memories brought about by the Overhead Railway's nickname.

He liked riding on the rickety old line because its elevation gave passengers uninterrupted views out across the docks and the countless ships unloading on every quayside. He gazed out towards the Mersey as the train sped along — Brocklebank Dock, Langton Dock, Alexandra Dock, Gladstone Dock — every foot of quayside crammed with shipping. The good dockers of Liverpool were keeping the country afloat — from this elevated vantagepoint, there could be nothing quite so sure.

By the time he arrived back at the family home in Crosby, his father was already there ahead of him, and was standing in the doorway smoking a pipe.

'I thought you might be back before tea, but this is pushing it,' William Hutchinson said, with a glance down at his watch.

'We deckhands can't afford taxi cabs, Captain,' Remmie said. 'I took the train.' He opened the gate and strode up the garden path — the site of a thousand childhood adventures, but which now seemed so tiny. He dropped his heavy bag and offered a hand for his father to shake. Unexpectedly, his father pushed the hand aside and enveloped Remmie in a bear hug.

'I saw the *John Holt* when I was at St Nazaire, clear as day. I knew you must have been there.'

'I saw you too, Father,' Remmie said. 'Did you not see me waving?'

Hutchinson rubbed his white beard as he released Remmie from his embrace and steered him through the front door towards the kitchen, where Eileen was waiting amid the steaming pots and pans.

A couple of hours later, after the meal had been cheerfully consumed and the dishes piled up in the sink, Eileen walked back into the dining room clutching an envelope. She handed it to her husband. 'It's from Rom,' she said. 'He's serving on the *Havelock* now.'

'*Havelock*?' Remmie and his father repeated incredulously.

'But HMS *Havelock* was with us at St Nazaire!' Remmie said, shaking his head in disbelief. 'You mean Rom was there too and we didn't realise it?'

'I suppose not,' Hutchinson said. 'It's a funny old world.'

'Well, I'll put the kettle on,' Eileen said, removing her pinafore and reseating herself at the table. 'But before I do that, now is probably as good a time as any to tell you both that I too have a bit of news.'

'Christ, you weren't there at St Nazaire too, were you, Mother?' Remmie said dryly.

She slapped him playfully with the rolled-up pinny. 'Don't be coming back into this house blaspheming, Remus Hutchinson.'

'Well, come on then, dear, spit it out,' Hutchinson said with a hint of exasperation in his voice.

'I've volunteered to do my bit for the war effort.'

'Have you now?' Hutchinson muttered suspiciously. 'In what capacity?'

'First Aid ambulance driver. They were signing people up in the high street when I was taking my library books back.'

'Ambulance driver?' Remmie was puzzled by the notion of his mother driving anything.

'I was exactly what they were looking for, they said. I had five years in nursing before I met your father, and Uncle Ernie taught me to drive when I was a girl on the family farm. I think Ernie had an idea that he'd have me driving the tractor, though I never progressed beyond the old farm truck. Still, it was all valuable experience.'

'But that was years ago,' Remmie interrupted with a chuckle. 'You'll cause more road accidents than you're sent out to deal with.'

'They're not thinking about sending us out to road accidents,' she said with a laugh. 'They're training us up for when the bombs start falling. Anyway, we're going to get plenty of training — including a refresher course for driving the ambulance.'

There was a long silence around the dining table.

'Do you think Jerry will really bomb Liverpool?' Remmie asked his mother.

'Too bloody right they will,' Hutchinson interjected. 'It's a matter of when, not if. This is the second city of the Empire and our docks are keeping the nation's bellies filled.'

There was another silence.

'Are you sure you'll be all right with that kind of thing, Mother? I'm mean, at your age.'

'Cheeky beggar,' Eileen said, once more finding a use for the rolled-up pinafore. 'I'm forty-five years old, not ninety-five! I'm certainly capable of doing my bit for King and Country in our nation's hour of need.'

'Of course you are, Mother,' Remmie said, looking sufficiently rebuked. 'I think it's marvellous that you're up for it.'

Eileen showed the flash of a smile. 'And what about you, Captain? What do you think about me doing my bit?'

Her husband rubbed a hand across his beard and shook his head with a smile. 'I agree with Remmie,' he said after a moment's careful consideration. 'It's a ruddy marvellous thing to be doing — especially with your nursing experience. I hope and pray that your services will not be needed, but I rather suspect they will — and sooner, rather than later, I'm afraid. But I for one am very proud that my wife is doing her bit.'

Another prolonged hush descended across the room, and Remmie could see the moisture glistening in his mother's eyes.

'Well, I'd better go and put the kettle on then,' she said, carrying her rolled-up pinafore with her towards the kitchen.

Rom was accompanied throughout the journey from Plymouth to Belfast by a little private from the Royal Army Medical Corps named Bill Bagwell. At five foot three, he was a sharp contrast to the stately six-foot-two figure of Rom as they lumbered along the railway platforms and later trod the decks of the ferryboat together, looking out at the unusually calm waters of the Irish Sea.

'These chaps will sort you out, get your head clear again,' Bagwell told him, as they both smoked woodbines while looking out towards the city of Belfast, edging ever closer on the horizon.

Rom nodded and took another drag on the cigarette. He didn't want to discuss his inner turmoil with anyone, let alone with this ruddy-faced little West Country boy. Bagwell was decent enough, but being accompanied by anyone made Rom feel like one of the small evacuee children he had seen at the station, heading off to meet their adopted countryside families.

Bagwell accompanied him all the way across Belfast and on the bus out to Purdysburn Hospital on the lower slopes of the Castlereagh Hills in County Down. It felt a long way from the war, with its quiet country lanes. Perhaps that was part of the Navy's reasoning for sending him there. But it did nothing to remove the sinking sensation of dread he felt as they got off the bus and walked up the long driveway towards the imposing mansion-turned-hospital. Three storeys of stretching bay windows on either corner of the administration block gave the impression of a fortress, with a cupola perched on the roof and an ancient-looking clockface high in the masonry adding to the sense that he was entering a formidable institution.

Once the home of the Imperial English aristocracy overseeing this northern corner of Ireland, it had been adapted to provide medical facilities almost four decades before — initially as an infectious diseases hospital. But now, the diseases being treated in this sinister complex were all diseases of the mind. He was handed over by Bagwell to an indomitable-looking sister with a sharpened Belfast accent, and an apparent inability to make small talk.

'You will follow me,' she said to Rom, making him feel ever more like an inmate rather than a patient.

'Cheerio then, chap,' Bagwell called from the doorway behind him.

Rom gave Bagwell a half-hearted wave, without turning for a last look at the little fellow. He was shown to his ward, provided with pyjamas, and inexplicably, given the time of day, was made to change into them and surrender his uniform. Once changed, he sat down on a chair that was placed beside his bed and looked along the ward at the other men. He presumed they were all there to receive psychiatric treatment, like him. They were all sitting quietly, reading newspapers and books, some just staring idly out of the window at the rolling countryside beyond the hospital's grounds. In their pyjamas and dressing gowns, it was impossible to assess their role or rank, or even to guess what section of the military they served with — soldiers and airmen and sailors all looked remarkably alike in a pair of striped pyjamas. It was, Rom told himself as he settled back into the chair, going to be a very long few weeks.

None of the other patients seemed in any way psychologically disturbed during the long hours of the late summer afternoon, with the sunlight streaming in through the windows and the regular ticking of a clock on the wall. There was no ranting or raving, as Rom had imagined there might be, and there wasn't a single straitjacket in sight. It was, in fact, all remarkably civilised. They ate dinner together in a large mess hall, all seemingly oblivious to the peculiarity of eating formally despite all wearing pyjamas and dressing gowns.

I suppose you just get used to it, Rom thought to himself as he wrapped the gown more closely around his torso and wondered briefly why none of the gowns were furnished with cords to act as belts. Then he remembered that he was now living in a mental institution and the penny dropped. Of course there are no cords or belts or sharp knives. He gave a shrug and settled into the meal of liver and onions.

While all the men had seemed perfectly healthy during the day, with nighttime and lights-out, sleep revealed the truth of the anguish that each had evidently worked so hard to mask. The ward became a ghoulish soundscape of anxious mutterings, whimpers and the occasional hair-raising, desperate scream. Unsurprisingly, Rom did not get much sleep. But equally, he did not succumb to the night terrors he had experienced in his cabin.

The following morning, he was feeling groggy as he sipped a cup of weak tea, sitting up in bed and gazing out of the big bay window. A ruddy-faced man with a pencil-thin moustache ambled across and without giving any kind of an introduction, handed him a rolled-up newspaper.

'Thought you might want something to read,' the man said with a shrug. 'A chap could go off his rocker in a place like this,' he added with a wry smile, before returning to his own side of the ward. The man walked with a slight limp and Rom guessed he was probably an airman. Peculiarly, it didn't seem appropriate here to ask anybody about their service. It was as if they had all taken a temporary step away from their lives.

'Thank you.' Rom nodded across the ward at his new friend and opened the newspaper. The Luftwaffe had bombed a "northern city", apparently, with "mercifully few casualties" according to the report. He wondered if it might be Liverpool and worked hard to try to read between the lines to pinpoint the attack.

Why, Rom wondered, were bombing raids over London reported in the press with their geographical location given, while bombing raids elsewhere in the country were shrouded in this ridiculous secrecy? What was the point? The people being bombed knew they had been bombed. The German bomber crews knew well enough where they had dropped their bombs. So, what was the actual benefit of such broad censorship?

The article included a brief interview with a bus driver, who seemed to believe that a Dornier Do-17Z bomber had been chasing his bus and his consignment of women factory workers through the streets of this nameless "northern city". The driver told the reporter how he had weaved and dodged the falling bombs and delivered his passengers to the relative safety of a public shelter, thwarting the bomber crew passing twenty-five thousand feet above. *It's bound to be Liverpool*, Rom thought. His reading was interrupted by the appearance at the end his bed of a pretty nurse with a softer Belfast accent than the sister.

'Sub-lieutenant Hutchinson,' she said with a smile. 'The doctor is ready to see you now, if you'd be good enough to come with me.'

Rom nodded, thinking that he would happily follow her to hell and back. She flashed another smile at him as he got to his feet, hoping that the doctor's consultation would not prove to be a new hell for him to discover here at Purdysburn.

In fact, the doctor seemed friendly enough. He was a small man with wire-rimmed glasses and a glinting bald head. He explained to Rom that he was a psychiatrist and a psychoanalyst. Rom wasn't really sure what he was talking about.

'Will I be medicated then, doctor?'

The little man shook his head with a smile.

'I've heard all about how you chaps like to electrocute people,' Rom added suspiciously.

'Electroconvulsive therapy,' the psychiatrist said. 'That won't be necessary in your case either, you'll no doubt be pleased to hear, Lieutenant.'

'So, what's the plan to get me out of the loony bin?'

The doctor smiled patiently. 'We're a hospital, like any other hospital. We'll get you better and then you will be able to get back to your very important work.'

'But how?' Rom demanded. 'What is the treatment?'

The doctor leaned back in his chair and steepled his fingers. 'Talking,' he said softly. 'You and I are going to do a lot of talking, Lieutenant.'

The ward was empty when Rom shuffled back after an hour with the doctor. He would return for his "talking therapy" every day for an hour at the same time. The thought of it baffled him — what earthly good could all this jabber possibly do for him? He glanced at his wristwatch. The other chaps must all have gone to lunch, he thought, and he was about to head straight on down the corridor towards the mess hall when he realised that the ward was not entirely empty. The portly silhouette of a man in the familiar uniform of the Royal Navy was outlined against the bay window in the far corner. The figure was looking out across the countryside of County Down, and seemed at first not to have noticed Rom's arrival. But then he spoke, and before he even turned his face away from the window, Rom felt his legs buckle beneath him.

'Good to see you looking so well, old boy,' the figure said, and as he turned and the sunlight illuminated one side of the visitor's face, Rom could barely believe his eyes.

'Chubby?' Rom whispered.

The man moved slowly along the ward towards him, but there was no mistaking that ambling gait.

'Chubby Smith. How in the name of God...?' Rom stumbled across to the chair that stood beside his bed and slumped down into it, just before his legs collapsed under him. 'Chubby. But Chubby...'

'I know,' Chubby said, raising his eyebrows. 'Who'd have thunk it, eh? I, for one, thought I was a goner for sure. Such a nasty business. I mean, machine-gunning the blasted bridge. It's just not cricket, is it?'

'But you were dead, Chubby,' Rom said, shaking his head.

Chubby shrugged and looked down at his own chest. He gave it a pat. 'We can all recover, given a little time, old boy.'

'No, you were dead, Chubby,' Rom insisted. 'We buried you at sea, for Christ's sake.'

Chubby's podgy face twisted into a squeamish grimace. 'Please,' he said, 'I'd really rather you didn't go on and on about it.' He sat down on the edge of Rom's bed and absentmindedly picked an invisible speck of dust from the lapel of his jacket.

The two men sat there for a few moments in silence.

'I know I'm a goner,' Chubby said at last. 'But let's not get fixated on that. I'm not here to talk about my troubles.'

'What are you here for, Chubby?'

'I'm here to help you, old boy. You need to get yourself together so you can get back out there and give Jerry a taste of his own medicine.'

'Yes,' Rom nodded. 'Yes, I know.'

'I know it's been a tough time, but really, Rom, you need to snap out of all this.'

'I'm having talking therapy.'

Chubby waved the idea away with an impatient hand. 'Talking therapy,' he laughed. 'If it was me, I'd be telling Sigmund Freud in there to shove his talking therapy back down his torpedo hatch.' His face softened. 'But of course, you must do what you need to do, my friend. Whatever it takes, eh? Do you understand? Remember — detail and compassion.'

Rom nodded and looked down at his lap. 'Yes, I understand, Chubby,' he whispered, and for the first time, he really did understand what he had to do to get himself back on his feet.

'Would you…' But Rom cut short his next question when he looked up to see that Chubby had vanished. 'I'll do whatever needs to be done,' he said to the empty room. 'Whatever needs to be done. Detail and compassion, Chubby. Detail and compassion.'

CHAPTER EIGHTEEN

As the late summer turned to early autumn, the nightly terror being delivered from the skies above Liverpool became more intense. Getting to grips with the unexpectedly complex details of driving an ambulance proved to be nothing for Eileen Hutchinson compared to the horrors of being first on the scene after a land mine had flattened a house or shop or school.

Eileen's first experience of facing large-scale death and destruction came in mid-September, when she was called out to Walton Prison — an unlikely enough target for the Luftwaffe — where a rogue bomb had obliterated an entire wing. First aid was a pointless offering on that occasion. The prisoners had all been sitting in their cells — no air raid shelters for them. All the ambulance crews could do was help to begin the process of removing the rubble and pulling out more than twenty bodies with as much dignity and compassion as possible. There was a strange equality in death between the prisoners and the prison guards — as though all their sins had been forgotten in that terrible, cleansing blast of light and heat.

Two nights later, the bombs hit Central Station. Eileen imagined carnage as she drove at speed across the city, but the rolling stock bore the brunt of the blast. She was still treating a railway guard who had suffered some minor cuts and bruises when she was directed to assist with first aid efforts elsewhere — an inferno was tearing through the Alexandra Dock, there was another major fire started by incendiaries in Byng Street, as well as a timber yard in Rimrose Street, Bootle. But it was a blast outside the T.J. Hughes department store in London

Road that had created the largest number of casualties, so Eileen found herself racing back across the city centre, where she treated the wounds of a special constable, who had been thrown by the blast a full seventy-five yards across the street. He had been found sprawled outside of Collier's department store, with his rescuers momentarily assuming he was dead, rather than unconscious.

'Jerry will pay for this,' the middle-aged Lazarous had muttered as she dressed his wounds.

A few days later the Cunard Building and Dock Board offices suffered considerable fire damage and there was widespread devastation across much of the city's docklands — Wapping, King's, Queen's, Coburg and Brunswick docks all took a hammering. Eileen looked out across the burning quaysides and wondered where on earth her husband and two sons would find to moor when they next returned home.

But it was a call out to a bomb strike in Durning Road in late November that really devastated her. A public bomb shelter had been hit at the Ernest Brown Junior Technical School with more than two hundred and fifty people crowded inside. It was a scene of utter devastation when she arrived and leapt from the driver's seat of the ambulance. It was impossible to know where to start looking for survivors beneath the enormous, smoking pile of rubble where a three-storey building had stood. But within minutes of her arrival, the mound was crawling with would-be rescuers, forming a human chain to remove the bricks as quickly as possible.

Eileen worked as hard as any of the men to frantically clear the debris. But there were many more dead bodies being pulled from the rubble than there were survivors. A few seemed to escape with miraculously little injury, while others had been horribly mutilated and must have died instantly. At least,

Eileen sincerely hoped that they had. It was the sight of a child's body — a boy of no more than eleven or twelve years of age, twisted and broken like a rag doll, that finally brought her to her knees, sobbing into her palms as she fought to regain her composure.

In the Irish Sea both Remmie, aboard the SS *John Holt* and his father, a little way behind him on the bridge of the SS *Robert Holt*, could see the glow as their home city burned. They could see the amber flicker on the horizon illuminating the underside of the rolling clouds miles before they reached the landmark of New Brighton's Fort Perch Rock where two six-inch guns had been installed to guard the mouth of the Mersey. Just four miles of sea separated the two ships, and their horror was shared just minutes apart at the sight of hell unleashed on the familiar quaysides of their city.

'God help us all now,' William Hutchinson muttered, removing his cap and rubbing his eyes wearily with the thumb and middle finger of his right hand. 'Dear God, help us.'

They could barely moor the ship amid the chaos, with warehouses well alight just a few hundred yards away. Hutchinson looked down the long quay and saw the SS *John Holt* safely tied up alongside. Stepping down the gangplank, he entered a world of rubble and smoke and frenetic activity with rescue workers jostling with dock workers as they all battled to exercise their respective duties — the former picking through the still smoking rubble, while the latter worked the ropes that harnessed the great ship, and almost immediately set to work on relieving her decks of cargo.

Hutchinson walked hesitantly down the gangplank, taking in this transformed world. On the quayside he picked his way across the dust and debris and scattered piles of rubble and stood for a long moment beside a blanket that had been laid over a body.

He rubbed at the grey hairs of his beard for a moment, before stooping down onto one knee and lifting the edge of the blanket back. He gasped softly to find himself gazing into the extinguished eyes of a familiar face. Old Jim. Dear Old Jim who wouldn't hurt a fly, and had worked the gates of this dock for so many decades in his quiet, plodding way. Hutchinson shook his head and felt a desperate aching deep within him. Somewhere in one of the little terraced houses of the Dingle, a few miles along the river, a pan of scouse would be bubbling on a stove — a pan of scouse dutifully prepared by elderly feminine hands; a pan of scouse that Jim would never get to taste.

Hutchinson heard the shuffle of feet in the dust behind him. He stood up and turned to face Remmie, whose eyes were glinting up at his. There was fear in them, a weary kind of terror. He opened his arms and embraced his son for a long moment, while the frenetic bustle of the quayside continued to unfold around them.

One hundred and fifty miles away across the Irish Sea, the doctor was looking at Rom through his wire-rimmed glasses.

'You have made a remarkable recovery, Hutchinson,' he said, rubbing his bald scalp as he spoke. 'I wouldn't have told you this when you arrived, but not everyone makes it back to a complete clean bill of health from this kind of thing — certainly not back to the kind of health that would allow you back on the bridge of a destroyer.'

Rom nodded. Purdysburn had become a kind of second home to him in the past few months. He hadn't exactly become fond of the place, but it had taken on a feeling of safety and comfort. Despite this, he was more than ready to step out of the door and never look back.

'There was a moment with you, a turning point quite early on — that was the key to your recovery,' the doctor mused, removing his spectacles and waving them across the desk at his patient. 'Something clicked, didn't it, Hutchinson? It was as if there was a moment when you suddenly realised what you had to do.'

Rom shrugged. 'I had a little help from an old friend.'

The doctor gave him a puzzled frown, but then waved it away with a dismissive gesture. 'Well, never mind about the whys and the wherefores,' he said. 'The important thing is that you are most certainly on the mend. There is a war on, after all. We need chaps like you out there fighting.'

'Absolutely, sir.'

'Feel up to it, Hutchinson?'

'I've never felt more up for anything, sir,' Rom said, with an expression of determination.

Back on the ward, he dressed in his uniform and carefully fastened the leather strap of his wristwatch back around his wrist. He looked at the distinctive twin watch face. It had long since stopped ticking, waiting silently for all these weeks. He took it back off and held it between nimble fingers as he wound up the mechanism before putting it back on and allowing the pressed sleeves of his shirt and jacket to fall over it. He turned and nodded at the man in the bed opposite, who nodded back a silent farewell. The long corridor echoed with the sound of his polished shoes and the big old oak front door creaked open.

As he walked down the driveway in front of the hospital, he paused briefly to look back at the imposing brick frontage, now familiar and strangely reassuring. There was a flicker of movement in a first-floor window, and for the briefest of moments he caught sight of a face in the shadows, almost obscured behind the net curtains. The chubby cheeks and slight twinkle in the beady eyes were visible to Rom even at such a distance. Rom raised a hand and gave a valedictory wave towards the window. He saw the face in the shadows give an almost imperceptible nod of approval, before Rom turned and headed for the main road.

Rom returned back across the Irish Sea on the ferry later that day alone — with no chaperone from the Royal Army Medical Corps standing at his side. His gaze cut across the granite waves as the wind buffeted his face. He leaned on the rail, quite alone on the deck, and closed his eyes. He sensed the great open expanse of the sea stretching out to the distant horizon with slate-grey clouds barrelling towards him. More than ever in his life, Rom felt at home.

He had a few hours to spare in Liverpool before having to catch his train at Lime Street, so rushed back to Crosby. But the family home was deserted. His father and brother were, no doubt, out somewhere on the pitching and rolling surface of the Atlantic. He couldn't imagine where his mother might be at this time on a Thursday morning. Perhaps she had taken up a hobby or had joined one of the voluntary services to do her bit for the war effort. Rom certainly wouldn't put it past the game old girl.

He walked around the empty house alone for a few minutes, taking in the strange familiarity of the kitchen, the dining room, the sitting room — but he felt like a ghost walking through his own past. He walked slowly up the stairs and looked in on his old bedroom. It was peculiar to see how little it had changed in the months since he was last here. The

Hornblower books were still on the shelf where he had placed them when last he had enjoyed enough leisure to read. The little wooden globe that his father had given him and his brother for their twelfth birthday was still perched on the side. He slowly turned it. Its open patches of blue did little to convey the enormity of the great oceans that were out there awaiting him.

Back down in the kitchen, he scribbled a note to his mother and placed it on the kitchen table, weighing it down with the pepper pot:

I have been a little ill, but now I am very well. I'm heading straight down to Plymouth to meet my new ship and all the untold adventures she holds for me.

He thought about writing a note to Charlotte, too. He had wanted to write to her previously, but he had been too ashamed to admit to her that he was in hospital. He had received more letters from her that had been forwarded to him while he was there, but they had all gone unanswered. He would write to her, he told himself, once he had worked out what he would say.

With one final look down the hallway, he closed the front door gently behind him and walked to the garden gate, smoothing down his sharp naval officer's uniform.

The next morning, Rom found himself walking along the quayside at Plymouth docks. Before him, looking like a work of exquisite beauty, was the angular, gun-metal form of a Royal Navy cruiser. Rom strode purposefully up the gangplank and met the captain waiting for him as he stepped onto the deck. He dropped his pack and stood to attention with a stamp of his shiny shoe, as his right hand moved mechanically to his forehead to give a crisp salute.

'Sub-Lieutenant Romulus Hutchinson, reporting for duty, sir!'

HISTORICAL NOTES

Throughout the Second World War, the Royal Navy's destroyers stood as vigilant sentinels of the sea. Agile, heavily armed, and endlessly versatile, these ships were the backbone of Britain's naval defence — protecting convoys, hunting submarines, and engaging enemy forces from the Arctic Circle to the Mediterranean.

In fact, the destroyer's lineage dates back to the late 19th century when navies sought a counter to the emerging threat of torpedo boats. The Royal Navy's early "torpedo boat destroyers" evolved rapidly, becoming faster, more seaworthy, and increasingly capable of independent operations. By the outbreak of the Second World War in 1939, destroyers had become indispensable fleet units, designed to operate alongside capital ships or independently in escort roles.

Britain entered the war with a mix of pre-war designs and newer vessels, but the demands of global conflict soon led to the rapid expansion and diversification of destroyer classes. Destroyers were the Swiss Army knives of the Royal Navy. Their duties were as varied as they were vital — from convoy escorts and fleet screening to torpedo attacks, U-boat hunting and shore bombardments as well as playing an important role in rescue operations. By 1945, the Royal Navy had commissioned more than 300 destroyers during the war. Many were lost in action, but their contribution was immeasurable. They kept the sea lanes open, protected vital convoys, and stood firm in the face of overwhelming odds.

In this novel, and its future series, I attempt to give a sense of the breadth of the destroyers' role in the period, as well as offering an insight into what it was like to be serving in the Royal Navy and the Merchant Navy during the Battle of the Atlantic — a time of peril that is almost unimaginable to us today.

Some of the characters you have met in this novel are based on real people and others are complete fabrications. Everyone from Commander Richard Courtenay-Boyle, captain of HMS *Grenade* to the affable Captain John Pelly, commander of the training establishment HMS *King Alfred*, were real people. The experiences of Bill Ridgewell, the gunner of HMS *Grenade* were recorded in detail by the Imperial War Museum oral history recordings. I recommend listening to the interview with Ridgewell, which is available online at:

https://www.iwm.org.uk/collections/item/object/800 20823

Where real names are used, please be aware that I merely present fictionalised versions of their real lives — a process I have approached with great respect and care for the dignity of their memory. As you may have spotted, there is also a cameo within these pages of my own paternal grandfather, Stanley Clensy MBE, chief engineer on the *John Holt*.

Wherever possible I have clung closely to the real events and the actions of real ships, but have sometimes deviated in the cause of storytelling, either to increase the dramatic impact on the lives of the fictional and fictionalised characters, or to amalgamate disparate real-life incidents in a manner that allows them to be recounted as a coherent narrative.

A NOTE TO THE READER

Dear Reader,

Thank you for taking the time to read *For Those In Peril*.

One of my earliest memories is of getting my head stuck between the railings on the Pier Head in Liverpool. I must have only been three or four years old. My grandad would often take me down to Woodside where we would catch the ferry over to Liverpool. For me, it was mostly about the fun of walking down the great, tube-like gangway leading to the floating landing stage — hoping the tide was low so that the walkway would be extra steep. Sometimes I would have to hold on to my grandad's big tobacco-scented hands for fear of tripping and rolling all the way down into the river.

My grandad and I would board the ferry and climb the steep steps to find a bench on the top deck — our perch carefully chosen for the best views while avoiding the sooty flecks coming from the funnel. Sometimes we didn't get off — we just took the triangular boat ride from Birkenhead to Liverpool, back across the river to Seacombe, before getting off again at Woodside. But if my grandad was feeling more energetic we would disembark at Liverpool and wander around the Pier Head, looking at the "Three Graces" — the Royal Liver Building, The Cunard Building and the Port of Liverpool Building with its great dome that made it seem more like an ancient temple than an office block.

I could look along the river to the Royal Albert Dock in one direction and Princes Dock in the other. Beyond for as far as I could see, there seemed to be docks all along the Mersey. I could imagine my other grandfather — my dad's father —

climbing aboard the great ocean-going ships he worked on as a chief engineer for the Liverpool shipping line John Holt & Company throughout the 1930s, 40s and 50s. If I looked back across the river, I could see the giant cranes and warehouses of the Birkenhead shipbuilders Cammel Lairds, where I could imagine my uncle hard at work, refitting a submarine in a great starburst of sparks from his welding torch. Sometimes my grandad would even point out the distant flame along the river that marked the Shell oil refinery, where he had spent the last years of his working life.

Even at that early age I was fascinated by the old buildings and the view across the Mersey. I sensed the history — the generations who had walked in the shadow of the buildings before me. Which, presumably, is how I came to have my head stuck firmly between the railings.

As I remember, my first reaction to the situation wasn't one of panic. I just enjoyed the view, wondering, somewhat academically how I would survive now my head was firmly trapped between these two metal bars. My grandad showed no outward signs of panic either, though there was some initial talk of phoning the fire brigade. In fact, all it took was for my grandad to lift me upside down, and with my ears facing the right way again, I was able to free myself, and cease to be a permanent part of the Liverpool waterfront.

I may have been freed from the railings, but still the Liverpool waterfront would always be a part of me — deeply ingrained into my brain, in ways I wasn't even aware of until I started writing this new series of naval adventures for Sapere Books almost half a century after the incident with the Pier Head railings. As I wrote, my imagination conjuring and weaving together a saga of a Liverpudlian seafaring family, the landscape of my own childhood flowed effortlessly back to the surface. The voices from my childhood, caught on a Mersey wind, echoed back down the years.

I hope you have enjoyed spending time with my fictional twins, Romulus and Remus Hutchinson, who will reappear in further adventures. Reviews are important for authors, so if you enjoyed *For Those In Peril*, I would be really grateful if you could take a moment to review the book on **Amazon** or **Goodreads**. You can sign up to my newsletter and find out more about what I'm working on by visiting my website: **www.davidclensy.com**.

David Clensy

Sapere Books is an exciting new publisher of brilliant fiction and popular history.

To find out more about our latest releases and our monthly bargain books visit our website: saperebooks.com